THE ROWING LESSON

Also by the Author

The Devil's Chimney

THE ROWING LESSON

A NOVEL

Anne Landsman

Published by
Soho Press, Inc.
853 Broadway
New York, NY 10003

Library of Congress Cataloging-in-Publication Data
Landsman, Anne, 1959–
The rowing lesson : a novel / by Anne Landsman.
p. cm.
ISBN 978-1-56947-469-3
1. Fathers and daughters—Fiction.
2. Terminally ill—Family relationships—Fiction.
3. Death—Psychological aspects—Fiction.
4. Americans—South Africa—Fiction.
I. Title.
PS3562.A4832R69 2007
813'.54—dc22
2007005193

10 9 8 7 6 5 4 3 2 1

For my father
Gerald Bernard Landsman

CHAPTER 1

I CAN HEAR the dirty blood inside you, the way that old fish, the coelacanth, spins on its head and can hear the heartbeat of its prey. I can hear the sea sweeping up onto the beach and back out again, as you breathe, and with it comes all of your past, the good and the bad, washing up around us like empty Coke cans and bits of driftwood and dead jellyfish. There's Maisie, your sister, the dark beauty, and the little one, Bertie, the baby brother you hate. They're standing on the shore and they're wearing funny bathing costumes. Bertie's pants are wet and he's crying and there's your ma, and she's laughing like a little girl because Wolfie is there, sitting under her umbrella, and he's flashing his perfect smile at her. He's the grown-up son of Ralph Isaacson, proprietor of Isaacson's Men's

Clothing. Wolfie can't stop telling her about J.L.B. Smith, the man who identified the coelacanth and yes, it was just yesterday when one was pulled up out of the sea and that East London lady kept it and showed it to Smith. It was going bad already and she had thrown the insides away. She threw away the viscera! What can you do. But still, J.L.B. Smith is going to find a live one, a live million-year-old fish and did you know, I've seen him in Knysna. He has a house there. I think it's near the lagoon and he loves the water, of course, and he has a boat. You are standing in front of your ma and Wolfie and you weigh one hundred and nineteen pounds even though you're eighteen and you never played one rugby game, never ever. Wolfie was a flyhalf for Outeniqua High and he's looking up at you as if you're a very basic form of marine life, something without a spine, something you can see through. At least the sun is behind you, and he has to squint.

I'm in the sea up to my waist and I'm waving like mad but of course you can't see me. I'm smaller than a pin, a memory of yesterday, a part of your life that isn't now, that isn't in the sun on a beach at Lentjiesklip. Betsy, Betsy, it's Betsy, I shout, but all I hear you say is Sorry, sorry, as you drip cold water onto Wolfie's flat stomach, as you stand over him with your own flashing smile, your hair that's still very, very black, and that long nose pointing East then South. Fantastic! you say. The water's fantastic! Your ma gives you a towel that's quite worn, really, even though your dad sells some nice bright ones in the shop, right there next to the buckets and spades. It's 1938 and the towel you have is the towel you keep. Your ma is still worried about you, even though you're not six months old or five or nine or thirteen. You've been rubbed in grease, wrapped in bacon and sent to Calvinia where the air is dry and the girls are prettier than the girls in George but nothing, nothing has put any fat on your ribs, on your bony, nosy face or those terribly thin legs.

Your ma is talking about going to Cape Town to see her sisters, Molly and Poppy, and you're asking her to bring back sprats. Sprats! Wolfie pulls a face and he says something rude about sprats and it cuts you, as if you're the sprat on his plate that he's frowning at. But then he laughs again, and you laugh too. How can you not when the sun shines on you, when this strong man with the sandy wave in his hair, and the chest and legs of a rugby player shines his light upon you. This peacock shuffling his tail like a deck of cards, dazzling your mother, your sister, Maisie, dripping right next to you. Maisie has her own light, in the velvet darkness of her eyes and in the mystery that's happened under that ugly old bathing costume of your mother's that she's wearing. No one can see Wolfie strutting alone into the future, a thousand girls lost and won and forever lost or Maisie, married young into your mother's dream, become a woman, a rich woman staring at the sea from an ocean liner heading towards Europe, staring into her life moving so fast underneath her.

Bertie is the one you don't think about, never ever, because his spot on your mother's lap is your place, the clothes he wears are your clothes. Even his filthy one-eyed monkey is your monkey. There's nothing that he hasn't taken from you. He's the sprat on your plate, the flea in your bed, the rash you got two summers ago.

But here you are. It's summer at the Wilderness again and your father's at the shop in George selling people sweets and coffee and combinations, the worst kind of underwear in the world, a one-piece top and bottom thing that itches and buttons and scratches and drives you mad. You wore them for a whole year once, to keep the fat in and the cold out, and it was hard to get them off fast enough. You soiled them once, outside the convent, and that was the worst day in the world for you, coming home dirty in dirty combinations. You can only hope nobody is buying them today.

That's a bad thought, because nothing is more important than people buying soap or stockings, beach umbrellas or chutney. You're in the sun, and your father isn't, selling everything from beans to furniture. He's always working, moving things on the shelves, or sweeping the floor or looking at the catalogues the commercial travellers bring in. Sometimes the travellers come for Friday night supper and everyone talks and laughs and there's dancing. You can tap dance, and so can Maisie and the two of you spin and whirl and tap until you can hardly breathe anymore. "Daisy, Maisie, give me your answer do . . . I'm half crazy all for the love of you. . . ." And there's more laughing and your ma has tears running down her cheeks and once she even wet her pants.

Ag, Friday nights. You had the lucky job of catching a chicken from the backyard and putting it in a bag, hitching the horse to the cart and driving the squawking chicken to the shochet's house where there would be a quick "*Baruch Attah Adonai . . .*," the knife swooping down on the chicken's neck and blood spurting into a bucket, as the *shochet* held the headless bird. There were two nice plump ones, one named Maisie and one Harold after you, and one day it was Harold's turn. Nettie, the maid, looked out into the yard and the bird was gone so she said to your ma, "Madam, Harold has been killed!" Your poor ma fainted, right there on the kitchen floor. The jokes that Friday night were even funnier, and your ma laughed like a drain, and even your dad, who was always the one listening and smoking, smiled.

Wolfie is reading the *George and Knysna Herald* on the beach and he's talking about the Great Trek they're doing, to commemorate the Great Trek of a hundred years ago. There's a picture of the two covered ox-wagons, the Piet Retief and the Andries Pretorius, arriving at the foot of the Voortrekker Monument in Pretoria, months after leaving Cape Town. Everyone's wearing long beards and carrying flaming torches. They're throwing the torches into an enormous bonfire and all that fire reminds you of the pictures of Kristallnacht.

You look at the golden beach, the hills curving around you like gentle green arms holding a treasure, and it's hard to believe that the world is tilting, slipping, that the Great Trek just happened all over again, that shops like your father's were burned in Germany. Bertie van Riet went to see the Trekkers and so did Hermanus Claassen. Lots of Afrikaans boys went and watched the wagons and the men on horseback tumbling through the Little Karoo. At every town they stopped, there were people waiting and cheering, the dominee praying and someone from the Broederbond talking.

It's not our holiday, your dad said, and he went and bought a car. A 1938 Chrysler Imperial called Charlotte. Charlotte is a dream, a white gleaming fish of a car, bigger and better than Lucas, the Model T Ford, or Charles, the Rugby. CAW 955. You attached the license plate yourself. Charlotte has a lilt to her, a rhythm, and you've sat in the back and looked out at the sea, as she hugs the coastal road between George and the Wilderness. Places catch you, they take your breath away and sometimes, if it was up to you, entirely up to you, you might be quite a trekker yourself, hiking here and going there, climbing this rock-face and swinging into that gorge.

It's a miracle he's alive, Doctor Brown once told your ma, and you look at old pictures of yourself with matchstick arms and legs, your five-year-old head balancing like a big, funny ball on those shrunken shoulders. Nobody knows why he's so thin, said your ma and pa and your two aunts, Molly and Poppy, and they sat you down (and strapped you down!) and tried to feed you milk puddings and *vetkoeke* and *gribbenes* and you hated all of it. You loved the saltiness of sprats, you loved fish caught fresh from the sea, and fruit. You and Maisie climbed over the fence into the neighbor's backyard one day and sat in their plum tree, eating their plums. The neighbor children sat at the bottom of the tree with a biscuit tin and everyone gave them a penny to sit and watch you eat plums.

"All things bright and beautiful, all creatures great and small. . . . All things wise and wonderful: the Lord God made them all. . . ." Singing hymns is when you look at Hilda Lewis's breasts, pushing against her school uniform, or Gertrude van der Westhuizen's black-stockinged legs. You have seen those legs swimming in the Touw river, the stockings crumpled and empty on the bank. There are girls everywhere, chattering and laughing, their hair up, their hair down, their hands carrying and fixing and stroking. Your teachers, your ma and your sisters, Nettie and her girls, the ladies giving shillings to your dad, their fingers opening and closing around the money like sea anemones.

In fact, you decided that you might just want to be a doctor one day in one of those brightly coloured huts on the beach in Muizenberg. You were five and your mother and your aunts were changing into their bathing-costumes and their breasts, all six of their breasts, were out at the same time and you never ever forgot the living, breathing sight of all that softness.

Your father's father was a carpenter from Lithuania and your ma, well, you know what they said about those girls from the East End of London. A lot of them fresh from the shtetl and only in England for a minute before a lady called Bessie Levin came looking for girls wanting improvement, wanting a better station in life. The station was Frenchfontein, Johannesburg, and it was the last station of all. The men came searching for gold, and when they found it they were tired and there were no women. So Bessie brought the girls to the Spire House, to Phoenix, to Sylvio Villa, on the corner of Rissik and De Villiers. The pimps were Russian and Polish Jews from America—how terrible!—Joe Silver and Lou Rosenthal and a lot of other Jewish names that could make you die of shame. Jews selling Jews to white men and black men and all the thousands of browns and pinks and greys in between.

Shame on them. Shame on those bad Jews who make everyone else hate the Jews, who give the Jews a bad name. That's why Bertie van Riet said that Hitler's right. It's Joe Silver's fault, and Freddy Gold's and you're never ever going to touch money. You're going to touch broken arms and legs, and fix them, and touch foreheads and listen to hearts, beating away under breasts, under flat ones and soft ones, with nipples like thumbs, under big ones, bigger that your head, bigger than anyone's head.

But your ma never came to Rissik Street. It wasn't her,

was it? By the time she came to South Africa they had cleaned up Frenchfontein. It wasn't quite so French anymore. It might have been your great-aunt Fanny but nobody really knows because she disappeared anyway, with a man twice her age and what happened before or after is anybody's guess.

Wolfie is smacking you in the stomach and curling his arms at you as if this is finally going to turn you into a man. You can have my boat, he says, and you can take the girls up the river. Have a picnic. The oarlocks are there. The oars are on the jetty. Maisie will bring her friends, Hilda Lewis and Gertrude of the long legs, and Bunny will come and his cousin, Morry Berelowitz.

So it's later, much later, and the six of you are crowded into Wolfie's red-and-white boat. The boat sits deep in the water and Gertrude is trickling her fingers over the side and no, you say, lifting the oars into the air for a moment, Stop doing that. I am the captain of this ship. The girls laugh, because you sound big and small at the same time, and it's funny. Gertrude says, I want to row and now she's getting up. The boat rocks and you grit your teeth. She almost falls down right next to you and takes the left oar. Hard on port! you shout. She crabs, her oar stuck. And now it's out of the oarlock, floating on the water's surface. With the right oar, you turn the boat around, grab the oar that's drifting further and further away. You chaps don't even know how to row! you say.

Gertrude moves back to her old seat, sticking her hand

even deeper into the water this time. You want to smack her on the head with the oar but you don't. You keep dipping the oars, the blades catching and pulling, followed by the little melody the drips play. Your sleeves are rolled up so that the girls can see the stringy muscles in your arms, as they bunch and release, bunch and release. If there's one thing you know how to do it's row. Maisie wants a turn now but you won't let her. Bunny and Morry are talking about the mad Germans and if there's going to be a war. Bunny says, I am going to fly, and Morry says, It's the sea for me, and you say, I am going to be a general. You tip the oars back, making a V. The boat coasts to a stop. The General of the Generals, you add, putting your hand inside your shirt like Napoleon. Gertrude takes a leaf, and she puts it under your nose, like a moustache, and you're Chaplin, Charlie Chaplin exactly.

We're going to Ebb 'n Flow, is what you said to your ma, and she boiled some eggs and gave you tomato sandwiches, spread with chicken fat and sprinkled with salt. They're in a brown bag tucked under the prow. The river is still wide here, and there's a campsite on the bank with canvas tents, and you row, row, row the boat under the railway bridge, a special railway bridge that cars can cross too. You've driven over in Charlotte and she's waited in front of the bridge for the train to pass, a panting buffalo of a train coming from De Aar.

You slip under the bridge between the pylons and there are black, long-necked birds on the bank, gazing at the six of you from a rotting tree. It's the only dead tree you can see. Everything else here is green, greyish green, or moss-green or blue-green or silver-green. The river flows between two soft green hills, and you and Morry and Bunny and the girls are going to follow the amber water up to its source, to the place where it trickles out of the mountain, to its secret hiding place, to Ebb 'n Flow. You have been up this river many times before but each trip is different. Sometimes the sky is as blue as a window flung open, other times, like now, it's grey like a mourning dove. There are so many sounds as you follow the river, folding itself between the ancient stinkwoods and yellowwoods dripping with moss. There's the plish-plash of the oars and you try your best to make the strokes even, to tell the girls to stop laughing so you can listen to the water, to the monkeys screaming above your heads, to the call of the birds. You're looking and listening for the rarest bird of all, the Knysna *loerie*, with its brilliant blue body and green head, its crest like a cockatoo's and the flash of red as it flaps its wings and disappears.

The river narrows and narrows, and soon you can see the rocks and pebbles gleaming under the water, which seems to have softened and thickened, insects, twigs and foam gently swirling on its surface. You have to be careful here, not to leave a red scrape of paint on one of the rocks. You use the oar to push away from a tree draping its branches into the water, a giant old hand reaching at you. You push the boat around a corner, and there's an orange rock-face on one side, pocked with *dassie*-holes and *dassies.* Sometimes you can even see one basking in the sun, a fat rock-rabbit minus the long ears. Gertrude shrieks at something Morry said to her and this time you almost hit her, with the blade of the oar. You can't hear the monkeys, that noise that makes you feel like the river and the sky and the rock are a million years old.

But the beach is there, on the right, a tiny swathe of white sand edged with miraculous ferns, the giant yellowwoods gathering themselves in the background, a council of elders, larger-than-life witnesses. Morry and Bunny jump out and the boat lurches. You shout, I am the captain! but no one listens. And the girls are climbing out, falling out, Maisie looking back at you. She knows how you like to make a perfect landing, how you like to let the boat glide onto the sand, a whisper, not the crunch and growl these overgrown boys are making, as they haul the boat up onto the beach.

Gertrude lifts her leg over the side of the gunwale. She sees you watching her and she gets stuck on the oarlock, the boat wobbling away from her. Bunny is in the water, his pants wet, and he lifts her up because he's strong as an ox. She screams *Eina*! and he puts her down on the sand. Gertrude is sitting with her legs pressed tightly together, her hand in between her thighs, and she's trying to make the best of it but there's a dark stain on her dress and nobody knows what that's from.

Maisie is spreading an old tablecloth out, and unpacking the picnic and soon everybody is sitting down and eating their sandwiches. Morry and Bunny want to go further up the river, to where you can see the water seeping out of the mountain but you are worried about Wolfie's boat. Morry starts walking up the river, his pants rolled up around his knees, a dent left in the tablecloth to mark where he was sitting. Maisie wants to go, and so does Hilda, and Bunny pulls them both up off the ground, as they hold their skirts. You raise those dark eyebrows at Maisie—what will Ma say when you lift up your dress?—but she's in the water already and has knotted her dress to one side. Gertrude won't budge and you stay with her.

Maisie's laugh is like bubbles, and the bubbles pop and fade as she and the others splash their way across their mossy rocks to the crack in the mountain where the water starts. You put your finger to your lips and yes, the monkeys are there after all, screaming and swearing at each other from the tops of the trees. Gertrude looks scared and you ask her if her leg hurts and she blushes. She uncrosses her ankles and then recrosses them and you see, you can't help it, the dark vee of her dress caught between her legs. Can I have a look? Your words are out and up, caught like flies in the long strands of light-green moss hanging off the trees. She parts her legs, and oh God, it's better than going up the river, because her inner thigh is the colour of milk, and there are scratches on it, like tiny red roads. You touch the raised red skin, and her thigh swivels in on itself, and your hand is almost trapped underneath her.

It's not bleeding, you whisper, but you can't help noticing, out of the corner of your eye, the other place, which is seeping, seeping, like the river trickling between the rocks. Inside you there's hot lava, something bursting and burning and climbing in your pants and now it's your turn to knot your legs. There's a spreading stain on the tablecloth and suddenly you give Gertrude a little push as you pull the tablecloth out from under her. The cloth shrieks as you rip it in two. You give Gertrude one piece which she stuffs under her dress and the other piece, with the blood stain like Passover wine, you ball up and toss into the bushes.

Aaagg! Ghh! Aaagh! You both look up above the spotted trunks, above the frills of leaves, above the damp feathers of moss, and there are two Knysna *loeries* in the sun, mating. There's a burst of laughter that you hold inside you, a flash of joy, but all you do is squeeze Gertrude's hand so hard that she pulls it away. Come on! Look at those birds! You're almost spitting you're so excited. Their undersides are bright red and they're flipping and swivelling in the light and they disappear and then they're back again, with their swooping and grunting, like squealing pigs instead of birds.

Morry and Bunny and Hilda and Maisie come tramping up the river towards you and the birds become black dots, then vanish. *Aaggh! Aaag! Ghhh . . .* ! You missed them. You missed the *loeries. Ggggh!* Gertrude is laughing and telling them Harold sounds just like the *loeries*. I promise you. Maisie's dress is stuck to her and you notice her nipples flashing at you and she says Morry threw me in the water, won't Ma be furious. Auntie Molly gave me this dress. Where's the tablecloth? She asks you and you don't answer. You just get into the boat and shout, All aboard! It's your captain speaking.

The clouds have come over and now the water is steel and the goosebumps go up on everyone's arms. Maisie is still asking about the tablecloth and why does it matter. It was so old anyway. You know how your mother is, she says, and you do. The time she slammed her hand down on the table and squashed a hot potato. The time she threw a bell at you, and it knocked some paint off the wall. You ducked and she was mad as a snake. She embroidered that tablecloth and everything. It's starting to rain and the raindrops are bouncing on the water and this is not good either. You're rowing and this time your arms are very tired but you don't want Morry or Bunny to row. No sir. Bunny can carry the girls in and out of the water as if it's nothing. Morry plays rugby and one of his ears got bent and it stucks out like a hand. But you have to row and row and row. You could never carry Gertude like that. She's bigger than you. And so is Hilda. Maisie is your size but then she's your sister. How about that!

The river widens and you slide back under the railway bridge, your oars pointing home. There's the Serpentine, a little river off the main river, that will take you to a string of lakes: Island Lake, Langvlei and Rondevlei. It's narrow and there are tall reeds on both banks as it meanders its way to Island Lake but you're not going that way today, not with Bunny and Morry and Maisie and Hilda and Gertude in the boat, and the rain pelting down. You pass the thatched bungalows of the Fairy Knowe Hotel and the river bends again, and there's another campsite, and Freesia's Rock, a bent elbow jutting into the water. Each place has a story and you can remember your ma and dad fighting in a boat about something and the time you went springer fishing at midnight. There's the boathouse that got flooded and the pylon that collapsed in the worst storm of the century so far. Maisie says, Harold, where's the tablecloth? She's mouthing the words at you in the rain, and you say, Remember the springers we didn't catch?

Maisie is shaking and Morry has given her his wet jacket and his big arm is draped on her shoulders like a log. This is trouble, you're thinking, this and the blood on the tablecloth, the one with the cross-stitched basket. Ma, please don't shout. Everything is special in your house, everything has roots and a place and when something gets lost there's a giant aching hole no one can fill. They came from Lithuania, from London, your pa's ma and your ma's ma, and they had their Shabbat candlesticks wrapped in sheets and even the fading silk robe you were circumsized in is wrapped in tissue paper and sits in a box in your mother's cupboard. When you were five you took it out and tried to put it on and your ma saw you and she give you a bloody good hiding. She was holding it up to see if it was torn and there was a tiny brown spot which must have been your blood, but she didn't see it or say anything. She folded it and put it away and that was that.

One day your son will wear the robe at his bris, and his son, and your daughter's boy but you don't know this. It will be the colour of tea by then, and the world will have capsized and righted itself, but none of this is what you're thinking as the wind blows and Gertude crawls into the little prow of Wolfie's boat. Bunny and Morry are singing, *Daar kom die AliBama* to keep warm and Maisie's teeth are chattering. It's a summer day at the Wilderness which can be a sorry, damp story for anybody. You have been rained on during picnics, in your father's cars as they climb over the hills, between here and George and yes, on the river, so many times on the river. Of course your ma will be nervous about you getting sick, about your lungs and your heart, not to mention your nose, which points East then South, and has its own shadow. And that's another reason why you want to become a doctor. You want to stop the consumption from galloping, the fevers from burning, your rickety knees from knocking. For your ma's sake. She worries and you can see all her fears written on the walls, invisible but burning.

YOU ROW TOWARDS the wide mouth of the river, where it flows into the sea under another, bigger railway bridge which edges a small golf course. For a tickey, you and the boys dive for lost golf balls from the bridge. But today there's no golf and no diving, and the little village is sodden and sleeping.

You are scared when you open the creaking gate, when you walk down the path to the front door. Maisie is behind you, her dress still wet. You and Morry and Bunny and the other girls pulled the boat up onto the grass near the mouth of the Wilderness lagoon and Morry drove all of you the ten miles back to George. It was getting dark when Morry's father's car struggled over the hills above the sea, when you looked down at the black water of the Kaaimans River. Maisie kept talking about the bloody tablecloth and you wanted to hit her, almost as much as you wanted to put your hand on the scratches, the thin red lines on the inside of Gertrude's thighs. Gertrude was sitting in front, next to Morry and you could see the outline of her breast in the dark, a small mountain right there, right inside the car, that you wanted to climb and hold and conquer. The sound of the crickets and the smell of sea, the bit of forest, then the lights of the small town pulling you into its center, along its quiet, dark streets right up to your parents' house, next to the shop, on the corner of Meade Street and Hibernia Street.

You pass the banks of hydrangeas, their pale heads drooping in the moonlight, and you can hear the crackling radio from inside the house, a pukka English voice slicing syllables the way Nettie chops tomatoes. It's ridiculous, you say to no one in particular. Maisie whispers, What? You say, One of these days I'm going to be a doctor! Maisie laughs, one of those infectious engine laughs that can make you wet your pants. You don't look like one, she says. You wait and see! You open the door and now the two of you are inside the house, peering into the lounge. Your mother, Yetta, has her trim ankles crossed and she's wearing beige shoes pocked with holes. You know her dress has big pale flowers and she has an apron over it but you keep your eyes fixed on the holes in her shoes. Joe, your father, fiddles with the radio and then turns it off.

The food is cold, your mother says, and she's shaking with rage. You sit down at the table, opposite Maisie, and her nipples are poking fun at you. You stare at them and Maisie shifts, covering herself. Harold! Your mother is shrieking at you, and what's in her hand? It's not a potato or the dining bell. It must be what's left of your little brother, Bertie, after she swallowed him whole and spit him out. Where did you take your sister? She's screaming so loudly that her breasts are heaving like twin whales. She has something balled up in her hand. Oh God, it's the tablecloth and you can see the streaks of blood from here. You are a dirty boy, the dirtiest little boy in the world. The nuns hit you and you tried to run away but they move very quickly in those big black skirts. They got you and took you home to your mother and she was so ashamed of you and so angry and now it's happening again, except this time your shame and your longing and your own dreams are so big that they're almost poking a hole right through your pants.

We went to Ebb 'n Flow and it started to rain, you say. Sit down and eat! Your mother shrieks and the thing in her hand is a dish towel not the tablecloth and you're immensely relieved.

Your father says something about going back to the shop to lock up and your mother glares at him. Eat! You sit down and Bertie walks in, in his pajamas rubbing his eyes, and up he goes onto your mother's lap. The food is cold. Your mother was right about that. Flat meat, and boiled cabbage and boiled potatoes. I'm surprised she didn't boil the table and the chairs and the flypaper hanging from the ceiling, you're thinking, as you pick up your knife and put it down again. I'm not hungry, you tell the beige shoes and they're so angry you can almost see steam coming through the holes. Your plate lands on your lap, and then the bowl with the cabbage and there's a tinkling and breaking and clattering as everything lands on the floor. Yes, she does have the tablecloth, but it's still half on the table, one corner in her hand, and there are no baskets on this one. No sirree! Yetta! your father shouts, as if the Ice Age just ended and he stepped into the world. Maisie has one hand to her face, and there's meat on her shoulder, a nice long piece, and suddenly you start to laugh. Your mother pulls the last piece of the tablecloth off the table. You can hear tinkling, the last plate breaking and an apple, a lonely apple, rolls across the floor.

Look at you. You won't eat. Your legs are like matchsticks and now this. Supper's on the floor. We might as well decorate the lampshades with cabbage, have a potato fight, toss the meat up into the air and catch it on our heads. You've never ever wanted to eat in this house, with its brown walls and brown food and brown couch, browning like the onions always browning, browning on the stove. You like salty fish and fresh fruit and the delicacies that aren't in the cupboard. They don't go on the table when all your father's trying to do is make sure you aren't the boy in the class with bare feet and ringworm and every other kind of worm that eats into the heart of poor people.

He's a *guter*, a good man, your father is. Joseph Klein, the House for Value and Quality. General Merchant, Direct Importer and Showroom Specialists. Dealer in groceries, crockery, millinery, dress goods, boots, shoes, socks, stockings, headache powders. Everyone buys everything in his shop. Everyone loves Joe Klein. Nettie, who has worked in your house since the day you were born, always tells you how she and her husband, Isaac, sleep in the bed your father gave them when they got married. He gives extras, an extra bag of flour, two more eggs, a chocolate for the baby, smelling salts for ouma, to the customers who come into his shop sometimes to buy and sometimes just to stand and talk. A man is buying nails and he tells your father about his blind son and your father gives him a hammer too. Your father comes home and he's tired and he sits low in his chair and you know what everyone says about him and you try to say something to him but he's too, too tired. Your ma is never tired and she's smacking things on the table and the clock is ticking and there's something giddy and wrong in the house. When there's a commercial traveller sleeping on the couch in the lounge, or your dad's sister, Rose, sleeping over or your mother's, Molly, then the house is a different place and there's singing and laughing and you can eat what's put in front of you without gagging.

Tonight is not one of those nights. It's just the five of you, Ma, Pa, Maisie, you and the bloody baby and now this. Food everywhere. Maisie is bending down and picking up potatoes and now it's her bum that's showing and of course you're not going to miss looking at that. Joseph! Your ma is screaming again. Teach your son to be a gentleman! Your pa tries to give you a look but he's also noticing Maisie and her wet dress and even Bertie walks over to her and looks up her skirt. Oh God. Your mother just stepped on something soft, some cabbage, and she slid right onto the floor. Your father says something no one can understand and it sounds like Rumpelstiltskin or Gorilla. Maisie giggles her engine giggle and winds up little Bertie and then it's your dad's turn and he's laughing so much the tears are plonking onto his shoes and you see this and you think it's the funniest thing you've ever seen. No one wants to look at your ma but you know what? She's laughing harder than anybody else. She's so full of laughs and smiles that you half-expect the ceiling to fly open and confetti to come floating down on all of you, tiny bits of white and pink that cling to your hair and decorate the lampshades and the armchairs.

There are good times and bad on Meade and Hibernia. Good moves into bad like fizzy drink up your nose. Smack, cough, choke. Bad slips into good like a monkey's wedding when it's raining and the sun comes out and the rain and the sunshine are caught together in surprise. Nettie is pulling open the curtains and it's the morning of the next day. There is a long line of sun coming in through the window, a spear that pierces the heart of the brown house and it's gold suddenly and you've floated into the life you're going to live next year. Harry, she says, Mister Harry, holding up a ribbon of cabbage, *Wat het gebuur*? What happened? Nettie, Nettie, you say, and you want to sweep this fat, ebony-skinned woman with hair that's almost white into your arms. You want to show her the latest dance moves, you want to dance with her to the moon and back. But you don't. You do a little tap-tap and a shuffle and she claps for you. My God, Mister Harry, that's fancy. Save it for *Tweede Nuwejaar.* You take the cabbage from Nettie, and twirl it around your finger. Just how sour is this kraut? You ask her and you're Harold Lloyd, not Harold Klein and what was the point of becoming a doctor anyway?

The radio is on and there's cheering from jolly old England. It's the Cup Final and Thomas Woodroffe, the commentator is saying, in his frosty voice, "If there's a goal scored now, I'll eat my hat!" Ssssh, you whisper to Nettie, the way you shushed the girls on the boat at Ebb 'n Flow so you could hear the monkeys. Sssh! It's the closing minutes and Preston scores and yes, he's going to eat his hat! The crowd is roaring and Woodroffe is chewing away! Maisie, you shout and she runs into the room. Woodroffe is eating his hat! Whoa! You spin her like a top and lift her and my god, those skinny arms are strong! MAISIE! She falls and you fall. You all fall down.

CHAPTER 2

WHAT ABOUT DIALYSIS? I ask the tall doctor with his white clogs and his silvering hair. Dr. Daniels looks straight through me and beyond, his eyes on the window behind me, framing Table Mountain, the Southeaster laying the tablecloth, a long expanse of cloud spreading and dissolving over the top of the mountain. The same wind has been blowing all night and it's still blowing at seven o'clock this morning.

Your mother says no, that's not what he would have wanted. And she's probably right. All his organs have packed up, everything's tired, worn out.

Just last week Dr. Daniels told me you were a bit cuckoo. I was on the phone with him in New York City, and his gruffness took me by surprise. Your father's a hard arse, he went on. He's not OK in the top storey. If we bring the urea level to below forty, we won't have the confusion, just the hard arse. Hey, if I put that amount of urea in your blood, you'd also go cuckoo.

By the time I got here, you had stopped struggling. I miss the flailing you, grotesque as it was. At least you were alive then and not laid out flat in death's waiting room, in an end-stage coma. His GFR should be 120 but it's less than 12, Dr. Daniels tells me, his gaze flicking from the tablecloth to my swollen breasts, and then lower to my abdomen. I cross my arms.

If we could only get it up to thirty or forty . . . he's almost hopeful, as if the old *chorrie* has a chance of springing back to life again. I'm the one escaping now, staring out of the hospital window, at the curve of De Waal Drive below, wide canopied trees mantling the lower slopes of the mountain, an aching blue sky above. Yesterday I was in the air flying over Africa and now I'm here, in Groote Schuur's intensive care unit, the same hospital where you learned how to become a doctor, where, in 1967 Chris Barnard performed the world's first heart transplant.

Aloud I ask the doctor, Can he hear? We turn towards you, shrouded under white sheets, the automatic sphygmomanometer, the ECG machine, the intravenous drip and the catheter recording and monitoring your blood pressure, the rhythms of your heart, your fluids, both incoming and outgoing. I can't look properly at your face yet so I look at your left arm lying outside the sheet. A small monkey's hand, laced with dark hairs, scrubbed clean as always, the line for the IV taped to your wrist and forearm. I carefully look over the white hump of your body at your right hand, fingers and thumb peeking out from a cast. All I want to see you do, just one more time, is sit up and wash your hands, one palm slipping over the other, raising a froth of foam, hot water pouring down on them from the tap, washing all the germs away. But the hands don't move.

I don't think so, Dr. Daniels shakes his head. If we did an EEG on him right now, the waves would be flat. No wind.

He could be asleep, I say. (I drew you once, when you looked like this, face hewn from rock, beak of a nose jutting out then down, eyebrows magisterial, thick shock of silver-black hair, fast asleep in an orange-flowered armchair.)

Last week he gave us a helluva time, Dr. Daniels says. He kept pulling out his tubes with his good hand and we had to tie him down. He was pointing at all these machines saying, This is a garage. I'm not a car. Take me to the hospital!

He clears his throat. It's better this way. He's not fighting us anymore.

Hot tears scald my eyelids. I blink, swallowing hard. He was a bloody good doctor, Dr. Daniels murmurs, his white clogs squeaking apologetically on the tiled floor. I turn to the wall, watching the ECG machine line-draw your heartbeat. Call me if you have any questions, he says. And then he's gone, white coat flapping soundlessly down the corridor.

I'm pregnant, I tell the bag of fluid hooked onto the IV stand, making sure I'm at least three feet away from you, keeping a wide berth now that we're alone together. Sixteen weeks the obstetrician says. I almost didn't come, you know. William didn't want me to fly. I look at you out of the corner of my eye and I imagine I see your foot twitch, that there's a light burning inside your head somewhere, changing the grey of your face to a soft pink.

Remember what you said when you came to visit us the last time? When I took you up onto the roof of our loft?

YOU CHAPS ARE in the crow's nest!

You weren't listening to William telling you how he'd bought the loft for a song twenty years ago or when he told you that the street below was called Bond Street because of the bond traders and merchants who lived here before the factories came. You were staring at the lumps in the tar paper covering the roof, at the wooden water tower, and then finally you gazed out at the skyline. I'm in Manhattan, for Chrissake! Hell's bells, man. That's where the Jews used to live, and that's the Bowery, and there's Wall Street, for crying out loud.

When William went downstairs, I pulled open the swollen door of my studio and took you inside. You barely noticed what I'd pinned up on the walls to show you, the very beginning of my series of extinct animals. You glanced quickly at the quagga, the bandicoot, the potoroo, the Great Auk, the rat kangaroo, the gelinote and the kaka. You didn't even comment on the mess, dabs of paint everywhere—on the walls, tables, as well as my palette—postcards tacked everywhere, shelves piled high with shells, tiny animal skeletons, rusted old toys, my drawings stacked on the floor, canvases leaning against the walls. Where are the naked women? you asked me. Dad! I could hear the plaintive mix of shame and fury in my voice. Come on Betsy, you said. You've got to have the big match temperament! Trying to recover, I pointed to my favorite, the quagga, extinct cousin of the zebra with its striped head and neck, the rest of its body plain brown, a creature that lived right where you were born. You looked at it as if you were looking at a rival. But I thought you painted nudes, you repeated. As we left, the Great Auk looked at me with a beady eye and I wondered why I bothered with him, big lug of a bird lost more than a hundred years ago.

Back on the roof, we were swept up into the buzzing, grunting, honking sounds from the streets below. I sat down on an upturned flowerpot, a relic of one of my failed experiments at roof gardening.

You pulled up a broken beach chair and sat down

right next to me, talking the hind-leg off a donkey about Freemasonry, and your lodge brothers, ma's repugnance at the lodge dinners, the Royal Arch, and the Third Degree. Of course I'm not supposed to tell you, you said. It's a secret. Those chaps take it too seriously, man. They don't have a sense of humour. Your mother hates the whole thing. But she and the other girls cook for us, and they do a damn good job. When I became Master of the Lodge, we had a big dinner. All the chaps and their wives came. I made a toast. It was quite something, even though I say so myself. I brought the house down. I should have been an actor.

You got up to look over the edge of the low parapet wall. Somebody's going to have a terrible accident, you said, backing away. You know ever since my fall, my shoulder's never been the same. *Wragtig*, that was something. I was at Tjoekie van der Merwe's house, examining one of the kids who had chickenpox and I was just on my way out of the door. One minute I'm standing and the next minute I'm on my arse, twisted sideways, in their bloody conversation pit. I knew I'd fractured something. It hurt like hell. Your face was riven with melancholy, the hardest of memories. It's hard when an old person falls, you sighed. Old bones take a long time to heal and they're never the same again. Did you know I have Paget's disease?

What's that? I said airily, staring at up at the empty sky.

My spine is turning into bamboo, for Chrissake!

Wait, you said, let me take a picture of you up here. You took your camera out of the old leather camera case around your neck. Stand over there, you told me. Not near the edge, for God's sake! Your mother wants lots and lots of pictures. Damn it. There's something wrong with the mechanism.

Dad! I said, waving my hand in front of my face. You're just like your mother. Impatient as hell. This camera is not as good as my old one. Hang on, chaps. Let's get those towers in the background. They look like giant tuning forks!

You caught me squinting, the sun in my eyes.

Carefully you put the camera back into its case. I was so small they thought I'd never grow up, you went on, My legs were like matchsticks. I've survived a lot of those buggers. Half of them dropped dead on the golf course.

The river was bad this year. I only went to Ebb 'n Flow once. It was too low to get very far. Hard to believe that we used to dive off the bridge at the mouth of the lagoon. Now you'd break your bloody neck on all that sand. Remember that time you curled up in the front of the boat? That was one helluva storm. Your mother doesn't go in the boat anymore. She never liked the water, not the way you did, or Simon. The last time he came from America, I took his girls up the river. They wore those headphones the whole time. What do you call them again?

Walkmen.

Betsy, don't forget to remind me about the penicillin. Later that night, you remembered anyway, parting the giant curtain that separated our sleeping area from the rest of the loft, a big ziplock bag full of bottles and bottles of different antibiotics in your hands. Here take these. Call me in the morning.

Dad! (I scrambled back into the jeans that I was pulling off.) I don't want your pills. What? They're not good enough for you? No, it's not that, Dad. When I get sick, I try to boost my immune system. Your immune system? What bloody rubbish are you talking? What do you know about immune systems?

You walked straight into the makeshift bathroom without knocking, straight into William who was thankfully just brushing his teeth. You handed him the bag full of pills. Compliments of the chef. Take in case of emergency. Wash down with a good Shiraz.

William had thrown up two Sheetrock walls and a door at the back of the loft, an instant bedroom just for you. You spilled out of the little room, telling us stories, asking us to help you read a map of the city, your glasses perched on your nose, your dressing gown gaping open. Dad! You looked down and tightened the cloth belt. You're a bloody Victorian, just like your grandmother, you scolded. William, did you know that my daughter used to be the president, secretary and treasurer of the Worcester Teetotallers' Society?

William's answer was an unblinking stare over the top

of the newspaper, levelled right at you. You as well! You said this with a sense of great injury. You buggers are against me, like all the rest of them. Your mother too! One day, when I'm dead you'll be sorry. You folded your arms, chin thrust out, feet crossed at the ankles. You know how I want to go?

I shot a look at William. This is an old one.

I'm in my surgery and there's a patient stretched out on the examination table. I go over, and I'm just about to put my stethoscope on his chest, when BOOM! Massive heart attack! I drop dead on the floor right next to him. No bloody hospital for me. No doctors, none of those clowns and cowboys you get these days. Jesus Christ man, they all specialize. The heart chappie doesn't know where the abdomen is. The neurologists don't go past the neck. Forget about the pathologists and the surgeons. They don't know what a patient is! They've never been to his house, met his wife and kids, his mother-in-law, his dog—some of those dogs, man, they eat a Jew for breakfast every morning! But you know what I mean. In the old days, we used to do everything, from obstetrics to appendectomies. There weren't all those bloody machines. You had to use the machine up here! You jab your finger at your head.

The old chaps were expert clinicians. They knew how to take a history. They knew how to listen to a heartbeat. They weren't painting by fucking numbers. You know what one of my patients calls me? A deaf Afrikaans woman whose five children I've delivered? *Dokter God!* (pointing that same jabbing finger up into the sky, making the sign for God.)

Two nights before you left, I took you to see *Guys and Dolls* at the Martin Beck Theatre on Forty-fifth Street, in the dazzling heart of the city. I wore big earrings, a swingy black dress, my hair pulled back. You sat tilted forward on the edge of your seat as Nathan Lane and Faith Prince sang and danced the Damon Runyon stories of your youth. Bloody marvelous! you said, turning to me at intermission, the high beams of your enthusiasm shining right at me. I can't believe I'm here, my girl. You did me a big favour. A wave of feeling spread across your features, black eyes softening, a rueful smile catching at me.

Harry the Horse! Nicely-Nicely Johnson! Mindy's Restaurant! Maxie knew pages and pages off-by-heart. Me and him and Mickey Levin used to go to . . . never mind. Before your time. Still, District Six was full of all kinds of characters. It's all gone now. Those bastards bulldozed the life out of Cape Town. Your mother and I saw it coming. It was not long after the war when the Nationalists came into power and the signs went up, *Blankes, Nie-Blankes*. Well it's all changing again. Who knows what's going to happen. It's bloody fascinating, though. I just hope I live long enough to see the *verkramptes verkramped*!

The curtain lifted on the Second Act. The lights sparkled on your glasses. We leaned forward in unison, uncomfortably twinned. Later, over a prized Pinotage you brought all the way from South Africa in your hand-luggage, you made one of your toasts, to mine host and mine heir! To my youngest. You swirled the black-red wine, took a concentrated sip. To Betsy Klein. President, secretary and treasurer. . . .

I waved my hands at you. Dad, please!

Chaps, you know what Hannes Laubscher, the wine-maker, said? This Pinotage isn't for sissies. I've had it for five years now, sitting in my cellar, waiting for the right occasion. I don't drink this kind of wine with everyone. You took a big sip, filling your mouth, your head tilted back slightly. It's their first crop from some new plantings. William held his glass to the light. Lots of red fruit, he reported, after tasting it. Sleek body. Vanilla and prune on the finish.

Bullshit, man, you told him, as you drained your glass. Here, have some more. Do you know what a Pinotage is made of? you barked at William. Well, it's a blended wine, Pinot Noir and Cinsault, you told him, topping up his glass and yours.

There are all kinds of wine drinkers, William. Those who like to talk, those who like to drink and then there are the chaps who make the wines. Those blokes are the ones you can trust. I've learned a lot, you know, even though I don't trample the grapes myself. I hear it from the horse's mouth, right from the farmers them-selves when they come into my surgery complaining about their wives and their workers, when they sit there with chest pains and high blood pressure because it rained too much or too little.

You know what makes Robertson special?

(Robertson is a town, I muttered to William.)

The southeaster in the summer, cooling off the vineyards in the late afternoon. Limestone soil. Where we are, the soil is mostly alluvial, with a little clay. Now they're starting to plant up in the hills. Maybe we should open the Meerlust Rubicon, let it breathe a little. Hell's teeth, man. Meerlust's a place to see. Those buggers have been in business since 1693.

William, I'd love to take you around, show you the Boland. You've got to meet the people, talk to them, seeing what's going on. Never mind the politics. It's the most beautiful place you'll ever see. Betsy can tell you about the mountains, the Hex River Valley. You haven't tasted a grape until you've had an Alphonse Lavalle, our Hanepoot, our Barlinkas. I had a patient once, in Sandhills. Farmed export grapes. We used to picnic near there. Betsy, remember the white, white sand and the little river with those smooth riverstones? Remember Ockert Pretorius? He was killed at a railroad crossing, train went right over his car. I loved that man.

Tears started in your eyes. You cleared your throat. We could go to the Wilderness. I could take you up the river in my boat. Now that's paradise. I've been going there every summer since I was a boy. Betsy can tell you. She and Simon used to climb up a tree with the other kids and grab hold of the rope and swing right into the middle of the river. Ssshwwwssh! Boomps! And then they would swim over and I'd pull them in. This is your captain speaking. Don't rock like the boat like that or you'll walk the plank. Remember the time we had eight in the boat and it sat so low in the water? Your mother doesn't like the river. She can't even swim. My wife comes from a long line of learned men, William. Chaps who thought they knew everything.

You moved your shoulder, wincing. It's never been the same since I broke it. Fell on my arse, I did. Rolled from the frying pan almost into the fire. Hey, I'm glad I gave those buggers a bloody big fright. I was screaming my head off. They should have put something up there. If it wasn't me, it would have been somebody else. I was in the middle of telling them that God was punishing them for their stupid laws. That's why it hasn't rained for months and months. He's trying to tell you something. One minute I'm up on my feet and the next minute I'm all twisted up.

You know what I always tell them? *Ek is 'n wit kaffir!* That fixes them!

I whispered "white nigger" in William's ear and he looked from me to you, then back to me again, still swinging on the rope over the river, not sure where to let go.

How many stories up did you say your restaurant

was? You were looking out of the windows, staring at the sparkling towers, your body tilted forwards on the edge of the couch. My wife is afraid of heights, She'd never go up there, not in a million years. Did I tell you we went to the Waterfront for my birthday? One of those fancy new places. I could have stayed at home but your mother really wanted to go. There's an aquarium near there. They have a plaster model of the coelacanth, the big fish they caught near East London, the one they thought had been extinct for millions of years. The chappie who found it kept his boat at one of the Knysna lakes. You can't imagine how hot under the collar people got in those days. No one wanted to believe we were related to a bloody fish.

In the morning, you were standing at the foot of my bed when I woke up, in your dressing gown and slippers. Dad! I shouted, pulling the covers over my head. Get out!

I was just looking for the light switch, I heard you telling William, who was up and drinking his first cup of coffee. I can't turn the lights on in the toilet.

What the bloody hell is this? Bladderwrack? Milk thistle? You were shouting from the bathroom, reading the names of the vitamins and homeopathic remedies stacked on a shelf above the sink. Scullcap? Devil's Claw? Nux Vomica? Belladonna? What's this one over here? Elderwort? I'll give you Elder Fucking Wort! Where are those antibiotics? BETSY!

The toilet flushed and flushed, spasms of water

gurgling, the old plumbing rattling. Dad! I was dressed in paint-spattered jeans and a shirt of William's, my hair streaming. You were standing over the toilet, pouring pills from a bottle of Butcher's Broom into the bowl. Empty vials and bottles littered the floor. Betsy Ilana Klein! You're a throwback to the nineteenth century! You flushed the toilet again, and the pipes thudded and whooped in a kind of death agony.

My pills aren't good enough for you? Penicillin would have saved your grandfather's life, you ungrateful little bitch!

Dad, you're not my doctor.

Of course I'm your doctor. I'm your father, for God's sake!

Stop! I was screaming now. Get out of the bathroom! In a flash, you picked up a razor off the top of the sink. I'm going to kill myself! Ridiculously, you waved the blade at your own throat. William! Suddenly he was in the tiny room with us, between us, blocking the light with his large frame. Give it to me, he said, and you handed him the razor, between panting breaths. Your mother was right. I should never have come. This whole country is for the birds!

You retreated into silence afterwards, eyes hooded, your beak of a nose a study in granite displeasure, the corners of your mouth drawn tight. William fixed you with another long, cool look and you stared past him, at the maze of buildings and streets, lost in the dense weave of your thoughts. This last day in New York City you spent packing and repacking your suitcases in the little room we built for you, wearing the solemn, silent dignity of an aggrieved Carmelite nun.

In the cab on the way to the airport, you turned to me, as if waking from a long sleep. But that was one helluva show, wasn't it? I bet my sister, Maisie, hasn't even seen it. Maxie would have loved every minute of it. The chaps would have eaten it up! What did you say that girlie's name was? What? She had a nice pair of legs, that girl. And what a voice! You know most of the buggers are dead now? They say only the good die young.

The cab pulled over in front of the British Airways terminal and we were on the curb now. You reached into the trunk for your suitcase and your carry-on bag, suddenly yelping with pain. My left shoulder! Bloody bastards! I tried to lift the bags and you shouted, No! No! Don't touch them! In one gesture, I paid the cab driver and took them anyway. Let go! There's wine in there! Don't hold it like that! You're like a bloody animal! I dropped both bags between us, took your shoulders in my hands, stared at you through the wrong end of a telescope, the familiar knots grouping inside me, the old cold panic setting in. The sound of my own voice was harsh, jangled. Dad, I'm going to get back into that cab and leave you right here all by yourself if you don't listen to me.

I slipped a dollar into the machine that dispensed luggage trolleys and easily lifted the bags onto it, my arms used to lifting and moving my own large paintings. We have to go over there, I pointed to the doors breathlessly, stating the obvious. A small smile played on your lips. I always said you were my strongest child.

In the long queue for the South Africa Airways flight to Johannesburg, you shrank into yourself again. I looked around for a familiar frown, the right set of shoulders, scanning the travellers gliding across the floor for any glimmer of recognition. It would please you to have someone slap you on the back with a Hello, Dr. Klein, Hello, Harry. You were known in the small Boland town where you'd practiced the art of medicine for over forty years. You were used to shopkeepers' greetings, uniformed schoolchildren nodding at you from their bicycles, servants and mothers and babies and schoolteachers, farmers, fellow Freemasons, nurses and garage mechanics all paying their respects, with handshakes and dimpled smiles, some shy, some bold, your friends and your enemies all noticing you when you walked down the street, when you parked your car, when you dropped into the same seat you always sat in at the local bioscope.

No one knew you here. We shuffled forwards towards the check-in counter, trapped in the vast desert of your loneliness. You were looking up, a large, grey-haired child staring at the signs and the flags and the lights, and it was hard not to feel the drift of your melancholy soaked reverie. We exchanged one last juddering hug, before you walked past the sign that said,

PASSENGERS ONLY BEYOND THIS POINT. You turned to look back at me one last time, lifting your hand, and my hand was lifted too, and I wasn't sure which one of us was which.

CHAPTER 3

IT'S BLOWING LIKE hell, Ma says, when she enters the room, patting her thinning hair into place, attempting to restore her Queen Elizabeth II do to its proper form. Oh, *chookie*, she murmurs, clenching me tightly in her arms. I'm seven again and I'm almost throttled by her but I grit my teeth and step back, almost stepping on the toes of Simon, who flew here from America just like me, only three days earlier, the good son, the better boy. He's looking at the screens and the graphs around your bed, trying to read the book of your body from the inside out. Bigger structures than you're used to, I say to Simon the scientist, explorer of the mouse genome, the human bitter-taste receptor, sea urchins, yeast. It's all relative, he answers, his mouth wan between the covers of his brown beard.

Betsy, you look tired! I brought some food for you in my bag. You know what they wanted to do yesterday? Take out his gall bladder! I put my foot down. I said, No! Leave him alone! Hasn't he been through enough already? And look how it's blowing out there!

Waves scud across Table Bay, trees stretch sideways, the *cape doctor* blowing everybody's germs out to sea except yours.

I checked the date on it. It's still OK. Ma hands me a strawberry yogurt with a plastic spoon.

I'm not hungry, I say, turning to Simon. Do you want it?

No, he shakes his head mutely. Unopened, the yogurt stands at your bedside between the tubes, trays, buttons and nozzles.

There's a yellow smell in the air, not medicine or machine but a whiff of what's lurking inside you, under the white mound of the hospital sheets. Funnily enough, his arm is healing really well, Ma says. When he fell right in front of me, I thought he was going to get right up and brush himself off. Instead, he just lay there groaning. I still thought he was up to his old tricks. Even when he said, Chaps, I'm buggered. You blighters have got me this time, I thought he was performing.

When they wheeled him into surgery, he was terrified, she says, her hands raised to her face.

All he had was a broken arm, I say.

It was a pathological fracture! Ma is loud, emphatic.

Was it cancer? I ask.

Shush! Don't ask so many questions! I was waiting for him to come out of the recovery room. Hours and hours went by. Five or eight, I don't even remember. Something terrible happened in there.

It wasn't here? Simon says.

Ma shakes her head. It was at the other place. They brought him here the next morning.

I notice a piece of torn paper lying near you, a white leaf flickering on a silver surface. Ma hands it to me. He wrote this down when they had him on a respirator. One of the nurses gave him a pencil and a piece of paper.

I read the extravagant swirl of your doctor's handwriting. "Not talking = madness."

Your face is the Brandwacht, Outeniqua, Langeberg, Hottentot's Holland, eagles screaming as they glide over its crags. Your thin sliver of a mouth is slightly parted, lips dry. Your lids are sealed, rimmed with short black eyelashes pointing straight down. I want to take that alligator clip I stole from a battery and clip it onto your ear lobe, the way I did when I was ten and you were taking a nap in your orange chair. You levitated then, as you suddenly woke up with tiny steel teeth digging into your ear. I couldn't believe my eyes, Daddy. I made you fly.

Everyone's been calling me, Ma says. The Laubschers, Aprils, de Wets, du Toits, Mr. van Rensburg, Lucky Mopane, the Griels, Mrs. Grobbelaar, Antjie Foeitog. All the patients want to know how he is and then the family keeps calling, Molly and Poppy, Bertie, Pamela, Ricky, Benny . . . the phone just rings and rings all day long. What can I tell them?

He's so still, Simon says, his voice cracking. If only he'd say something. He's crying, and I'm crying and Ma has gone to get tissues and tea and talk to the nurses and call people back. Outside the southeaster still blows and blows, whistling, wheezing through the leaves, through the bricks in the walls, making the roofs creak and the dust spin.

Remember the old cottage hospital before it was torn down, white walls and a green roof set on a rise above a stream and a terraced garden, Dad leaving us in the car while he made his rounds? First we played under the giant *kaffirboom* collecting lucky beans and then we followed the stream under its tiny bridges, racing leaf-boats, the sun sparkling through the trees, on the water, turning the leaves into gold green stars. I can still see the beans in my hand, kidney-shaped with a bright red streak in the center. Si, there were three and sixty-seven? More like five hundred, Bets. Remember the big medicine bottle we kept them in?

There were scented trees in that garden. White blossoms? Pink?

You've got to have something to eat, Ma says, coming back into the glinting room. Did you have anything on the plane?

I'll be alright, I say, and then I swear your foot moved

and you almost turned over. Simon, Ma! I'm shouting now, and it seems as if you're smiling ever so faintly, as if you know I'm here. Oh *chookie*, she says again, You must be seeing things. It's the jet lag, Simon offers.

I half expect you to sit up bolt upright and say, *Ag*, bullshit man, to your only son, but the wall of your face stays closed, eyelashes pointing straight down, the snowy mound of your chest barely stirring.

The doctor said they might be able to get his GFR to a thirty or forty . . . Simon shakes his head when I say this and he's talking now, about congestive heart failure, and the kidney not being able to filter enough extra salt and water out of the blood to lighten the heart's load, the body's total fluid volume increasing instead of decreasing.

WE'RE BACK IN the sea of bad blood and I wish I had a net, a fish net or any kind of net to clean up the mess, to strain the poison out, to fix you up. The great saphenous vein, the small saphenous vein, the inferior vena cava . . . all your roads are buggered up. I make a left, taking the carotid artery, and now we're driving a car together, the new turquoise and white Vauxhall you bought from Frank de Vos when you turned forty. We're going to Slanghoek on a house call because one of the le Rouxs is sick and you think it's pneumonia. You leave me at the turn off in the dark, and I look at the National Road which heads North towards Joh'burg, and then at your road, the Slanghoek road to the le Roux's farm. The rain is pelting down and your car, your turquoise and white Vauxhall, slips into the shadow of the Brandwacht mountains like a deep-sea fish, like our old coelacanth friend. I'm praying for you, Doctor Dad.

Hennie called at nine o'clock and he's the young one, the young Mr. le Roux. He was having trouble with his breath. "*My asem,*" he said on the phone, "*Maak my seer.*" "It hurts when I breathe." You looked at Ma who was sitting with her feet up and the sock basket in her lap. Those le Rouxs are animals, you said to her, clearing your own throat. Still, you took your black bag with a penicillin injection and some cough mixture. You left the ECG machine behind. It's dark, pitch-dark and you remember me asking in the car last Sunday, Why is it called Slanghoek?

In the rear-view mirror, you could see Simon making a thousand snakes with his fingers. Then he reached over to tickle me. You could hear me giggling like a giggle machine and now what's in your head as you drive is me laughing and the words, Snake Corner. You love the rain driving at the windshield and the madness outside, the trees bent over double in the wind, and the grapevines like arthritic fists, their trunks stripped for the winter. Those buggers were praying for rain, and now they've got it and perhaps the Breede river will flood and you and Ma will take us there to marvel at what the water has done to the land. The river is usually as wide as this narrow road but when it pours down like this it spreads and that's why the bridge is so bloody long. You and me and Ma and Simon will stand at the side of the national road, and watch as the brown water surges around tiny islands of land, around trees caught in the suddenly expanded river. We will stand in silence, a kind of prayer for the skeletal trees, for what's gone and what's coming.

This isn't the George rain, the Wilderness rain you grew up with, the long, sloughing sigh of wetness that crept into the cupboards, the blankets, the long-lasting sea smell that's still in your nose. This is the Boland, and your life and your life's work is circled by mountains. There are long, dry spells, blistering summers where the grapes swell and ripen, and the fruit trees get heavy with their fruit. The winters are wet and cool, and occasionally it rains like this, a kind of furious drumbeat of water on the roof of the car, on the corrugated iron roof of the house, a shout of Yes, to the prayers of the churchgoers begging for rain, the grape farmers and the wine farmers on their knees before God.

It's the wrong kind of begging, you tell them. You better ask God to forgive you for Sharpeville four years ago, for pass laws, for your rotten divide and conquer, separate but equal, your rubbishing apartheid laws. But no one really listens to the Jew who's good for driving out in the dark, for twisting dislocated shoulders into place, for listening to breaking hearts. You fix anyone for a cent, a tickey, ten rand or twenty. Doctor God makes you feel better, and you can go back to beating your dog, or your wife or your *klonkie*. Doctor God will fix your *klonkie* too. He'll fix anyone. He doesn't mind touching white skin or black, and all the brown shades in between.

The blinking, shifting windshield wipers are all that stand between you and the soaring rain-soaked Brandwacht mountains. Here there's a cluster of *pondokkies*, a trail of smoke lifting into the air. There's one le Roux's farm, the older le Roux. You pass the turnoff to Hennie's farm because it's impossible to see everything on a night like this. At least the Vauxhall is dry and you don't have to sit with water dripping down your neck. You make a U-turn on the lonely road and now you're driving on a dust road that's becoming mud. With a lurch in and out of a ditch and a rev of the Vauxhall's engine, you drive into the heart of Slanghoek, a crisscrossing of wine farms, of veld, of twisting snakes and whatever else wasn't shot and killed by the farmers years ago. Once in a while someone spots the eyes of a leopard in the dark, a child steps on a scorpion, a baboon tears open the arm of a motorist who stops to take pictures. But the real night monsters are the people, who fight and claw at each other when it gets dark. Hennie is a drinker and you never like to go out on a night like this to someone who has been drinking the way Hennie drinks. But when he coughed on the phone, a drowning, lung-sounding cough that caught you, you shouted, *Ja*, I'm coming. Put the bloody dog away.

In the car you're thinking of what Hennie's wife, Marietjie, said about his soaring temperature, and his struggling to get out of bed to lead the water into the garden even though it was pouring outside. *Roes, dit lyk soos roes*, she said, when you asked her what he left on his hankies. Phlegm that looks like rust. Dad is sick as a dog. Doctor Harris is at his bedside and there are no goddamn antibiotics. The mould hasn't sprouted in Fleming's lab and your own father is dying. Your hands clench on the wheel and now the dark is suddenly as black as death. You're driving inside the belly of eternity and there's nothing but boiling terror in your veins.

You're at the river now, an offshoot off the Breede, and you drive slowly over the causeway. The tires are in the water. What was is it that floated past the two-headed dog? The boat, the floating leaf, the little ship that goes straight into the endless end? Rome is divided into three parts and the Germans are marching to Poland. Or is it Pretoria? The water is spraying the car doors. Ssssssh.

The car stops. You turn the key in the ignition. Click. And then you laugh. You're buggered now. You look out of the car window and it's hard to see where the water begins and ends. Suddenly you're pushing against the door with your shoulder. It opens and you're crossing the causeway, your black bag on your head, the water gripping and tugging at your ankles. It's blind man's buff but you're Sarah. No wait, you're someone's *nonnie* carrying a petrol can, a water boy diving for golf balls, Moses high-stepping it across the waves. Lucky you have gills and a tail on a night like this.

You're out of the water and into the woods. A kind of scrub, really. Low trees and the shoulder of a hill in the semi-demi-starlight, the washed-out moon covered up with clouds, wrapped like a newborn. Mewling from somewhere. A barking, pleading and then a cough from deep within the lungs and the final ugly spitting of all the *roes* that was inside your father for all those years. All the years of rusting up in the shop on the corner of Meade and Hibernia Streets. The bags of nails and the sign outside and the till rusted up, so you couldn't even bust it open with a hammer. Sold for a song. Everything that was anything is gone. And your feet are terribly wet, unbearably cold and you're the one that's going to pay for this bloody game in the night, for that animal Hennie le Roux who probably breathed in his own vomit and got it into his lungs and now this. Fucking pneumococcal pneumonia.

The syringes are in the bag. Penicillin and then erythromycin and tetracycline, since you're almost sure it's bacterial. Not a coronary, you decided when you left the ECG machine behind. You can tell from the sound of a man's breathing, the timbre of his cough, the way he complains and sometimes what he doesn't say. You listen all day long to people saying, Doctor, I have a pain and you know that pain has many faces, and occasionally wears a long, pointy hat, with frills and bells. Sometimes it's dull and other times it lights up like a bloody Christmas tree.

Hennie slurred on the phone. There was drunken shame in his voice, and terror at the pain. *Roes met die hoes*. Rust with the coughing. You've come to love the shades of Afrikaans, the language that's a mirror into the soul of these earthbound people who tower over you. It's also the heartbeat of the *volkies* on the farm. Their voices pluck at you in the dark, as one squelching foot follows another. *Onnosel. Onnosel.* Bloody idiot. Hennie's not yet forty-five and his liver's grey with scars. A dog starts to bark and now your heart is suddenly beating in your ears and the Hennie fear is completely gone and it's you on the block. There's a racket on the farm, not one dog but ten and a door slams somewhere. Hennie's screaming. You know it's him because there's a flurry of coughing and his croaking voice shouting, *Voertsek*! Then a leaden crack, the sound of a gun.

This is it, Harold. The pee dribbles down your leg and you look into the sky racked with clouds, scarred like Hennie's liver and your own failing courage. You put down the black bag. Hennie thinks it's a *tokolosh*, a bogeyman, a *skollie*, a *tsotsi*, someone dark as this velvety night, coming to get him, his wife Marietjie, and their two little boys, Petrus and Kosie. Help, help, you shout, but the dogs don't listen. Oh God, you're walking past the convent again, and your pants are soiled and the nuns are coming to get you, sailing towards you like a thousand black ships. They're going to tell your mother. HELP, you scream, Hennie, you bloody bastard! It's me. It's the doctor!

You've stopped walking. It's you and the cocked gun and Hennie drawing a circle around his family. He's scared of the *impis*, the *swart gevaar*, all the bumps and the lumps in the night. Hennie, put the gun down. Put the bloody gun down. This time, the dogs stop and you can almost see their ears pricking. Help! Help! *My kar is in die rivier.* My car is stuck in the river. Hennie coughs and he asks, "*Dokter?*" "*Ja,*" you shriek, "*Jou blerrie onnosel!*" Hennie laughs.

You're standing in the kitchen drinking tea from the saucer and the kitchen smells of warm milk and wet dog. Hennie's gone back to bed and you're wearing his huge pants tied around your waist with a rope and his *veldskoene* are on your feet. It's a big joke because you're two bricks and a tickey high and Hennie was a scrum-half for Western Province once, and he's six foot four. Your feet, not much bigger than your wife's feet, are lost in these big man's shoes. Hennie's blonde, red-eyed wife, Marietjie, is standing over you and she has your clothes in a plastic bag. I told you to put the dogs away, you tell her, your voice gruff. They eat a Jew for breakfast every morning.

Hennie's flat on his back in the bedroom, waiting for Doctor God and when you come in, his hand reaches for you. *Ekskuus tog*, he apologizes, his cheeks flaming red. You fill the syringe with penicillin, and Hennie's eyes watch you. Don't worry, man, you tell him. It doesn't hurt me. Then it's over and he's rolling down his sleeve. What about the car, doctor? The battery got wet, you tell him.

He's coughing again, and he shows you the rust-coloured phlegm inside his hanky and you look at it carefully. It's your father's five-penny hanky. It's still raining at the Wilderness and you and Morry and Bunny came home late with Wolfie's boat and the tablecloth was gone and your mother shouted at you and your father shouted at you and you never ever forgot where you threw the tablecloth. Years later when you took Simon and Betsy up the river to Ebb 'n Flow, you went looking behind some bushes for the tablecloth but it was gone. Even the picture of the basket.

We can pull the car out with the tractor. Hennie coughs again and you give him the cough mixture. Two tablespoons every four hours. You call Mrs. God on the telephone and you tell her about the car and how you screamed help, help, and Hennie thought you were one of the *volkies* drunk in the night. You don't say anything about the pants in the plastic bag and already you've put them in the same place you put the tablecloth with the basket picture. It's past midnight when you drive into town past the blue gum trees, over the railway bridge. Mrs. God is asleep and you walk into Simon's room and watch your son sleeping and then you go to my room and you stand at the door. She looks just like Maisie, you're thinking as I roll over. Then you tiptoe away.

In the morning when you've already gone to the hospital, I see the farmer's shoes, *veldskoene* so big they must belong to a giant and then I see Hennie's pants, hanging over the chair. Something happened in the night and my father grew so big that his head burst through the roof like a beanstalk. Ma says, no, his car got stuck in the causeway because of the rain. These are the farmer's pants. I smell them and they smell like farmer's pants and the big shoes are caked with mud. Even when the pants and the shoes have left the house and gone back to the farm in Slanghoek, I can see their shadow in your bedroom, the shadow of a father the size of a giant.

CHAPTER 4

MA PRESSES A Saran-wrapped hospital sandwich into my hand, white bread, white butter, a thin slice of cheese folded back. Eat! She says. I peel the layer of buttery plastic off the bread, and roll it into a tight ball which I place next to the unopened yogurt. We are living in the garage with you, Dad, and the nurses are here to look under the bonnet.

Outside, the wind has shifted from the southeast to the northwest. The *cape doctor* has packed his bags and gone home. Rain is sweeping across the slopes of the mountain and on De Waal Drive the cars have their windshield wipers going. I'm looking out of the window and behind me Simon is talking to a nurse about the cardiac arrhythmias on the computer screen. Yees, she says, fluting and elongating her vowels. It's the potassium building up.

You're supposed to be eating for two, Ma says, after I take two bites of the pale sandwich and toss it in the rubbish bin. I'm not hungry, I answer, as I always have. She looks at the small carry-on suitcase parked near the foot of your bed. Is that all you brought? She pulls the suitcase over to her by its pull-out handle. It falls on its side with a soft thump. She props it up again, and unzips it. Her hands are on my clothes, searching for the right things. She holds up a simple dark red shift and matching pants with an elasticated waistband. Not bad, she says. If it still fits you. You can borrow one of my jerseys to wear with it.

I don't tell her that I bought it the day before yesterday. When the shop assistant asked if I was looking for something for a special occasion, I said, the occasion I'm looking for is a service, of the religious kind. I want something that's a little bit solemn but definitely expandable and I'm taking it in a suitcase on a plane, that shouldn't be too crushable. I'm pregnant you see. The service is for a person I know very well who isn't feeling so very well, who isn't, in fact, feeling anything very much at all, in the current situation he's in. At least that's what I've been told. And it's not a prayer meeting. The religious service, I mean.

(He's not an old friend although he could be, but never has been. He's older than a brother, but sometimes just as jealous. He's close to my mother but he's not her sister, or her best friend either. Married he has been, and to her, but it's been on the wry side, with its own twist of bitters. So, festive the dress should not be, celebrating an occasion as spartan as this, but he never was too serious, and he was capable of lots of laughs, both giving and receiving, as well as all the other ills, which he could both incite and cure, in his very best mode.)

I know just what you need. And it's not something you crush or chew, or take lightly. She handed me a deep-red dress, with three-quarter length sleeves and a scooped neckline. When I looked at myself in the mirror, I saw a woman from overseas, who left donkeys years ago.

The saleswoman sang from the cash register, snipping the tags, You'll get so much wear out of it. You can dress it up. You can dress it down. You'll be able to wear it after the baby comes. See, you can lift up the top and nurse!

He knows you're pregnant, Ma says. I told him last week when he still had the breathing tube in. He jiggled all his wires and cords and hoses.

You don't budge when she tells me this, not even the slightest quiver of the IV or tremor of the blood-pressure cuff. How about his eyes? I ask, Were they open? Yes, she says. Very.

I look at the stage curtains of your eyelids, ready to roll them back with a fingertip, to see if you can look at me just once more time to let me know you really heard what she was saying.

They thought it was the *horries*, Ma says. When he was thrashing like that. At one point they even poured whiskey down his throat to try to calm him down. Simon lifts his eyes off the heart monitor. Uremia is like a kind of drunkenness.

I wouldn't wish this on my worst enemy, Ma says, with a shiver. No one should have to suffer the way he did, not even a dog. Outside, sunlight still gleams on the wet road, and there's a tangle of clouds and blue sky swirling around the mountain. A chill sweeps over me, and now I'm shivering too in this icebox of a room, with its stainless-steel surfaces and dials and gauges. We could be in the deep freeze, I tell Simon. Here, take my cardigan, Ma says, and she hands me something light-blue off the back of her chair. Thanks, I say, putting my arms into the sleeves of the cardigan. It's loose on me, several sizes too big and smells of camphor and old perfume, the smell of Romanze, the only dress shop for ladies in the town of Worcester that had black-velvet blazers from Paris, and jerseys that fell between your hands.

THERE WAS ALWAYS a tea tray on the antique table where Fay Sampson sat, her long hair twisted in a sleek, brown bun, dark red outlining her full lips, often dressed in a cool shiver of a blouse, dark pencil skirt and perfectly angular jacket showing off her neat waist, black-and-white sling back shoes dressed with rosettes sharp as

French pastries. If I'm not mistaken there was a knot of big pearls at her throat, catching the soft interior light. Wherever you looked there were dresses hanging, flat and empty, waiting to be filled with dreams. Some glittered with gold thread, others announced their presence with swirling, promising paisley and a select few shied away from immediate attention, dark and sultry, waiting to cling to the right shape. There was a faded pink chaise lounge where Stan the dog slept, an ancient asthmatic poodle, the fur below his eyes damp with rheum. I sat on the edge of the chaise, finding a biscuit on the tray as Fay poured a cup of tea for my mother. There were no windows.

A curtain separated a room where the Malay alteration hands sat, the clatter of their sewing machines and the occasional glimpse of their presence a comfort to the ladies sweeping in and out of the dressing rooms, sashaying backwards and moving in closer to the big mirrors, finding many faces in their reflections, their heads tipped, their arms akimbo. No this one's too tight. *Kyk hoe vet ek lyk!* Look how fat I look! This one's just perfect. *Pragtig!* Fay was a careful presence, cigarette in a cigarette holder, never ready to lie. She was the high priestess of Romanze and would only tell you the truth. At least, that's what all the ladies believed, even the hoity-toity farmers' wives from the Valley. When Fay approved of the way you looked, you bought whatever you were trying on, no matter how much it cost.

My mother was thickening at the waist, middle age congealing like a slow-cooking stew. Fay cast an expert eye through the racks, precise as a surgeon. Stella, try the yellow and white linen suit. It looks good on. And the red one as well. I patted the dog, trying to avoid the sticky parts while my mother stepped out of her skirt, her legs still girlish. Betsy! She called me in to help her with the yellow suit. She couldn't reach the bottom of the zip. I was in the dressing room with her, the air still with talcum powder, stale lipstick. At ten, my head bobbed close to hers, the fresh extremity of a two-headed monster. In the mirror, we glided past each other's eyes like midnight rowers. I won't see you if you don't see me.

Then I was back on the couch with Stan, sinking into dull contentment, watching the dresses rise and fall. There was no end to the places the dresses would take you. Romanze was on the other side of paradise, where there were no screams in the night, no knife wounds. Even the smoke from Fay's cigarette breathed elegance, the promise of leaving your own skin and travelling far, far away.

She picked the yellow linen in the end. The red dress had a lopsided bow at the neck and the black lace dress Fay handed to her through the curtain was too small. There was no need to ring anything up because Stella had an account at Romanze. She was one of the lucky ones who got a special box at the beginning of each season, delivered to the house and filled with dresses wrapped in tissue paper, hand-picked by Fay, I thought these would look good on you, on a creamy notecard in Fay's long longhand. She tried them on and you and I nodded or shook our heads. Buy it or put in back in the box, sighing between its wrappings. We watched without watching, you bustling in and out of the bedroom, walking your doctor walk, clearing your throat. I was on your bed, head cupped on one hand, raised up on an elbow.

OUTSIDE THE HOSPITAL, water drips from the wide-canopied trees on the lower slopes of the mountain. The monkeys are throwing confetti in the wet sunlight. It doesn't matter to them that ma has lost her looks and that we can't find them hidden in the tissue paper in the box of dresses. Her looks have just upped and gone, folded into her disappointment at living a country life with a country doctor, at living with you.

She's looking past you now, to the other side. And you're quiet, finally. The years of your voice have ended. You've stopped shouting, calling all of us names, swearing and joking and needling, talking about George and the War and the Freemasons, your favorite songs, the doctors you hate, the patients you treat and everything else in between, from the stock market to a film you once saw, to *The Water Babies* which your mother loved and read to you over and over again, and your father, your poor father, who could barely make it past the first page. What we can hear in this room is a very faint echo—hell's teeth, poor blighters and *wragtig, mense!*—whistling between your lips with each breath you take. Your watery reflection shimmers on the damp window, and I can almost make out that madcap twinkle in your eyes, or is the headlights of the cars, turned on in the middle of the day because of the rain?

I think we should get a second opinion, I say to Ma and to Simon as they watch the nurses move you and turn you, as if you were an oversized doll. *Ekskuus tog*, I say to the older nurse, her grey-streaked hair tucked and folded under her white cap. *Is dit te laat vir die bloodversuiwering?* Is it too late to purify my father's blood? To turn the headlights back on?

Betsy! Ma takes in a breath, the corners of her mouth drawing down, her side teeth lengthening. Why do you want to do this to him? What for? He's suffered so much already!

Simon looks at me, his eyes clouding over. Listen, he says. That door is closed. We made a decision. We had to.

(Funny you should talk about doors, Si-Si. All the doors that were never shut, the parade of doctors marching in and out of our house, my body and yours. You never go there, Si. And maybe you never should.)

I still think we should ask! My voice is tight, louder than it means to be. There's a second engine whirring inside me, a motor just reserved for you.

* * *

OUTSIDE, THERE'S A soft summer rain falling that's good for the hydrangeas and the lavender and all the trees in the Kynsna forest and maybe some of the last Kynsna elephants too. Harold is going to leave the forest forever and he's going to climb into the dusty pages of the *Encyclopedia Britannica, Fourteenth edition, 1929, A New Survey of Universal Knowledge,* right here in the George public library, this last summer before medical school.

He's diving straight into "Medicine, General" and "Medicine, History of" and it's very, very deep over there. It's going to be a helluva long time before he comes up for air, with or without golf balls. The pages are very thin and the encyclopedia is very thick. It's Volume 15, Mary, Duchess of Burgundy to Mushet Steel, that's making you sneeze and you don't even have a hanky. Mrs. van der Vyver, the librarian who showed you where to find this volume, has a squeak in her skirt and you wonder if you're going to see a mouse running down her leg anytime soon.

"Influence of the World War. Since 1910, the progress of medicine has been much influenced by the four years of the war. . . ." You're staring at the page so hard now that it's almost making you *naar.* Trench fever and shell shock, boetie. Paratyphoid fevers. Maybe it's her foundation garment that's going to snap. She's walking around reshelving books and you can see the wisps of hair pressed against her neck as if they've been flattened between the pages of a book, pressed like violets or pansies or something.

Under the encyclopedia, you've hidden *Gray's Anatomy,* which you slowly withdraw, turning to page 1,025, "the External Organs of Generation in the Female." A face with a hairy bonnet yawns at you, all folds and holes with its own backyard fouchette. You're settling nicely into the froenum of the clitoris when you hear your father's voice drifting towards you, a curl of smoke from the old country. Oh God, he's asking Mrs. van der Vyver for something. She's even smiling a little, patiently listening through his Lithuanian accent, the way he can't help raking words like "please" and "Can I have?" through the coals. But Mrs. van der Vyver doesn't speak the King's English either, even though she has a nice sing-songy voice and likes to flute "Yeeeees?" at all the people who come past her desk.

"This way please . . ." Joseph Klein follows the squeak-squeak of Mrs. van der Vyver's thighs, and her rising voice, which flows backwards, the trickle eking out of the mountain, to the tiny high place that's green and pure, where spinster ladies sing and do crochet work in the still afternoons. Your father is following this fold-up rose lady to the children's section and he's pulling up a small chair and putting on his round glasses. Joseph Klein is reading to himself, softly, carefully, and you're not sure if it's *Treasure Island* or *The House at Pooh Corner* but it's words written for children. Your father, your poor father, who was almost trampled by a Cossack once, is trying to read your old books and sit in your old chair. You can't leave and you can't breathe and you'd like to break every chair in this place over your father's stupid head.

You can't see *The Water Babies* in your father's hands, the pictures with babies sleeping in oyster shells, an underworld of plump children and silvery fish, angels and seaweed, girls round, pink and untouched and do-as-you-would-be-done-by. You can't see the beads of sweat on your father's lip, hear the sea swell of his breath, the chair too small and the words too big, the words his children spill into the house, the long English words on the wireless jabbing their fingers at him. He thinks of you and your long nose, pointing East and then South, your scorn when he talks and you don't listen, you never listen, you're tap dancing away from all of us, tap-tapping right down Hibernia Street, right out of town, this boy who wouldn't eat. He wants to slam the book on your head but he doesn't. He folds the tissue carefully over the frontispiece and up he gets, his body not quite young, not yet old. Water Baby is what your mother called you, and now he knows why. You're not the chimney sweep, up in the dark the way he was, you're playing on the ocean floor, with the pink girls and the pink shells. You don't know snow falling on your village, the quiet before the pogrom, the hooves that scar and the upset house, and a long, terrible trip in a ship that almost killed your grandmother. You don't know what it's like to leave and never come back.

He doesn't see you, slumped over the apex of Douglas's pouch, until his coat brushes you and he says he's sorry. Your head moves and of course it's your nose that catches him, and "Harold!" he shouts as if he's never seen you before. He's a tall man in a suit, with a shop, and a bicycle propped on the wall outside, near the big oak tree with the long, long chain, where they used to tie up the slaves. It's the bicycle not Charlotte, not on weekdays, never on weekdays. Charlotte is for drives on a Sunday, on the dust road to the Wilderness. You stand and it's not like you're going to drive anywhere together, no father and son to the shop together. He won't let you work in the shop. You've never even opened the cash register. For all you know, there are mice inside, or marbles.

You slip *Gray's Anatomy* back under the *Encyclopedia Britannica.* No point in telling him about the Hippocratic Oath because he doesn't know anything about the Father of Medicine. The oath he knows is the covenant with God, the promise to circumcise your sons, and the mysteries of the Five Points of Fellowship. Your father is a Jew and a Freemason. He loves both his temples. He's a man of mystery and friendship, do-as-you-would-be-done-by. Shame and love swirls between you, and you almost want to laugh when he gets on his stupid, wobbling bicycle, this father of yours who's not Doctor Brown, the elegant English doctor who comes to your house when someone's ill. He comes in his car. So what if the boys on the street touch the windscreen and stand on the running board. He doesn't care.

He doesn't care! You want to run after your father

and shout, He doesn't care! But you can't really shout these days, not too loudly, since across the seas there are blackshirts and brownshirts and here there are greyshirts, special South African Nazis, picked and pickled in our own backyard and they're on the streets and at school and you don't even know where else you might find them, marching and goosestepping and acting like the sour Krauts. It's no joke when you're two bricks and a tickey high and you turn the corner and there they are, thick and blond, a band of Afrikaans boys furious about the Boer War and the Depression and English money and Jewish shops. No one has thrown the first stone although you've seen plenty of glass all over the newspapers, Jews in Germany sweeping up glass and of course the ones who died that night, the Night of Broken Glass.

You can't look at the window of "Joseph Klein" on the corner of Meade and Hibernia without hearing the sound of glass breaking. Of course, nothing is going to happen. How could anything bad happen in this neck of the woods, where necking in the woods is all you really want to do, with Gertrude or Hilda or any other sweet girl who will do the Lambeth Walk with you. She'll be the Peanut and you'll be the Toffee King and you'll walk the Lambeth Walk.

Mum left the East End when she was ten but even then she loved musicals. Her half-brother, Sam, still sends programs and records from London and you've just learned to sing "Any evening, any day, when you're walking Lambeth way. . . ." It's a tuck-arm, roundabout, happy-go-lucky dance-and-dip, lift up the leg and laugh a lot. Knees up, Mother Brown, and you poke Mum in the ribs and she has her happy face on, smiles for miles. You and Maisie go to Mrs. Giles' Bioscope and Oh, God, that's where you can see women! Ten pence on a Saturday, usually seven and a tickey to get house seats. Jean Harlow slipping in and out of your dreams, the smoke from her cigarette sharp in your nostrils. She moves and your heart flops. She swaggers and you stop breathing. Maisie laughs at you in the dark and she has the same smile as Mum, and the same mad up-and-down temper. You're all up-and-down people and Look, it's a monkey's wedding, a sun shower. After the film, you and Maisie walk home together in the lances of rain with the sun poking through the clouds and don't you just wish this black-haired, brown-eyed girl was your girlfriend and not your sister!

Maisie's up early listening to the wireless and once you caught her practically upside down. Physical Jerks was on and she was touching her toes and standing on one foot and then she bent over backwards and that's when you came in and she almost choked on her foot. Chamberlain saying "it's peace in our time" came on after Physical Jerks and you remember both together, the promise of peace and your sister's foot halfway down her throat. It's amazing what the human body can do.

* * *

WHO IS THE little girl standing over there? Is it my sister? you asked Ma last week before I came, before the coma dropped you into the pitch-dark. You were still cuckoo then, not OK in the top story. But now it's me not Maisie standing at the foot of your bed waiting for the lights to change, waiting for you to wake up. If you don't open your eyes soon, I'm going to take pliers and some tape and fix those damn kidneys myself. You didn't know I was an expert at plunging toilets, did you?

It's 1967 and we're back in the Touw River, a web of green slime floating on the surface of the water. The sand has crept up so high that you can walk across the river at its widest part when the tide is out. The golf balls are gone and forgotten and I'm in the boat. Well, almost forgotten. I'm holding an imaginary golf ball in the pocket of my shorts.

The boat is a special red-and-white handmade wooden rowing jobbie that you bought from a furniture salesman who liked to go fishing on the Knysna lagoon not far from the place where J.L.B. Smith had his boat. The coelacanth man. You mention the coelacanth and the boat, which is a collector's item, in one breath, and the time you went up the river with Maisie and Bunny and everyone. All the old roads. Putt-putt, goes the five-and-a-half horsepower Johnson engine, lubb-dupp, lubb-dupp goes your heart. That summer you couldn't start the boat your heart broke, but that's later, when I'd already flown away and the boat was empty.

I'm sitting on the prow, my feet slipping into the water every so often and you tell me not to but it's impossible to talk to children. They don't listen and they don't care. All she cares about is dipping her feet in the water so that the spray wets your arms and your sleeves and you wonder why you're in this boat at all with your youngest child, a dreamer and a *loskop*. She walks into walls and once she even walked into a moving car. Sometimes you think it could be something neurological but Mrs. God says, *Ag,* rubbish. She's just a *loskop*, that's all.

You and Simon and me and Simon's friend, Andrew, went up the river after lunch, to Ebb 'n Flow, past the little white beach where you used to have picnics, where Gertrude scratched herself getting out of the boat. You always look at the white sand, and still to this day you remember the milk-white of her inner thigh revolving against your hand. The tablecloth must have rotted by now. You never let the children get out. You're the captain of this ship and now that area is completely overgrown. It's a thicket of tangled branches and matted leaves and you are sure there are snake holes and snake nests and snake parties in there. It looks so much more dangerous than it used to.

Is it the web of dark-green, thickening against the flank of the mountain, the river slowly curdling, or the Sharpeville massacre four years ago when I was still a baby? Property values dropped and you and Ma bought a house in the Wilderness suddenly for half what it was worth a few months before. The couple who owned the cottage on the banks of the river left South Africa for good. They live in England now, somewhere in the North. They weren't the only ones, of course, fleeing the pictures in the papers of black bodies strewn in the road, shot in the back by the police. Then the rioting in the townships, share prices on the Johannesburg stock exchange plunging as white people sold and left, sold and left.

You didn't sell. You bought. The house has a view of the lagoon as it fans out into the sea. Behind you, mountains, in front of you this glittering sweet river slowly going bad, and the roaring sea. This sea is the breath in your body, the tide going in as you breathe in, the tide going out, as you exhale. Now and forever. You are bound here, caught in this crook of land. The river runs straight into your heart, the vena cava bringing blood without oxygen, to be renewed and restored, renewed and restored. Every summer you come back here, where you follow the river up to its source, to the miracle place where you shush-shush all of us and make us sit quietly in the red-and-white boat listening for monkeys.

You listen, there's a plash in the water (I can't sit still) or Simon gets tickled and he laughs and the monkeys scatter. Then it's back down the river to the Rope where we clamber onto a mossy bank and swing into the middle of the river from a gnarled, knotted rope that looks like entrails and hairs and an elephant's trunk. Another coil and a slither of river and it's Fairy Knowe where you dropped Simon and Andrew this afternoon, to play tennis. You stopped at the jetty and let them off and Mrs. God was supposed to pick them up later. Clouds were stacking up in the sky but it was still warm. You decided to take the boat back, with me.

I beg you to teach me how to row and you maneouvre the boat into a quiet spot, away from the speedboats and skiers and swimmers. I sit on the seat next to you, and you put my hand on the left oar and cover your hand with it. I can't see my own fingers. We dip the left oar in the water together. At first, it skitters in and out of the water, bouncing unevenly, what Simon calls "catching a crab." The little boat jerks like a marionette bobbing on the end of its string. I feel your warm, dry hand tightening on mine, my fingers slowly going numb. Your mouth tightens too, as if I should know how to do this already. But your movements are slow and steady, and I try as hard as I can to follow them, bracing my feet against the wooden bar set up on the seat in front of us. Hold water! you shout, when a speedboat comes too close to us and I'm not sure if you're talking to the driver or to me but I freeze anyway, squaring my oar. Back pedal, back pedal, you hiss when we start drifting towards the reeds. All the time, your hand stays clamped on mine, small and square, the skin a reddish-brown, hairs crisscrossing the knuckles. I can smell the scent of Prell in your hair, the sweat dampening your armpits, mixed with the whiff of petrol coming from the orange fuel tank on the floor of the boat.

Finally, you let go of my hand, and I start rowing by myself, just with the left oar. You have the right one, and every time we dip the oars into the river, you say, Catch, and then Pull, Catch and Pull, Catch and Pull. The oar-locks creak, I breathe in loud, big gusts, and you suck air in between your teeth as the boat slips through the water sweetly and easily. On the other side of the railway bridge, you say, I think we've had enough for today. We lift both oars into the boat and you pull-start the five-and-a-half horsepower engine. I climb onto the prow, my favorite place, and try to keep my feet from trailing in the water.

We chug-chugg past the aerodrome where I once sat on the wing of a small plane and you took a picture. As we round the bend in the river, near the caravan park and the other bridge with the storm-tossed pylons from your own childhood, there's a low growling in the sky, grey dragons of clouds heaving one on top of the other. The first drops sweep across the surface of the water. I swing my legs into the boat and sit on the seat near the front where you tell me to sit. The boat has to be steady at all times. You can't have everybody doing whatever they please, especially at times like this, when there are waves in the water. They're not big waves, but the water isn't smooth anymore.

You look at me and I stare back at you. I have black eyes too, black hair and a long nose that won't be as long as yours, thank God. I'm wearing red shorts, a short-sleeved shirt with puffy sleeves and no cardigan and I'm shivering. You say something about the storm that brought down the pylons in 1926. I look blank. I'm cold, I say. You can see the goosebumps on my arms and the star-shaped scar on my knee where I fell into a rose bush. There's nothing in the world like looking at the face of your own child but you can't tell me that. You throw me your old jersey and I wrap it around my legs. Then I crawl into the tiny space right under the prow where I was sitting before.

She's curled in there like a hedgehog or a rolled-up centipede, you think as you pass a houseboat moored near the caravan park. In the distance you see lightning crack open the sky for an instant. The thunder grumbles, a lion pacing up there somewhere. The waves are much bigger now as you steer the boat through the choppy water. This could be a bigger storm than '26 or 1914 or the one just before they reenacted the Great Trek. No wait, it's still summer, you think, stopping the flood of panic and excitement in your chest, that same mad thrill you get staring at a bone piercing through skin, or at a wound as open as a flower. Betsy can swim, you're thinking, but for how long. This is the first year Mrs. God packed away the orange cork-filled lifejacket Betsy hated so much. But the boat won't go over and if it does the river is deep only in certain places, not nearly as deep as it used to be when you dived off the bridge for golf balls. Of course there's the lightning flashing now here, now there, some mad giant in the heavens playing pin the tail on the donkey.

What if you're the donkey and that long crooked spark lights up you and your boat and me, hidden but not safe? What if your heart is the one that stops? You don't say anything to me about electricity or hearts that go bump-bump, lubb-dupp, bump, putt-putt, bump-lubb. Putt. Stop. I know you're worried because your face has that slightly grim, serious look, the look I remember when you bent over my knee and extracted a rose thorn buried deep in my flesh. You washed off the blood and laid the thorn on a white towel and the two of us stared at it, as if it was a moon rock or a secret talisman or a hook that could speak.

At the top of the right atrium is the sinoatrial node that sends out the electrical impulses that keep the heart going. Through the fabric of your short-sleeved shirt, you feel your own heart, its right margin under the right side of your breastbone. I watch you, as if I'm watching a magic show. I'm all curled up, your own offspring turned into a small black fox before your eyes. You're torn between the miracle of nature crashing all around you, the bang bang of your own electricity, and me, so small, so curved, that it takes you back to the day I was born. You remember walking into the delivery room, Mrs. God and the fancy obstetrician from Cape Town smoking and cracking jokes. You shouted at them and tried to wave all that smoke away, to protect the tiny, folded life that was on its way. Now I'm here and I'm big, my scarred knee blinking at you. You have so much you want to tell me but you say nothing. You can never speak what's in your heart because no one understands. Gertrude is probably married or dead—or married and dead!—and Bunny was killed when his plane was shot down in '42. Remember when there were soldiers everywhere? Remember those days?

I suck my knee and Don't do that is what you tell me. Your knee has been all over the place, collecting germs, wet ones and dry ones, ones that sit and ones that fly.

I'm cold, I say again, tired and slightly accusing, my teeth banging like castanets. You clear your throat and try not to look at me, as if I'm going to leap out of my hole and bite you, or even worse, move closer to you so that the front of the boat lifts up and you almost sink. Stay where you are, you say. It's not so bad. Not like the one in '26. You crack a thin, crooked sort of smile and I rearrange myself. You can see that every part of me is shivering. My cheeks are glazed with tears or rain, you can't tell which. I suck my knee again, looking at you defiantly. Good, you think, she doesn't seem sleepy or confused. No hypothermia. And then my eyelids flutter shut. Betsy! You shout. Pull yourself together. Buck up!

Are we there yet? I say, and then I laugh. You look funny. Your shirt is all wet. I giggle, the same giggle engine Maisie had, or still has, for all you know. It makes you giggle too and then I put my head upside down and now I'm really a baby hedgehog, some queer furry creature damp and odd at the bottom of the boat. Your mother is going to be furious. Wait until she sees you. She's going to be mad as a snake. I should have left you at Fairy Knowe. I'd be sitting inside drinking cooldrinks and watching the rain, I say. Not stuck here. With me, you say. With you, I answer.

The boat chug-chugs past Freesia's rock, wet and slick, the back of a dinosaur about to head for the trees. Funny old rock. I shift again. I'm asleep now, my face pale, the colour of the air and sky. You stop the boat, edge forward and feel under my armpits. Still warm. You take my pulse, the beat of my life between your fingers, the rush of my very own river. Your light shines right at me, your ears listen for engine trouble. Then you back away, start the boat again with a pull of the cord.

You sit down, heading for home, the river spread wide in front of you, houses, boathouses clustering the edges. Some of the houses have been there for donkey's years, Tudor style cottages with thatched roofs. Some are new with arches and porches and stuccoed walls. The sky is clearing and a rainbow stretches over the hills and into the sea. Tomorrow will be a good beach day. You want to wake me and tell me but you can't. You want to tell me lots of things but you can't.

She won't understand, you think. She walks into walls and she laughs just like Maisie and sometimes she's her own little animal, the way she is now and it makes you sad and happy at the same time. Nothing happened but you know this rainy afternoon will paste itself into your life as a special day, the day you taught me how to row and you and I got stuck in the boat in the rain and I crawled into the front and made myself so small you thought you could keep me forever, huddled under the prow right where you sometimes keep the petrol tank. Ma is standing on the jetty with Simon and she's waving and furious, an SOS going with her arms. For crying out loud, you want to say, we weren't captured or chased or beaten or anything. The lightning left us alone and the river's not deep and here we are. *Môre is nog 'n dag.* Tomorrow's another day. Look at the horizon line, blue and light as a dream. A good day for the beach.

CHAPTER 5

EXHAUSTION GLITTERS BEHIND my eyes, a thin silt I can feel under my lids, lining my throat. Get some fresh air, Ma says. Go get a cup of tea.

My shoes glide on the red floors, down the hallowed, yellow halls of Groote Schuur. I'm remembering the old cottage hospital in Worcester on Christmas Eve, the nurses in their white hats and black capes, the squeech of their rubber-soled shoes, singing *Stille Nag, Heilige Nag*, floating down the corridors in the dark, holding candles in paper doilies. I'm sitting on your shoulders probably for the very last time. *Ag,* shame man, one of the nurses says. It's her only Christmas.

The sour tang of hospital food wafts through the cafeteria, settles around the pile of plastic trays. There's steam and macaroni and green beans in the air, cabbage and boiled fish, and burst hotdogs. I'm struggling with everything, my tears, my tray, my tea, this honoured place where you became a doctor, the riot of sea, city and mountain just outside the windows.

The cup slides on the tray and the hot water burns my hand, drips onto my shoe. There's a quick place at a table between young doctors, men and women bulging with stethoscopes the way you must have, and a clatter of nurses to the left of them.

They're singing a kind of song I'm straining to hear, Afrikaans and English and the magical Latin and Greek of medicine braided together, leukonychia, hypoalbuminemia, *Meneer Kafaar en sy rooi gesig*, the laryngeal mask airway. Daniels' patient was cyanotic by then, a young woman wearing the tag, Dr. Marlene Matthee, says. *Hy't net sy arm gebreek*, a dark-haired boy who could be sixteen and not twenty-five, says. A fracture of the upper humerus.

The bobbling white coats rise and fall like piano keys. They're playing your song, the old talk on the phone about cardiac arrests and murmurs and babies with strawberry birthmarks, ECGs and haemoglobin and porphyria, not uncommon in the Afrikaner population. He was hypoxic, Dr. Marlene says, and there's a murmur, *Hy het nie genoeg suurstof gekry nie.*

A fracture of the upper humerus. I'm leaving now. *Ek is baie jammer*, I'm very sorry, as the cup spills the last of the tea on one of the housemen's coats. They've barely seen me, a patient's patient reeking of airplane and long distance, and now I'm travelling the halls again, my feet skimming the glistening floor, always two steps ahead of myself, a dark, curly-haired woman almost as short as you.

There are white faces and brown faces in the lift, white coats and white shoes, and sturdy brown legs, next to khaki pants. This isn't the kind of hospital you spent forty-three years in, with separate entrances and exits for *Blankes and nie-Blankes*, Europeans and non-Europeans.

Sy was baie bekommered. She was very worried, a blonde nurse with tight lips whispers to her colleague, an Indian nurse with a long, lustrous braid down her back. *Sy't Dr. Daniels gebel. Hulle het hom hier gebring.* She called Dr. Daniels. They brought him here. I'm looking at the numbers lighting up on the panel. Who was worried?

There's a knot of doctors outside your room, and Dr. Daniels, the anaesthesiologist, is there again. He approaches me with Afrikaner courtliness, his voice gruff but warm. He's fought one helluva fight but I think it's tickets this time. Somehow he's got one of my hands sandwiched between his large, dry palms and I'm lulled, as if he's putting me to sleep just by touch.

I retract my hand carefully, murmuring, Thank you for everything you've done, Doctor. I'm standing at the foot of your bed again, staring at the cliff of your nose, the folded swallow's wings of your black and silver hair. We're on the beach at Lentjiesklip and you're showing me a bluebottle lying dead on the sand, with periwinkles crawling out of their holes to come and eat its blue, stinging tendrils. They don't get stung, you're telling me as you pop the bluebottle's bubble with a long spear of dried kelp. We watch the periwinkles, shells pointing up, swept forward by the circular motion of what looks like a tongue and a leg and a sucker, as they ingest the bright blue of the bluebottle. You point up and out with your kelp spear towards the sky and the mountain, towards the old road from the Wilderness to George, snaking over the mountain, near the Kaaimans River gorge.

I CAN'T HELP going with you, all the way to the station to say goodbye to George, the town, and Mum, your mother, and to Maisie, eight-year-old Bertie, and your very own Dad. We're all crammed into Charlotte and we just travelled along the hepatic flexure, the beginning of the transverse colon. Whoopsa-daisy, there's the sharp downturn, the splenic flexure, which is scenic not splenic in the middle of summer, with the smell of lucerne in the air and no one's crying yet.

There's a knock-knocking sound underneath the car and your father stops dead. He gets out and his head pokes under the bonnet, checking. Time drizzles between your fingers, drips from your clenched knees right to your ankles locked around each other like cuffed hands. Your mother screams, Joseph! We're going to miss the train! And your father waves his grease-stained hands at her like a drowning man. Now you're out of the car and checking too and your father is so furious he almost slams the bonnet down on your head. Mr. Expert! He's shrieking. You think I'm a fool. You think I can't see what's wrong. Come on, Charlotte. This time he does slam the bonnet and you jump back, as if escaping the guillotine. He's in the car and Charlotte leaps into life but somehow he's thrown your suitcases into the road and is pulling away without you, taking you to the train station without you. Bertie is laughing and he's waving a spanner that he tip-taps on the roof of the car and you suddenly see that he's the noise, the broken twang, the bloody reason your mum threw you out of her bed and out of her love and out into the yard to catch the Friday chicken. All those years of blankets and special baths and special meals and special treatments for your stick-legs and your tiny arms gone in a flash.

The car stops and you've pulled Bertie out, headfirst out of the window, and you're choking him, and he's biting you and Mum screams, Joseph! Your father is driving away again and you and Bertie are running down the road after the car. And then it stops, like a funny silent film, and you run backwards to get the suitcases and Bertie hops up and down and then onto the running board. You jump up too and push him back through the window. The car swallows you and Bertie and the suitcases and swerves a little. Maisie is at the window, with her hanky to her mouth, green as a cucumber. She's sick of you! Mum is screaming and you say nothing but now the tears are rolling down your cheeks and you should be ashamed of yourself, a young man of eighteen crying like a baby. Buck up, man. Buck up!

Mum is talking like a wind-up toy and her head is bobbing and she's saying something over and over again about her cousins and her sisters and her brother in London and the wind can be bad in Cape Town, the southeaster blows dust into your mouth and the northwester brings rain and don't sleep with the door closed. What if the house is on fire or the street or if the war does come here but that won't happen. They won't let it. I never slept alone, mind you, she says, never ever. My mother and I slept in the same bed until the day I got married. She smiles as wide as can be.

Maisie looks up from her hanky, and she says, And your dad? My father was dead, Mum says and her head bob-bobs in a little-bit-sad kind of way. Of course, Maisie settles back into her hanky. I forgot.

You're looking out of the window. Your tears are drying in the wind and no one really cares. So what if your mum lost her father when she was three or four or six. She had all those lucky uncles and funny half-brothers and the whole of London town. Oh to be in England now that April's there and old Westminster Bridge. The earth has nothing to show more fair than the beauty of the morning. Who can be sad in a place like that? Great

Britain is pink on the map, always pink. Half the world is pink, you know.

You see Maisie out of the corner of your eye, across the madness of Bertie, who's sucking on two of his fingers, not one but two, and your mother is reaching across to slap his wet fist and she almost clocks you instead. Say the wrong thing and you'll be back on the dust road again, back with the suitcases, Charlotte's tires spitting stones at you.

I need to go to the lavatory. That's the only thought in your head as Charlotte stops at the railway station right at the end of Hibernia Street, past the High School, past Rosemoore, the Coloured location where Nettie lives, past all the houses and lives that you've known since the day you were born. You can't think goodbye anymore. All there is is the pressure in your bowels and the thought of the train, the colon, the colon-train that will carry you in and out of this old life where Mum toilet trained all three of you. She and Nettie held your tiny bottoms over chamber pots and lavatories and in water closets for years and years and years. It started early and it's never ended, this glint in her eye about clean bottoms.

Mum's talking the hind leg off a donkey now, about the tea dances and the southeaster, again, and don't look out of the train window, you'll get soot in your eye. You don't want to start Medical School with a patch like a pirate. The train is steaming into the station and there's a blur of movement around you, Bertie suddenly clinging to your legs with his head in your groin, Oh, God, not there, and Maisie seems to have vanished. The train has eaten her and it's grunting and panting and you look for her in the steam that's billowing and disappearing, billowing and disappearing. Your father is handing bags to you. You're in the second-class compartment with two old men and a stringy boy, taller than you, with bristles on his head, and a running sore on his wrist. You see the sore as he lifts his own suitcase up, and puts it right next to yours.

The steam engine bellows, once, twice, three times and you're out of George, Mum and Maisie up in smoke, your father clapping old Bertie so hard he nearly falls over. You run through the narrow passage, past the second-class compartments, desperate to find the toilet and when you get to it, someone's in there, and you bang on the door almost crying. The train lurches. Where are you? Great Brak River or Little Brak? You're stumbling over villi, over Peyer's glands and watch out, don't fall into the crypts of Lieberkuhn.

You can't go forward into first class or backwards into the third class, with the Coloureds and Natives. Dirty and bad, dirty and bad, that's what the wheels are singing, that's what's going to happen to you if you don't find the lav, the john, the loo, the place to poo. There's a baby crying so loudly that a seam opens up behind your eyes. You're jiggling up and down in your new big suit, holding your water, your waste, your baby tears, sad and bad, not big enough, too wet, too dirty, too sad. Your legs are twined like vines gripping an old, old tree and there are frog sounds, frog sounds at the Wilderness. Oh God, the frogs are going to get you through this, the night sound of all of them in the soft rain as you walk back in the dark to the *rondavel*, the lagoon black and soft in the dark. I'm leaving, you remember, I'm leaving and out of the window, the places you have planted your heart roll past, one love-place after another. Herold's Bay and Victoria Bay, the bluebottles and periwinkles, the curling waves and a thousand eggshells, all the picnics on the sand washed up and gone. Pacaltsdorp, where your grandfather *smoused* ostrich feathers, where there's one road and a graveyard, a small town heaving itself up onto a hill and Blanco, another tiny place where you stopped, once, to fill Charlotte with water. And the baby's still crying as the train thunders towards Mossel Bay, straight for the sea.

The cecum is the cul-de-sac where the small intestine ends and the large intestine begins. You're crouched now, a C shape, and you trip over the bristle-haired boy as he edges out of the door, the train throwing him this way and that, his running sore flying at your cheek. You recoil and fall into the water closet which is more vapour than water. The running sore boy has left a mess, and you are careful, now, a man in a minefield of microbes, a soldier covering the seat with garlands of toilet paper so that no part of you, not one inch of skin will touch the place where the sore boy sat. The baby's scream is a gurgle and a sigh and the baby feeds. You can breathe again, and the sheepshank inside you loosens. The next stop is Mossel Bay and suddenly a new fear sits down next to you. The train will stop and they'll put the engine that was in the front at the back and everything will be swung around. You'll be sitting here, shitting onto the tracks in front of the railway station and everyone will see.

The train groans and stops and it doesn't go into the sea. If you were in the mood, you could twist open the window and take a last look at Seal Island, a tiny hump of land not too far from the harbour just seething with seals. But you're frozen, waiting for the switch, for what was in front to go to the back and what was in the back to be put in front. You're in the cecum or is it much, much farther in the narrowest part, the sigmoid flexure? The tracks here are of course much narrower than the tracks in England, with a three-foot-six-inch gauge which makes the train slow, a day-long train with lunch on both ends. They curve forward, downward and inward and then form a loop, which ends in the rectum.

The third-class carriages are now in front, and the first-class carriages are at the back. The long line of panting elephants lumbers back, makes a left, heads inlands towards the looping mountain chains of the Western Cape. With a groan and a sigh, you leave the last breakfast you ate in your mum's house neatly on the tracks, a mile outside of Mossel Bay, next to the battered skeleton of a *dassie*. What is the better part of valour? What is it? What is it? The train wheels hiss at you and you search outside in the veld for the lost word and there it is, an *akkertjie*, an acorn, a tiny *miggie* inside the folded leaf of a succulent. Discretion. Discretion is the better part of valour.

Albertinia is the next stop. It's not much more than a railway station and a hotel with shade, a handful of farms with prickly pear fences and a few old ostriches who survived the ostrich-feather boom and then the crash, and watch the trains with hooded eyes. But the big thrill is just outside Albertinia, the Gouritz River bridge, a rickety wooden structure that spans a deep rift in the earth, with a sly trickle of brown water at the bottom. The train is on the bridge and there's creaking galore, the wooden supports swaying and groaning under all that steel and panting machinery. Bertie would love this, you're thinking. He'd throw something out of the window, down, down towards the mud puddle so far down below. But there's no Bertie. There's just you here, alone in the passageway of the swinging train, afraid to go back into the compartment with the infected boy who's not your brother, who is not despised, loved-to-death Bertie.

The train is off the bridge now and everyone is still alive. You must go. You can't stand here in the middle of the train all day, stuck inside the coils of your own colon, stuck like the shilling you once ate and then vomited up, your mother's white face hanging over you, big as the moon. When you get into the compartment, it's not the three you left, but five now, the two *ou toppies*, old ones, and the long boy and a couple of rough-looking extra ones, two *plaasjapies* from Albertinia. It's going to be Afrikaans all the way to Cape Town. And why not? *Waarom nie*?

Mum never learnt to speak Afrikaans properly. She tried in the shop and it was the sound of a *Rooinek* through and through, her tongue stepping gingerly over the hard g's and the rumbling r's. Your father was a different story, with his Russian and his Yiddish and his funny English, he took a dive into Afrikaans and never really came up. *Ja, meneer!* He loved to say when one of the hops farmers came into the shop. Then he was off and it always reminded you of those World War One flying aces doing double backflips in the sky. He didn't care. He made double language mistakes and then he corrected himself with a fine, fat Afrikaans idiom, just like the fine, fat-tailed sheep you see out in the far Karoo. Of course you learned Afrikaans at school and although it wasn't your best subject, you liked the sound of *vis* in your mouth instead of fish, *vuur* instead of fire, *vuurhoutjie* instead of match.

Albertinia, Riversdale, Heidelberg, Swellendam. Suurbraak. Sour Vomit. Nothing more than a siding where the train stops. *Waar is jou pappie?* Where is your father? The pipe-smoking white-haired *oupa* at the window looks at you with watery eyes, his pipe clenched between stained teeth. *Ek is alleen*. I am by myself. He is looking at you curiously, those watery eyes fixed on your long nose and you clench yourself for the next question.

Hoe oud is jy, my kind? The old film is burning inside you. It has edges so hot they're curling and setting the whole world on fire. Outside the sun is leaving the sky and suddenly the train is diving through flames, long ribbons of ruby and bright orange. The train window flashes like a thousand burning mirrors. God is fuming! He's going to poke his fingers into the old man's eyes and blind him forever!

Ek is agtien, oupa. I am eighteen, grandpa. Everyone in the compartment is looking at you and you're the one who's going blind. You can't see them because the sun is staring you down. The shadow of your nose falls between your feet and there's nothing to shade your eyes from these rude giants with their halos of glittering veld and sky, their weeping sores, their big, earth-slapping feet. How old did they think he was? Twelve? Thirteen? A tiny Jew they could fold up and stick in their pockets, right next to the tobacco pouch and the smashed packets of cigarettes.

The sun dips and is gone. You are left alone with these men in the ash-coloured light, caught between the day and the night. *Ek kan nie meer so goed sien nie*, apologizes the *oupa*, tears dripping into his beard. I don't see so well anymore. The fire inside you burns out. Soon you will be able to climb onto the old man's nose and fix those overflowing gutters. You will be able to dry the pus on the sore boy's arm. You will fix these people and they will say thank you. Thank you, doctor. *Baie dankie.*

The lights go on and there's newspaper rustling in the

compartment. The *plaasjapies* have taken out their supper. It's bread with a bit of *boerewors*. Of course you have a chicken and a half, and some boiled tongue just in case. You're reading the back of the newspaper wrapped around the *plaasjapies'* food and it's all about the South African cabinet meeting to discuss Hertzog's proposal that South Africa stay neutral if there's a war in Europe. *Ag*, that's old news isn't it. Smuts agreed but then he got worried when Czechoslovakia was cut up just like the chicken you're sharing with the runny-eyed *oupa*. Now Smuts is going everywhere to talk to people, to try to get them to change their mind if there's a war. Smuts, Hertzog, Smuts, Hertzog. They used to be together and now they're not. The train is singing a new song as you drive into the night, the lights of Bonnievale twinkling like fairy lights.

The other older man must be a schoolteacher or a deacon in the church but wait, he's the one with the brandy bottle and now he's pouring everyone a *dop*. The stringy boy lifts his glass to yours and God, that wrist looks terrible! You colour in the rest. Poor white. His pa was a *bywoner* and then he got a job with the railways. A salary of ten pounds a week, not twelve shillings like the Natives. Maybe he's riding for free on the train and doesn't even have a proper ticket. Maybe he has ringworm like Fanie Viljoen who used to sit in front of you in Latin with a handkerchief on top of his shaved head, knotted at each corner. Once you lifted up his hanky with your ruler and set it down again so softly he didn't even notice.

The steward comes with the bedding and now it's time to go to sleep. The blankets are brown and raspy and the sheet is so stiff it could slit your throat. The *ou toppies* are talking about Smuts and one is a Smuts man and the other isn't. *Tweede Vryheidsoorlog*, the Second War of Liberation, is what the Hertzog man says, talking about the Boer War and the whole compartment crackles, just like the sheets. How is this talk going to end? The *plaasjapies* start singing something dirty about *poes* and wine and old men's teeth and it's the brandy bottle that caused all this trouble. Stop it, you want to say, call it whatever you want but the bloody Boer War is over and you can all go home now and go to sleep.

The train swings this way and that. Will there be war, or won't there. Smuts wants to fight and Hertzog doesn't. You're in the top bunk and it's hot up there, the smell of sweat and pants and tobacco and brandy in your hair, up your nose. Smuts was in the Boer War, wasn't he? You want to tell the *ou toppie* with the dry eyes, who likes Germans and German beer and German everything, He's an Afrikaner just like you! But Smuts went to England and that's where the devil took him, and put an Englishman in his skin. In Cambridge they stole his heart. They turned him into wood and sent him home. He doesn't remember his brothers anymore. They put the King in his brain. The *blerrie* English will smile at you and steal your whole life.

The sore boy is snoring, his bad arm buried under

him, probably stuck to the bed. You pull away from the sheet that lies over you, thinking of all the bad hands and arms and legs that have touched it, that have lain right where you are, in this dark, smelly compartment, swinging and puffing through the darkness, stopping and starting, stopping and starting. In Bonnievale the train wheezes, then comes to a standstill. The Langeberge lie still, dark mountains washed by the cool moon, giant soldiers bent over in sleep. The raggedy velvet sky has a million holes in it. You stare at one star in particular. You pray for it to move, for the earth to shift, for the train to roll towards Cape Town, like a stone rolling down a cliff into the sea. But you're here forever and ever, lying awake, breathing and waiting for the train to move.

The cloth shrieks as you rip it in two. You give Gertrude one piece which she stuffs under her dress. Oh God, the boat is going backwards, and it's almost back in the water. Remember after that, when she opened her legs? In the dark, there's your own Langeberg under the sheets. Your heart is banging like a moth against glass. Bang, bang, bang. The louder it beats, the harder you are, and there's nothing you can do except rub and push the printed sheet, turning the South of "South African Railways" into ou, outh, out, outh A. You can't help noticing what's seeping out of her, and slowly seeping into the compartment. Her long white thighs are floating over you, opening and closing, like the large wings of a real-life angel. The inside of her thigh is a miracle, a pale valley that slips into another darker one. You squeeze your eyes closed, and you're the one with wings now, and you land on her mountains, right on the soft red beacon of her right nipple. You stay there, shaking and invisible, and you raise your flag.

Gertrude takes your hand. You're sweating, wet lines of panic down your neck, into the hollow between your shoulder blades. She's going to steal your flag! She's going to take everything you've got and run screaming down the mountain. But she takes your hand and pushes it inside her and suddenly you burst, a sticky mess all over "Railways." The men snore and the train puffs and grunts and it's goodbye Bonnievale. The lights are still out in the bioscope and when you get outside, it's burning bright but you're tired. So you sleep. The train rubs itself against the mountains, coiling and hissing, its tail almost touching its head on the five chain-reverse curves. The sleeping *koppies* and the sleeping farmers don't even wake up.

In the morning, the steward comes in with railway coffee, medium brown like the veld. The *ou toppie* with the runny eyes is waiting like a child, his lips pink and shiny. You climb down from the top bunk and the steward pushes the bunk up, and fastens it. You give him the messy sheet and the blanket in a big confused ball and his eyebrow lifts at you, up an inch.

Everybody sips the hot liquid. Everybody loves railway coffee. You breathe it in, and the heat reminds you of last night and flying Gertrude. You cross your legs and drink. Outside, the Langeberge clasp hands with the Brandwacht mountains and beyond Tulbagh, it's the long chain of the Koue Bokkeveld. Peaks, *kloofs* and gorges blushing the pinkest of pinks, waiting to deepen into blue, purple, then blue again, as the day goes on.

You pass through Worcester, where the George train meets up with the train going North, to Johannesburg. It's wine and grape country, the country of your future, but you don't know this, as you look at the green patchwork of vineyards and the gabled Cape-Dutch homesteads. You don't know the difference yet between the Barlinka or the Alphonse Lavalle grape, or the special sweetness of a Hanepoot and you've never tasted a Pinotage wine. The names of the grapes and the cases of wine, purple and cherry red and white-yellow, the gables on the labels and the farmers tasting and drinking, paying their Coloured workers in drink and yes, selling you cases at special prices, lies past you, past Nuy and Rawsonville, somewhere lost in that swirling finger of cloud shifting and moving, as the train chortles past. The mountains never end and now you're looping right through the middle of them, going up and around, Wolseley to Tulbagh, Tulbagh to Wellington, straight through to Huguenot, Paarl, Cape Town.

The *ou toppie* takes your hand when you tell him you're going to Cape Town to become a doctor. Clever *boytjie*, he says and you wonder if what's dripping down his cheek landed on his hands, whether you're going to catch it too, and dissolve into a pool of water before you have a chance to become anything. Clever *boytjie*, he says again. Clever sounds like cleaver, cleaver sounds like clobber. Clever, cleaver, clobber. Clever, cleaver, clobber. You're in the song, on the train, and flying up there with every goddamn bird in the sky. "All things bright and beautiful, all creatures great and small. All things wise and wonderful, the lord God made them all." You're going to see everything and make the world whole and look at bodies and babies and breasts, and touch and smell and feel every ounce of life that ever walked or rolled or crawled on this funny old planet!

CHAPTER 6

THE NURSES ARE back again, rolling and flipping you like a pancake, making sure one side doesn't get more cooked than the other. Simon is staring bleakly out of the window, and Ma is talking to yet another doctor, a colleague who remembers you from the old days, his face breaking into a smile between liver spots and patches of red, flaky skin. The skin is the mirror of the mind, you always said, and I'm looking at the old gentleman's sad-happy face as he remembers you from long ago, what you were and what you've become, putty in the nurses' hands, as they unwrap you and twist you and wrap you up again. A *dominee* has come and gone. No thank you, Ma said, in no uncertain terms. *Ons is Jode.* We're Jews.

Missus . . . Klein? A very young nurse with dimples and pimples is at my elbow. There's someone on the telephone. From America. I'm walking through the Valley of the Shadow of Death, past rooms and rooms of men and women just like you, stacked in snowy white rows, a blur of grey faces, some breathing through masks, some staring at television sets, mounted above their heads, or a godly God high above the heads of their beds, above the red roofs of the hospital, above the roiling waters of the Cape of No More Good Hope.

I thought it was all a hoax, William says, as I'm crouching now, in the nurse's station between computer screens, clipboards and trolleys. I thought he was up to his old tricks. I'm nodding even though he can't see me bobbing my head furiously, Yes! I keep thinking he's going to sit up and say, Got you, you buggers!

All he had was a broken arm! A pathological fracture, I tell him, a Fracture of the Upper Humerus. But still, he says. Why is he dying from a broken arm? I bite my lip, give the telephone cord a little pinch. It's too late to ask anything, I say, tears bubbling in my throat. William's quieter now, reminding me of the baby we saw floating on the sonogram screen the day before I left. How's our little fish? he asks, and I'm smiling through wet lashes.

You're arranged a little differently, your face bent towards the door, mouth slightly open, as I step back into the room, fresh from the phone. This time you're really going to wake up. What the hell's going on here? I can hear you shouting. Let's get this bloody thing out of the river and back onto the road!

Simon's got his reading glasses on and is studying a print-out of your bloodwork as if he became a doctor after all, and not a scientist, as if he can save you just by reading. I can't figure this out, he says finally, putting the paper down next to the upopened yogurt, which he hands to me. I'm spooning it down in big gulps, tasting sour strawberries. Simon's voice is faraway in 1965 and he's telling me how you woke him up four Saturday mornings in a row to listen to rugby test-matches on the radio. It was three or four a.m. our time and the All-Blacks were playing the Springboks. They creamed the Springboks in the first two games. The third test the All-Blacks were winning 16–3 at halftime. Then the Springboks came back to win 19–16! He's looking at you, and he's looking at me and we can see you cheering and screaming in the room with us, part dervish, part doctor, hopping and laughing and slapping your only son on the back. Hell's teeth, man. Now isn't that bloody marvelous!

It was one of the best times of my life, Simon says, as the echo of your excitement still rings in our ears, those times when the sun burst out of your black eyes and we were all dancing at the same party. They came back to win 19–16! I say out loud, just in case you're listening.

Simon looks over his shoulder quickly. I spoke to one of the nurses who told me what it was like when he came here from the other place in the middle of the night. Ma doesn't know that I know and anyway it was all over by the time I got here. Uncle Bertie's right outside, he whispers.

Bertie's suddenly in the room, your bad baby brother grown big and fat and he's in a blinding white coat like all the other doctors except he has the grandeur of a chief about him, his hair wilder than yours, leather tassels gleaming on his Italian shoes. I got him the best, he says, squeezing me in his arms. Those chaps do more shoulder surgeries than anyone in the country. They're the specialists' specialists! If it had been his heart I would have done it myself! He's at your bedside now and this time I know you're going to sit bolt upright and spit in his eye. For crying out loud, man, say something to us, he shouts. Tell us to go to hell just one more time!

Then he turns to Simon, and to me. I told your mother to go home and get some rest. Maybe you should go too. Simon looks at me and I look at him and we don't move a muscle. We're waiting for Bertie to tell us what he always tells us, about the times when he worked on Chris Barnard's team and they transplanted the first human heart into Louis Washkansky and later, when they did the same for Philip Blaiberg. Christ man, when Chris Barnard came to Medical School, he didn't even have shoes!

For once, Bertie stares directly at me, almost as if he's seeing me for the very first time. Betsy, your mom says you're going to have a baby. His eyes fall to my breasts, and below. You've got to look after yourself, my girl. Do you still live in that factory, with the fellow who is a waiter or something?

A sommelier, and it's a loft, Uncle Bertie, in what's become a very nice part of Manhattan. That's not what your father said, Bertie goes on. When he had to walk up all those stairs. And your paintings? I always wondered who would buy a picture of a quagga or one of the dodo-type animals and birds you always paint. But your mom says you sold one to a museum or something. He looks at his watch, then he gives me another quick embrace. I've got a ward round on the cardiology floor but I'll be back later on.

He did the same thing to me earlier, Bets, Simon says, as the slap and crackle of Bertie's shoes fades slowly away. What's new in the great big world of science, *boetie*? Split any more atoms lately or you are still cutting up sea urchins? No point in telling him that was my doctoral thesis donkey's years ago. He's a prick, that's all.

Runs in the family, doesn't it? I think but don't say, as I watch the still peaks of your face, as a ray of light from the window falls on your forehead, and the formidable arch of your nose. The sun brightens the grey pall of your cheeks, glossing the bad blood with a sudden radiance, Bertie's voice still echoing in the starched corners of the room. I'm thinking of Uncle Wolfie, an uncle who wasn't really an uncle, but a doctor too, remembering how I used to believe that all uncles were doctors and all doctors were uncles.

THERE WAS A drought in the summer of seventy-one, when the sun just burned and burned. Crops were lost, and they let us off school one Friday so that the farmers could go to their Dutch Reformed churches and pray for rain. Despite their prayers, the rain never came. But something else came that summer, what Ma called the curse and it happened to me.

We were on our way to the Wilderness and just before I got in the car I went to the toilet with its stack of *Lancets* and *British Medical Journals* piled up behind me on the tank, a juicy pantheon of ulcerated legs, disfiguring boils, elephantiasis deluxe, lesions and carcinomas for every mood and season. There was a red smear in my panties, the sign of sure death. Everyone whooped and cheered although I knew I was doomed. The skies stayed bright blue but I bled and bled and bled. Menorrhaggia, you said and it sounded like men are raging at you.

We were in the Wilderness and Ma covered the mattress in my room in our holiday cottage with a rubber sheet because every morning I'd wake up drenched in my own blood, having soaked through two pads in the night. I was eleven and it was more blood than I had ever dreamed of. Ma went into George and bought me waterproof panties from the babies' section of the shop and I bled through those too.

We went to the beach one day, and I almost fell down the stairs at Lentjiesklip, dizzy from sun and loss of blood. Down below, under a blue floral umbrella, Uncle Wolfie, a gynaecologist now, was sitting with his wife in big black sunglasses and a straw hat while Warren, his freckled son, played beach bats with Simon on the sand. You and Uncle Wolfie had a little talk at the edge of the water, waves curling around your ankles and later that afternoon you and Ma drove me into George to Uncle Wolfie's rooms at the side of his house just like yours. His waiting room had a gurgling fish tank near the receptionist's desk with blue-streaked neons, gouramis and a pale, pale fish without eyes. A blind cave, the receptionist said, used to swimming in the darkest of black caves, in the blackest of deep seas.

Uncle Wolfie's examination room was painted light yellow, with an examination table covered in tight brown leather, with a paper sheet over half of it. You and Ma and Uncle Wolfie were all in the room together and Ma told me to take my clothes off, and I handed them to her, blue shorts and a red-and-white checked shirt. I wasn't wearing a bra yet but my breasts were just beginning to grow and there was hair under my arms which I was terribly embarrassed about. I didn't know whether to hide my titties or my underarm hair so I just rolled over onto my stomach, face right up against the leather. I was still wearing the waterproof panties over the sanitary napkin which was held in place by two loops and an elastic belt around my waist. Take that off, Uncle Wolfie said, pointing to the panties and Ma put a beach towel under me so that I didn't get blood all over Uncle Wolfie's table. Then he asked me to open my legs really wide the way the dentist asks you to open your mouth really wide and I closed my eyes pretending to be the blind cave swimming in the black sea, not seeing anything ever.

It was the same summer Simon had worms and I remember a similar thing happening to him, you and Ma examining him with a flashlight. He was almost fourteen and he looked like a very big insect upside down with his legs all over the place and the two of you looking for the tiny threadworms in his bum, ready to scoop them out with cotton buds. So between Simon and the blind cave it wasn't so bad, lying there with the three grown-ups standing over me talking about girls getting their periods and how this sometimes happens in the beginning when the hormones are sorting themselves out. You were talking loudly, almost shouting, saying something about Gertrude and blood on your mother's tablecloth at Ebb 'n Flow. Ma got really furious and said Harry, You're talking rubbish again! And Uncle Wolfie said, Of course I remember Gertrude. Those were the days, old chap. Then he put this shiny metal thing that looked like two big spoons inside me and opened it. I saw this from between my shuttered eyelids and then I felt it, as if something had torn away my skin and was sitting right inside me, a big new guest of some sort. I was not sure whether it was better to breathe more or breathe less so I thought of the fish again, and Simon's bare bum in the air, that I just caught a glimpse of, as I was walking past his bedroom on the way to the toilet in the night.

It's going to be fine, Uncle Wolfie said. Everything looks alright in there. In a doctor's quick second, you shifted places with Uncle Wolfie and it was you holding the thing with two spoons. I swallowed one breath on top of another, and then it was all over, Uncle Wolfie telling us as we were on our way out, She should take some iron pills in case she gets anemic. Ma was still angry when we drove back in the car, to our house on the river's edge. She hated it when you spoke about the past, which you did all the time, and how jolly it was, life without her, life before her, life when you were just a boy from George. You got even angrier, calling her superior and her brothers even more superior, with their fancy, lah-di-da ways and their bullshit wives and how they looked down on you from their dizzy heights, looking down on everyone who wasn't a Sacks. You started to drive faster and faster over the mountain pass between the Wilderness and George, faster and faster on the single lane road, as it swept higher and higher to the summit, with its breathtaking views of the long beach below. I could see our car flying off the road, and falling into the sea and all that would be left of me would be a baby's blood-soaked rubber panties.

Soon after our trip to George, the bleeding stopped. The rest of the summer I looked away whenever I saw Uncle Wolfie on the beach. He mostly didn't notice me but when he did, he leaned over and made this funny squeaking, whistling sound in my ear, his old trademark. It never used to bother me before but now it did.

A CLOUD CROSSES the face of the sun and you slide into the cold again, and I'm pulling Ma's cardigan across my shoulders and shivering. She's back in the room and Simon's gone now. She's reading the newspaper, searching perhaps for the comic strip from the old days, Modesty Blaise and Willie Garvin up to their tricks, scaling walls and deep-sea diving, flushing out evil wherever they go. But it's a different time, and a different place, and I can't even find the tongue that will ask, Do you remember Modesty?

Instead she's plunging into a litany of terrible crimes, the four-year-old girl who was raped by ten men, the white housewife who was stabbed and thrown into her own pool to drown. I'm shouting, Stop it! And she says, I'm just telling you what it says in the newspaper.

I'm hanging onto your every breath, the faint whistle as the air escapes from your lips. The pause, where time stops, and so do you, and then the next inhalation and the merry-go-round spins around and around, and I'm flying backwards with you, leaving Ma and her newspaper and the screens and machines behind.

* * *

A WHISTLE BLOWS as your train pulls into the station. Nobody helps you with your suitcases. Hell's teeth, Harry, you're a man now. You look up and there it is. Table Mountain. Look at the famous tablecloth of cloud spilling over the top! Look at how flat the mountain is!

You're standing in the middle of Adderley Street, the city humming and swirling around you, a current that's pulling you this way and that. The mountain is not saying anything but the seagulls are screaming and the air is sharp with the smell of the sea. The flower sellers are sitting with their buckets and their blooms and this is what your ma told you about, the swirl of yellows and pinks and oranges, reds and purples. You want to buy a thousand daisies, a million roses, all the white blossoms in the world because today is the first real day of your life, with your hand on your suitcase, and your suit almost fitting but not quite. A little big in the shoulders but the pants are cuffed and straight and how can you worry about anything on a day like today.

It's noon and the cannon bellows from the old castle. The birds skitter and dip. And look what happened! The sky got even more blue, and that tablecloth keeps rolling over the top of the mountain, rolling and disappearing like magic! You can't stop watching but you have to. You have to find your way to Men's Residence.

You see women walking up and down the street,

their skirts bouncing around their hips, wearing gloves and hats and jackets, crisp and city smart, city slickers with their heels clicking on the pavement. They're smoking and laughing and talking, their lips are red and their hair is soft, and they're all city girls. Their scent drifts past you and it makes you dizzy and you almost faint. Lead me into temptation, please lead me there, you're begging them but they can't hear you. They keep on walking and talking and they don't see you standing there, your eyes big and dark, your nose pointing East then South. A regular old compass! That should help me get around you're thinking, as you pick up your things and try to find your way to Groote Schuur. I'll just follow my nose.

You're on another train, to Mowbray this time, each crunch of the wheels bringing you closer and closer to the hospital. People are sitting on benches and smoking. The windows are streaked with grime, and you peer out. The mountain's still there, I was just checking. There's a girl sitting opposite you and her knee bumps into yours. You say you're sorry but it's her leg that did it, that scraped your pants and took the skin off your heart. She's wearing stockings, isn't she, and where do they end? Your eye lands like a fly on her skirt, in her lap. Her hand is there, resting, and she could brush you away, just like that, but she doesn't. There are flecks of white and yellow and pink in the brown of her skirt, stars floating around in the brown night of her lap. You feel yourself sinking and swooping into the folds, floating and swirling, until you get sucked in, doing somersaults all the way, right down the drain.

Isn't that a French roll in her yellow hair? A twist, a loop, a plum bun? She lights a cigarette and the smoke billows at you, not a tablecloth but a whole bloody blanket. You climb out of the blanket into the fresh air, onto the platform of the train station. So that's where the smoke is now. The Mountain is lifting its cloud-covered hip at you, rocks cocked sideways. Or is it Devil's Peak?

There's a mournful trumpeting sound in the air, a sound that you've never ever heard before. It leads you past the rows of little houses, with their *broekie* lace and tiny front yards. You cross the street, and there's a shop on the corner, the mountain towering ahead, the mad trumpet still ringing in your ears. You're beginning to get worried that it's something loose inside you, the same piece that vibrates with joy, rattles with fury. *Ag*, there he is. It's the fish man, with a pole across his shoulders carrying baskets filled with fish. He's blowing a fish horn, a little trumpet made out of seaweed. You're close enough to see the veins in his forehead as he blows for his customers, the way the rabbi blows the shofar to call his congregants at the New Year. A fat housewife comes out, with an apron full of shillings. She calls the fish man Gatiep, and stands beside him like a sergeant major while he rifles through the *stokvis*, the *kabeljou*, the *snoek*, looking for a fish that's good enough for the madam. You feel the saliva pool in your mouth, the tang in your nostrils, the smell that's linked, now and forever, to the wail of the little fish horn, calling all fish-lovers to come out and buy.

You're five again, shorter than your father's knee, and you're standing in the waves at Buffels Bay watching the Coloured fishermen coming in with their catch. He lifts you up to look, and you want to jump into the middle of the pile of fish. You want to have scales and a tail, and you want to swim. Your father laughs and says, it's tickets for those fish. They're flopping, not swimming, and soon somebody will buy them and cook them for supper. You watch the fishermen scale them on the rocks and it's like watching the stars get scraped out of the sky. Their eyes are ringed in silver and if you look into the middle, the black middle, you can disappear. A wave knocks you down and you come up gurgling, sea water spurting out of your nose.

Joseph! Your ma is suddenly there and screaming, He'll drown! And she has you up in her arms like a housecat, up in the air, and down on the sand. Plop. You can see her breasts wet and heavy under the ruffled part of her bathing costume. They almost knocked you over.

Gatiep is holding a *snoek* in front of you, the famous fish of the Cape. Do you have any coelacanth? you ask, and Sorry, he says, we don't have cedar camps. The housewife is looking at you as if you need your mouth washed out with soap. I just wanted to know, you say. You know that's how they caught the first one. In a fishing boat. It has a puppy dog's tail. *Ag*, that one, says Gatiep. Old Fourlegs. He laughs a hacking laugh and the housewife backs away, as if he's got rabies.

Where's the new hospital? you ask Gatiep, and he points up the road, across a big street. Fresh white buildings with red roofs, a slow curve under the mountain. The Palace of Sickness. Men's Residence is a few blocks away. This is what the warden told your mother on the telephone. The fish horn is fading, fading, as you carry your heavy suitcase and your trunk towards Groote Schuur. The Hippocampus is not far from the Descending Horn. The place where you will live and eat is not far from the place where you will take a sharp knife and cut into the body, where you will lift the veil of the skin and peer in.

But that's next year, after botany, chemistry, physics and zoology. There's one last gasp left in 1938. Soon 1939 will be yours.

CHAPTER 7

Nooi, nooi die riet-kooi nooi	*Girl, girl, the reed bed is made,*
Die riet-kooi is gemaak	*The reed bed is made,*
Die riet-kooi is vir my gemaak	*The reed bed is made*
Om daaroop te slaap . . .	*For me to sleep on.*

YOU LOOK UP Adderley Street, towards Table Mountain and the klopse are coming, made up in blackface, white rings around their eyes and mouths, wearing top hats and satin costumes, in yellow and purple, bright orange and lime green, turquoise and pink. It's *Tweede Nuwejaar*! The day after New Year. *Boem*, pffff, *boem*, pffff . . . *"O Alibama, O Alibama . . . die Alibama die kom oor die see . . ."*

Listen to that bubbling banjo. The Coon Carnival is here. Mickey, who shares a room with you at Men's

Residence, is standing next to you and he's shaking he's so excited. Mickey comes from Kimberley and he is not used to wearing shoes. He shifts his weight from one foot to the other, and claps and sways just like the *klopse* coming down from the mountain. Mickey Levin, he said, with a cigarette dangling from his lips, when you met him a few days ago. Are you the chap from George? He has a pencil-thin moustache and is about a foot taller than you. His face is in the way but you don't even care. The music is fantastic!

The first group has sequins on their top hats, shimmering pink frock coats, white satin trousers. Even their shoes are white. They are so close you can see the beads of sweat dappling their black and white faces, the wetness under their arms. You can hear the creak and rustle of their costumes, the sound of their breath between songs. It's bloody marvelous the way they double shuffle and shoulder shake, the way their bodies tremble and dip with that mad minstrel sound, African ragtime and American jazz, dancing and laughing together under that blue, blue sky, the fairest Cape in all the circumference of the earth, so said Sir Francis Drake.

And Mickey. He loves to quote, and drink Scotch, and sometimes he takes you along, like today. He says you're his right-hand man, his batman, his swan's foot, his croix de guerre and you're not quite sure what it all means but you say yes, and you take the bus or the train or you walk, taking two steps, and sometimes three for every one of his.

Moppies and *sopvleis*, funny songs and serious ones, love songs and marching tunes, all the way to the Green Point Track, where there's a big singing competition. *Boem*, pffff, *boem*, pfffff, the *ghomma* drum beats the hot sun right into your bones. You can feel a line of sweat curling into a road across your scalp, then dripping down your neck into a wet field across the middle of your back, soaking that stiff new shirt from your father's shop on Hibernia Street. Harry, Mickey says, this comes from when the slaves were freed. When was that? You remember the tree outside the library in George, and Maisie and Ma and Bertie and your father, and suddenly the sun dips behind the mountain.

1834? Something like that. You look at the Coons and the colours are so bright that you want to scream. Let's go back, you say to Mickey, I've had enough. But the *klopse* keep coming, waves and waves of flaming colours, and stamping feet, cascades of satin, whole mountains of song and dance. Come on, man, Mickey says, I thought you were a song-and-dance man. What's wrong with you?

Suddenly the river comes to you. You're on a boat again with your old friends and it's not so hot anymore. The sky is grey, threatening rain, and you're rowing and rowing and rowing. Someone is tickling you from behind and it's that Gertrude. Damn her! You've just lost the oar and over you go, straight into the water, rocking the boat and turning everything upside down. But when you turn, it's Mickey and the water is your own sweat, not the river. He looks down at you, blocking the sun, and you want to hit him for being there, just standing there like that, bigger and taller and better.

What's wrong with you? He gives you a big *klap* on the back which makes you grind your teeth. He put a canna leaf in your beer two nights ago and you will never ever forget how horrible it tasted. Now he wants to go for a drink somewhere and he'll probably put something else into your drink. Don't growl at me, Harry, he says, save that for the Krauts. Krauts, what krauts? You had almost forgotten about them since you came to this city, with its tablecloth and fierce winds and crowds of high-heeled girls click-clacking down the streets. Mickey likes to bet and he's got one going with another new chap, Sam, about what happened in September. Mickey says Hitler will not stop and Sam says of course he will. He's got Sudetenland and now he's happy. That's enough *lebensraum*, don't you think?

You remember Maisie doing Physical Jerks and then, Yes, I believe it is peace in our time! Your ma was happy although your father grumbled about what happened to the Czechs. Come on, Joseph, she said, the prime minister's such a fine-looking gentleman! *Fein Shmecker*, he said. I'm sure they had caviar on toast while they signed away the whole bloody country. Your ma stared at him in that English-English way. Your father crumpled, sat behind his paper and you could hear her seething inside, Look at him, he's from the shtetl. He didn't even pass Matric.

You're walking down Long Street with Mickey and it's blazing hot. Your ears are still stinging from the drums and the songs and there's suddenly a Coon right in front of you, washed in green and gold. He flashes a big smile in your face, his front teeth missing. You bump into him and his head darts up and down, his face against your shoulder, as he dips and twirls around you. There's a black-and-white streak on your new jacket, where his makeup came off. He blows a big, fat kiss when he sees you rubbing the spot. Now you and Mickey are standing in front of the Blue Lodge, a big old cake of a building. It's light blue and dark blue and white, with a dark blue roof and filigreed Victorian balconies light as an Irish girl's blue, blue eyes. Mickey's father is in the hotel business and he knows the man who owns the Blue Lodge. Blau is his name, blue just like his place. Harvey Blau. Just ask for him, he told Mickey, tell him you're my son and he'll give you and your pals a free drink.

Drinks on the house! You're in the ladies' bar, and it smells like Sunday afternoon, cool, a little damp, the rose-red carpet sticky under your feet. Old smoke is still in the air, and a few glasses have a bit of drink left in them. The bartender, Moses, has his dark arms in the sink, washing tall beer-glasses with steaming, soapy water. Blau is there, a cigar between his lips, and his eyes the colour of whiskey. He's wearing suspenders, girding his round stomach like exclamation points. He rocks back on his little feet, looking at Mickey as if he's a godson. Mickey

Levin, he crows, You're going to be a doctor! Mickey pushes you forward, and you hold out a hand, embarassed. Harry, pleased to meet you. Blau winks at Moses, Where are the girls? Miss Lily is sleeping, and so is Koeka.

The clock ticks heavily on the wall. Four o'clock. The paint on the walls is reddish, like the floor, with dark, sweaty patches. Mickey has found a newspaper and is sitting on a sagging, bow-legged armchair. You try a cigarette but it tastes like ash in your mouth. Blau left and now it's just you and Mickey and Moses in the back, restocking and reshelving the bottles. You ask for water and Moses smiles and gives you a huge glass filled with warm water. It's as big as a bathtub and you raise it to your lips. Cheers! You say but Moses has ducked under the bar and Mickey is almost asleep, as if this is his own house. There's a sound on the staircase like the twitter of birds and your throat catches. You almost drop water all over yourself but you put the glass down, and move it away. Let someone else drink up this lake.

You look into the forest of mirrors and glasses because you don't want to look the other way, at the creaking, laughing stairs. Up goes an eyebrow, as you catch yourself in the mirror, between the Avocat and the Richelieu. Blue-black brows, slicked down hair, another wing of the same bird, and that damn nose again. You point it up, not South. That's better. You can smell the girls from here, your mother's lilac mixed with brandy and sweets and comics. There's one in the mirror now, and it's probably Koeka. Her yellow hair is coiled and twisted as if she just fixed it. You notice all the hairs that didn't make it. The tiny bushes and thickets still sprouting all over her neck. What happened to her eyebrows? They're so thin, that it looks like someone polished her forehead and scraped them off by mistake. She's sticking her tongue between her teeth and your ma would scold her for that. *Ag*, she's just licking off some lipstick. She catches you watching her in the mirror and she whirls around, twirling her tight, tight skirt. Bottoms up!

Her eyes are muddled and covered with makeup and her blouse is one of those frilly jobbies, in brown and black and grey, and you can't tell whether it's sliding off or not. It's all shifted and tight, her body struggling against the fabric. Your eyes leap onto her breasts, nesting there, as you wrap yourself around the bar stool, holding it between your legs as if it's going to buck, and knock you to the ground.

Wragtig, Mickey really is asleep. There's a soft, puffing sound coming from his chair and the newspaper crinkles a little. The other one, her hair black and loose down her back, is in a dressing gown and slippers. She lights a cigarette and whispers in the yellow one's ear. On the house. Moses looks up, and he has a boiled egg and a slice of bread on a plate and the dark one goes over to eat it. He calls her Koeka, and so Lily is the blonde, with the twisting clothes and the fluffy neck.

Nobody talks to you. Maybe they don't notice. Or they're busy. Mickey is the man, the one who everybody is waiting for, the one with the key in the door. You can see dust dancing in the doorway, a shaft of light coming in from a window in the passage. If you stare for long enough, the specks turn into light green and orange dots, pulsing in front of your eyes, in time with the lubb-dubb of your heart. Your lips are dry and you can't even remember if the wind was blowing outside anymore. Koeka walks over to you, sits down right next to you on a bar stool. She has something in the right corner of her mouth, a bit of bread, or a smear of fish and all you want to do is tell her to wipe it off. Instead, you try to stare into the distance, except there is no distance. Koeka leans close to you and you can really smell her now. Her hair drifts across your arm, and it looks like the seaweed in the Wilderness lagoon except it's black not green. You never liked that seaweed. She even smells lagoony, you're thinking, as you consider trying another cigarette. God, there's some food on her hair! You have to do something.

Let's go, she says, and she takes your hand as if she's marching you off to detention. She's winking—or blinking?—at you over her shoulder and that long lagoon hair is flying into your eyes and you're walking up the stairs into the dust and the light, past dying flowers on the walls, into a new smell altogether, blocked drains, sea water and urine. Where's Mickey? You look back and Oh, my God, he's necking with the other one, Lily, and his hand is in her brown shirt. You're going to die of fright. What does this lagoon lady expect? What the hell!

You wanted the fluffy one, the chicken girl, not this one, touched with the tar brush. Her hair drips into everything, flies into everything, moss trailing into brown water at Ebb 'n Flow. What if it gets into your mouth. You run the back of your hand across your lips, checking. She's opening the door. It sticks a little and she gives it a shove. *Ag*, no. Not this place. It's got water on the walls, a wobbling lopsided flower stain that's probably someone's toilet overflowing upstairs. She's undoing your belt! What did Mickey say when you weren't listening? What was he telling you on the train from Mowbray about Harvey Blau's funny hotel. You were looking at a nice-looking girlie then, and she wasn't wearing a bloody dressing gown. In fact, she was getting her stockings right and you were watching. Mickey's mouth was moving but you must have ducked because the words didn't touch you. They kept going and going like a tune in another room, in another house.

Is she really laying your pants out like that, as if she's your maid or something? Maybe she's going to iron them and this was really an ironing trip, and you're in a special ironing hotel. Come here, *boytjie*, she says, and she puts your hands inside the dressing gown right on her ta tas.

Corpora Cavernosa! You stop, in terror, in front of the Roman guards. They tear off their breastplates. They have breasts! You hold Koeka's breasts in your hands, and they're beasts not breasts. They snuffle at you, red-eyed and heavy, luminous moles, night animals. You can see tiny blue roads in the semi-demi dark. You trace them with your fingers and the world explodes around you. Everything goes. You're alone, *stoksielalleen*. Even Maisie is finished. Over and done with.

You follow your hands, your mouth, your throbbing fishtail. Your mother called it that, uncovering you on chilly mornings, your penis erect under your pajamas. You laughed at it. My long penis, you said and she covered you with a sheet. Put that fishtail away.

It's driving you now, that fishtail, corpora cavernosa, with its crus and its bulb and its fossa. Oh, God, vessels of pleasure filling and overflowing, your hands holding the sacred gourds. A coelacanth is driving you from here to eternity. You're holding its scales, its funny legs, its puppy dog's tail and it's pulling you under, into the blackest part of the ocean. Koeka's face swims above you, someone staring at you from dry land. You want to stop but you can't. You've lost everything. Don't go, they're shrieking, the voice of your mother and your sister and Bertie. Don't leave us behind. Your dad is waving and screaming and he has his hand out. Koeka takes something from him. It's a French letter and she's wrapping you in it. The tightness makes you scream. She covers your mouth and you're on top of her now, and the fish goes in.

The window's all cockeyed and Table Mountain's upside down. You lift yourself, looking at Koeka from inside out, your lungs buried in her chest, your heart stuffed into her throat. The burning, beating sound is coming from outside, from the drumming Coons, beating and banging their drums as you slide in and out. *Eina!* Koeka is talking to you but the words float past like balloons. *Eina!* Your hand is wrapped in her hair and her face twists. A tear squirts out of her eye, hot and sad, but you're too far gone. She arches her back and grabs her ta-tas and they're all over you. It's raining nipples and soft skin and God, this is too, too much! The fishtail lifts you up, raises you, and you're almost there, edging off the cliff, still hanging, not quite fallen, still holding on. Koeka brushes her left nipple, squeezing it and you tumble off the burning cliff, lost in lava, man eaten by fire, torched by his own sword. A thousand gleaming fish scales settle on your head, slowly settle, as you land.

The crowds are cheering. You run around the arena, the laurel wreath circling your forehead. Harry, Harry! You can hear them shouting your name. You close your eyes. Peace. Peace in our time. Koeka blows her nose on a greyish handkerchief, which she stuffs under her pillow. She gets up, and on goes the dressing gown. The way she's wrapping the cloth belt around her waist you'd think she was tying up a prisoner. She leans out of the window to watch the last of the carnival and her back makes you randy all over again. Go, she says, out of the window, just go. The *klopse* are coming again. *Boem*, pffff, *boem*, pffff. . . . And Koeka's waving.

It's all over. How about that. *Boem*, pfff, *boem*, pffff . . . Koeka comes towards you with your pants as if she's your ma and she's going to dress you. I'm not a baby, you tell her. Sorry. I have a boy in Matric, she tells you, opening the door before you can say anything.

You're back in the passage and this time there is hair in your mouth, a long damp string of it that you almost swallowed. Where is Mickey, the canna man? You hear a woman's muffled scream and a groan from someone's gut. Mickey? Mickey? You almost whisper.

At the bar, this time, you have a real drink. Whiskey. Koeka's probably back in the window, smoking, but you're down here now, and it seems like wonderland, soft lights, glowing bottles. Moses has a little shine to him. He's standing in a cup of light and he's pouring gold. Here, have some gold!

Mickey is back, his shirt browned a little from the yellow one's makeup, and he says to you, Let's take a walk by the sea. You're on a bus again, rumbling past Signal Hill, towards Sea Point and that's where you get off, to walk along the beachfront with your pal, looking at girls again, watching the waves suck and gurgle around the black rocks. Where is the world? You think, staring out to sea. Where is the rest of the world?

CHAPTER 8

~

DR. DANIELS DOESN'T want Americans asking him a million questions! Ma's hands are flying to her ears. All I want to know, I'm saying between gritted teeth, is what went wrong? Why can't I ask him that?

Your father knew he wasn't going to make it, she says, rocking backwards and forwards in the chair. If something bad happens, he told me, I don't want them to bring me back.

He'd just fallen and broken his arm! I say, but she shakes her head. No, no. It wasn't a simple break. Because of the Paget's Disease, his bones were brittle. That's why the operation took so long. He said, Stella, this is a balls-up, just before he went in to surgery. He knew!

You're still her husband, even with your loud voice

suddenly quiet, all your thoughts and your stories and your bad moods swirling in the room with us. Perhaps she knows that this is how you wanted to go but as I look at your still, closed eyes I have trouble believing it.

She's fidgeting now, with the engagement ring on her bony finger, telling me how she's thinking of giving me something for my fortieth birthday which came and went several months ago. Wouldn't I like this diamond reset into a necklace? I'm staring into it, the unblinking hard stone of your marriage, and I can hear ma's screams in the middle of the night, when you came at her with your bare hands and you woke us up with what you threatened to do but didn't. You needed us there, the boy and the girl to stop you when you had your hands around her throat and she glared at you, eyes ice-cold and withholding. I was sobbing my eyes out and Simon was screaming and kicking you in the balls and then you let go and we all traipsed off to bed and went to sleep and that was the end of that. The next morning, she read the newspaper with a scarf around her neck, her lips painted bright-red and she didn't look up when you came into the room to have your breakfast. You drank your tea standing up, pouring the tea into the saucer to cool it down, making a slurping, sucking sound. When she shook the newspaper, turning it inside out, I almost jumped out of my skin thinking you were going to fly at her neck again, black eyes bulging, eyebrows on fire.

Betsy, Ma says, would you like to have it? And I'm

back at your bedside looking at Ma's diamond and I can't say no and I can't say yes so all I do is nod.

THE FROGS ARE roaring in the Wilderness lagoon, a croaking so loud it's bound to wake you up, make you shake off your coma like a bad dream. Did you know frogs and toads never eat with their eyes open? They have to push down with the back of their eyeballs to force food into their stomachs. You and Mickey and Mattie and Chris, Louis and Tom are having breakfast before Botany, loose eggs on toast, in the big hall at Men's Residence. Tom is talking and he gets coffee on his tie. *Ag* no, he says, and he doesn't swallow with his eyes closed. He just dabs and dabs his tie. He knows the professors look at you up and down when you go into the class. They notice spots and stains and dirty pants. You all wear suits and ties and they have to be clean, clean, clean. No one wants a dirty doctor.

You try closing your eyes and yes, it works, the horrible egg slides down and maybe it'll stick to your ribs or your legs. Maybe you'll get a little fatter, a little bigger. Maybe Dorothy, the only girl, the clever girl, will move her frog next to yours. She doesn't mind the smell of formalin. She likes to cut. When she sits, her leg twitches and Mattie says it's because she likes frogs so much she keeps a spare one under her skirt. Just in case.

Anemophily. Pollination where pollen is carried on the wind. Anemophilous flowers are usually unscented.

The male flowers have numerous exposed stamens. The female flowers have long, feathery stigmas. You can't help laughing and Mickey kicks you under the table. Don't expose your stamen, old chap. Don't give away our secret.

And the class hasn't even started yet. For a moment, the room vibrates and you wonder where you are. The man's clothes on your body, even your hand cupping your shaven chin seem to belong to someone else, someone living the life of a grown man, someone who isn't you. You are a *pikkie*, still, holding onto the chair leg to pull yourself up, looking up at the world from under the table. The day you heard the *klopse* sing was a dream. It wasn't true and all you really remember about Mickey is that he once put a canna in your beer. Don't ever do that to me again. You give him a thick eyebrow look, over the top of your nose but he's getting up already. He doesn't care.

Everything is new here, and there are rules about everything. There is a warden called Smithy and you can't come back too late, and you can't bring a girl past the front door unless she's your mother or your sister or your aunt. You have books galore and a nice brown suitcase to put them in. You share a bathroom with a lot of other young men and sometimes there's mud from their rugby boots all over the floor or no hot water or the toilet gets blocked and you can't even walk into the place without feeling *naar*. You miss the mists of George, the hydrangeas, Maisie and Mom, and even your bicycle father, with his gaiters and his shop and his friends, the commercial travellers. The small streets run through your heart, a map of love and remembrance, places and faces grown in your bones, Hibernia and Meade, Dean and Church, the old road to the Wilderness, Wolfie and Gertrude and Bunny and all the boats bobbing on the lagoon, the dip of the oars and the journey to the beginning of the river, the moss dripping and the throbbing quiet of Ebb 'n Flow.

You are homesick, sometimes sick with longing for the old home and sometimes sick of the home that is sometimes sick with its misery and whirling fights and ma mad as a snake and dad puffing under the counter, hidden in the shop like his very own mouse. Still, you miss them all, especially Mum's God Bless, without a King or a Queen or anything. Just God Bless.

Epiphora, an overflow of tears. You saw the word one dusty, rusty afternoon, deep in the leatherbound *Home Physician,* in the back, back room of the George Library. Watering may be caused by excess tear production due to emotion or to conjunctival or corneal irritation. You can't have epiphora right now, with the others stamping and growling like young tigers around you, their heads cocked above yours. Drop the amphora on the ground, and let all the tears run out. The old man on the train had it, you tell Mattie. The bugger had amphora and he wasn't even sad.

The chairs scrape the floor and it's all up and away we go, off to Botany. You leave your tears, uncried, in the crumpled serviette. Under Flora, look for the forest of the heart, tiny flowers that are paper thin, mantis coloured, and grow just beneath the surface.

Miss Simmons calls you Mr. Klein, Mickey is Mr. Levin, Chris is Mr. Smit. Dorothy, of course, is Miss May. Miss May has her finger inside the book. She's got the right page, and she knows the xylem-phloem story off-by-heart. There are thin dark hairs on her pale arms and under the desk, one of her legs rattles. You aren't the only one who's watching her breathe. Gentlemen, Miss Simmons calls out, and Dorothy May looks up, along with you and Chris and Mickey and the Kimberley boys. One of them, Petrus, is a member of the Ossewabrandwag. He marches once a fortnight with the rest of the members, holding a flaming torch up high, and he wants most of the Jews to jump off Cape Point and drown in the sea. The rest of you can tumble down Table Mountain and die on the rocks. At least that's what he said last Sunday, when he and his pals came to Men's Residence, filled up with liquor, wearing their brown shirts. The warden was there and said he would call the police so they marched off, backwards, forwards, full of threats.

You have to listen if you want your name on a brass plate. Dr. Harold Klein. Not plain old mister. Doctor.

Miss Simmons is saying, Now gentlemen, even though the men aren't gentle and one is a girl. There are two rooms. One is full of big cats and the other is full of little kittens. Between the rooms, there is a membrane through which the little kittens can pass. Osmosis occurs when there are the same amount of cats and kittens in each room . . . and continues until the two solutions are of equal strength unless the movement of the solvent is opposed by applying pressure to the stronger solution. The stronger solution? What is the stronger solution? You write this on a page to Chris. War, he writes back and both of you stare at the board again, where Miss Simmons is resting the point of her chalk, her tall, bony body converging on that one tiny tip. She's purring now, and yes, she's the big cat in the room and you are all the little kittens rushing towards her to restore equilibrium, to osmote. Let's osmote. Your place or mine? Chris laughs and you know he's thinking of dancing tonight, a girl pressed tight against him, her skirt swirling and lifting, her legs following his, back two steps, forward and then back again.

Diffusion is the spread of a substance (by movement of its molecules) in a fluid from an area of high concentration to one of lower concentration, thus producing a uniform concentration throughout. You drift back to the Blue Lodge, and your own diffusion, the sound of the klopse in your ears. You remember how Koeka tried to put on your pants at the end, buckle your buckle. She called you *boytjie*, didn't she? There's a knot in your stomach, rage wrapped around pleasure, and you can't get it undone.

Mr. Sloan! It's Maxwell Sloan, the fellow sitting behind you. Simmons is ready to pounce but Maxwell has all the answers. He's the chap who knows about naked mole rats, Russian cinema and the Antarctic. He has a stamp collection with first day covers from the Boer War. Mickey drawls, He must be pulling your leg. I don't think so, you say. Look at him. Maxwell has the skin of a boy, with old man's eyes behind glasses. He throws and catches sentences like a juggler tossing knives. His mother lived in Brighton when she was a girl, and she tore tickets for her dad at the bioscope. Now she and Mr. Sloan sell shoes in Kenilworth and everybody comes to their shop, even *Ouma* Smuts. Maxwell's brother, Lawrence, is in the poker-*klawerjas* crowd. They're all studying law or history or accounting and they're not dreaming about diffusion or phloeming the xylem. That's another Maxwellism, you tell Mickey but he doesn't blink. He just looks through you the way Wolfie did, that day on the beach when you borrowed the boat.

Another knot tightens on top of the first one. Another bugger spits in your eye. Mickey took the wooden slatted bath mat from the bathroom yesterday because he and some of the rugby chaps are going to toboggan down the steps in front of Jameson Hall. It's Rag, the varsity festival with floats and dances and costumes, boat races with tankards of beer, and the toboggans bouncing and bumping down the stone steps, dozens of steps, then a landing, the men picking up their toboggans and then diving again, bumpity-bump all the way down to the bottom, Devil's Peak frowning behind them. Maxwell told you about *Battleship Potemkin* and the theory of montage, the baby carriage bouncing down the stairs and the broken glasses. His own glasses are never broken, or even smudged. You like to watch him clean them, almost purring as he stares through them, a man looking into his own bright future.

By the time you and Maxwell and Chris get to the top of the steps, there's a crowd there, stamping and chanting, Go, go, go!

It looks like two of the Ossewabrandwag men are in the crowd, in their uniforms, breathing fire on everyone. But then you're not sure if it's real or not because one of the older fellows from Men's Residence is dressed up like Hitler. And there's Haile Selassie in some sort of cape, his face covered with a woolly black beard. Anthony Eden and Mussolini are right in front, and they're about to pick up their bathmat toboggans. Mussolini swaggers a bit first, salutes everyone with a stiff arm. Anthony Eden hands someone his bowler.

The chaps dive down the steps—and Haile Selassie's in front! There's a wave of shrill screams, girls with their red mouths open, but they're lost in the sea of young men, chanting Go, go, go! as the toboggans bang and scrape on their way down. No, wait, it's Hitler in the lead, he just lept off that last landing, his lean body lifting into the air for a moment, then cracking down, wood against stone, bone against wood. He's at the bottom, everyone's around him, raising his arm victoriously, but he can't stand up, he's slumping. He's bleeding.

Maxwell leaps his way down the steps, two at a time,

with you behind him. God, it's Mickey! Mickey dressed up as Hitler! His jaw slopes off to one side. He looks like a broken monkey, drool mixed with blood dripping down his shirt. Serves you right, you silly bugger. Mickey looks at you, his face askew. He can't even wink. He's trying to ask, Did I win? but he spits out a tooth instead. Jesus Christ, man, you say, kneeling down and picking up the tooth. Of course you bloody well won.

There's mist in the air, a celebration spray of rain. Maxwell has his palms on Mickey's face, one on each cheek, and for one mad moment it looks as if they're going to kiss. It's dislocated, Maxwell says, and he pops and twists Mickey's jaw back into place. Mickey gives a grunt from the bottom of his chest.

You make mmntch, mmntch kissing sounds. Mickey grabs your arm, twisting it so hard the mountain almost cracks. You can't make jokes when a chap's done in, Maxwell says. Bastards, you're thinking, bloody bastards, dressed up and everything. What if I was the one lying here dead, or at least in a few bad pieces? What then?

Maxwell looks at you, spots of blood on his glasses, the Battleship man, Mr. Montage. Don't be so paranoid. We love your Royal Lowness. And with a couple of hail-fellows-well-met, they have you back under their wings, their own bright young chicken.

Who needs a mascot when you have Harry, your very own prince of George? Maxwell tells you this, and of course, you're looking up, not down, at the extra inches of his head, balanced on a longer than normal neck, stacked, bone after bone, all the way down to his femur that you could almost fish with, it's so damn long.

Dorothy May, Dorothy May, alert, Dorothy May. Mickey's still taking the Mickey out of Miss May, behind the Hitler moustache, which is jagged now, with dried blood. She looks at the three of you, as if you've all stood upright for the first time, Homo Sapiens Australopithecus, fresh out of a smelly cave. Show us your froggy, is what you want to say but can't. Show us the little green one in its froggy pond. Mickey is lighting a cigarette in the wind, cracked-up jaw and everything. Maxwell's on an island somewhere, in a burrow with his beloved mole rats, all naked. It's up to you, now. It's do or die. Mole and toad, three men in a boat, and who would you think they'd be?

Towed in a Hole, Maxwell says. Laurel and Hardy. It's showing at the British Bioscope in District Six. Care to join us, Diss May? Dorothy's a little troubled. Maxwell isn't a subject she's ever studied before and she's worried she might fail. Don't worry, you tell her, I always get an F. She flashes a lucky smile at you, and you almost fall into her lap. She's wearing spots, tiny white spots dancing all over her breasts and her thighs, with a belt in the middle, like a drawbridge. She's walking next you, and it's not so bad. You can make her laugh. You can make all the girls laugh.

Mickey says, Watch out for *skollies*. I'm going home. It's you and Maxwell and Dorothy May and suddenly, the wind has changed again, Devil's Peak is shrouded, clouded, and Dorothy's eyes are on Maxwell's glasses. She's chasing her own reflection, as she tells him about goat moths and slug moths and loopers. The looper caterpillar! Maxwell acts as if the bloody thing is his long-lost uncle. And bagworms. Did you know that the female is wingless, maggotlike and remains in a bag for life? There's the Maxwell plumebag dotlooper, you tell Dorothy, with a very large head. The male loves to tell lies, especially to the female bagworm. He's an interloper, that dotlooper. A brown playboy, more common in summer.

The one with the delicate tail, the single eyespot? Dorothy's in your hand now, her tiny tongue licking up traces of sugar. You're dying to cross the drawbridge, carry her into the castle, swim the moat if you have to. Maxwell's hovering, his bloody mole rats in his pockets, and one up his sleeve. Sergei Eisenstein's right behind him, montage and all. Tell the Russian to get lost. *Vat jou goed en trek*, Ferreira. Back to the steppes.

You're very funny, Harry. Dorothy's leaving, and it's you and Maxwell at the bottom of the steps, being left like this, high and dry. Unseasonal, unreasonable, two men and no boat. Let's look into a tube, Maxwell says, study the female brain stem and all its attendant fistulae, as the sun drops into its socket.

CHAPTER 9

HE'S A GREAT man, Ma says wonderingly, handing me a pile of letters and notes from your patients. The Cronjes, de Wets, the du Plessis family and all those Schoenraad children. All the teachers from the School for the Deaf! A whole street of houses in Zwelentemba! They all want to know how he is. I flip through the pictures of pansies and roses, the marbled sheets, the hands folded in prayer and then the simpler ones, pages torn from an exercise book, the writing painstaking and spidery correct. You were always our friend. You were always there to help us and now we are praying for you, *Dokter* God.

Outside this window, cars stream along De Waal Drive, the way the blood still flows through your veins, except in your case there are traffic jams and pileups and smoke streaming out of the bonnets of cars, whole sections of road that have been closed.

The room is suddenly full of uncles again, Ma's brothers arranged like long, grey birds in white coats around your bed, First Prize, the oldest, rocking on his heels and looking particularly grave. I'm digging my nails into my palm because they're talking your language, First Prize murmuring about a possible iatrogenic fluid overload in theatre, the others asking, Did he have an MI? Did he have kidney failure going in? Perhaps he shot an embolism. Their hypotheses unfurl into the air around you, circle you, enfold you but you can't understand a word they're saying. What I'm trying to hear is what you're whispering to me in your sleep, what happened that night they brought you here in an ambulance, struggling to breathe.

You're calling me to come over. Look, Betsy, at the cover of *The Lancet,* all my medical journals. See that symbol, the intertwined snakes? That's Asclepius' stick. Asclepius would put his patients to sleep with a magic potion, an ancient sleeping pill, and then he would put his ear to their mouths and listen to what they said. What he heard told him what had made them sick, and then he would find a cure.

I'M WATCHING YOUR dreams, Daddy, as you murmur to me. You're dreaming of dancing knives, dancing girls, the mountain on top, Rock of Ages, a slip of a dream, when the warden comes into your room at Men's Residence. It's as if a billy goat is there, all woolly and unkempt, stumbling into the middle of the night. All he can say is, The Telephone. It's bloody cold in the warden's office in your flannel pajamas from your father's shop, the last drizzly morning of the last day of August, 1939. The clock says two and that's not a good sign. Nobody's ship comes in at two unless it's a pirate ship, all black and hulking, slipping into the harbour, hiding between the rocks like a big old bat. The same bat is in your chest, your lungs turned into something grisly and folded, your heart a frightened mouse trying to run away.

You see your breath, your own life puffing in front of your lips, as Uncle Oscar speaks to you, your mother's oldest brother who lives on the other side of Muizenberg. You've seen the train from his house. He tells you that your father got influenza on his way back from the wedding in Johannesburg. There's a whistle and rattle in the phone as if the phone has influenza and you shake the mouthpiece. He died, Uncle Oscar says. Just now. The whole bloody mountain lifts up and sinks into the sea. Far, far away you see your mother's old letter dancing in front of you, the one you got today with its happy news of the wedding and such, and her birthday wishes to you, and her funny line, Like all good things, it is all a good old has been by now. Yes, she mentioned a cold on the train but it was a cold alright, a sniffle or two, not Death.

You tell Uncle Oscar. But it's not true, he had a cold in the head, a cold in the nose, nothing but a bloody cold and this must be your idea of a joke to wake me up like this and I'm going to fail my exam and it will serve you right. Your voice is very small (the mouse is talking) and you're shrinking inside the pajamas which were two sizes too big anyway, just in case you grew and grew while no one was looking.

No, you say. No. The billy goat is back in the room snuffling and shuffling and he sets a big cup of tea down in front of you. That's when you know it's true. The message is floating up to you in the steam from the teacup, in the uncommon kindness for something very uncommon. You sit down next to the tea and Uncle Oscar is telling you about another letter which your mother wrote two days ago which is on its way to you but now it's too late. He's dead already. Yes, she did make a telephone call but you were at a Botany class looking at Dorothy May's frog and you heard that he was sick but sick isn't dead. Sick isn't even dying. There's a problem with the tea because you're crying now and the tea is heaving over the side, not really a storm in a teacup but a real storm, a real fight in your chest between the black bat and the mouse and it looks like the mouse is winning.

The goat has an overcoat over his pajamas and he brings you a Scottish blanket which you pull around your mouse shoulders. Uncle Oscar is coming to get you in the morning, with Uncle Herman. Pull yourself together, Uncle Oscar says, Think of your poor mother. Maisie's been in the shop while your father was so sick and Bertie was lost yesterday and they almost thought there were going to be two funerals but then they found him in the kist, all crumpled and wet. Silly bugger, all crumpled and wet. A little flicker of light for a second, and then back to the general dark, the vast blanket of misery that seems to have dropped down onto everything. Buck up, Uncle Oscar is saying, You're the man of the house now. It's raining in George. (You can't help remembering the George license plate CAW, Cold And Wet.)

You've turned into the Snow King, your heart shot through with icicles, your feet two frozen paddles slapping and cracking against the cold stone floor of the courtyard. Your room is nothing but notes and books and the signs of former times. Tickets to the British Bioscope which you saved—possible collector's items, when all is said and done—and the letter dated early August about Auntie Lieba and the wedding. You collect all the pieces and put them in a drawer which you lock. If you lose the letter and the tickets, you'll be sorry.

Of course the wooden bathmat is gone—used for the toboggan races—and there's no hot water to shave with. Shaving cleanly is your forte. You leave no hair unscythed. But then, what? Looking at your face in the mirror is like looking at someone's ugly brother, the one with the terrible nose and bloodshot eyes, the one who didn't really grow up properly, with one foot on land and the other on a boat that's drifting away from the dock, the one who always lands up with his arse in the bloody river. You see your father pedalling away from you on that stupid bicycle and you suddenly want to kill him, even though he's dead already. Who said you could go and die like this, just take a breath on a train and die like a fly. Your pointy face looks back at you. I was the one who was supposed to die. I was the one with scurvy and rickets and crickets and every kind of cough and scritch and rash, blephiritis and pneumonia, epiphora and meganoma.

You sit, slumped, on the edge of the bathtub. You've lost a leg or an arm, a big chunk of Harold has just gone down the drain. Your father told you once Harold means "Powerful Armies" and that's a big joke. You're never going to be ready when Uncle Oscar comes.

Dad's Dead. It sits on top of you all the way to George in the car. It looks out of the window with you, at the Garden Route washed in grey, blue-grey, dove-grey, lost love–grey. Of course you don't eat and Uncle Oscar doesn't even *skel* you out. He just gives the chicken sandwiches back to Herman, his brother. You can't eat chicken that's been cut up, laid flat between bread, stained with tomato juice. You can see the bloody thing walking across the yard, the one called Harold and his soulmate, Maisie. They should never have killed Harold. They should have left the poor bugger alone. Mickey packed for you, although he was still drunk from the night before. Who knows what he put in your suitcase, probably empty bottles of Scotch which you're never going to be able to wear to your father's funeral. When he barged into the bathroom to take a piss, he said you reminded him of Sad Samuel, his boy cousin, He helped you get dressed and everything, the drunk helping the bereaved. Grieving, dream, wheat, is what you're thinking as you drive through wheat country, fields of winter stubble, the opposite trip, the backwards birth, the horrible return.

You don't know what was on that train that roared across the Karoo from Johannesburg to George. Was it the boy with the yellow sore, the *oupa* with his wet, wet eyes, or something from the ground, a tiny germ that went from the ground to a sheep, to a piece of sheepskin somebody wrapped around their gun that they cleaned on the train, just in case. You never know what flew in and out of the compartment, or the stinking toilet, or what your father touched or rubbed against or breathed in, or whether it was the tummy thing your mum mentioned in the last jolly letter from George. Thank God you're in a car, even though Herman smells of chicken and pickled tongue and the only way you can stop thinking about the smell is to press the tip of your nose hard against the window. How green is my deviated septum, how long and steep is the Valley of the Shadow of Death?

Riversdale, Heidelberg, Albertinia. Mum, Maisie and Bertie. You're scared of their faces. You're scared of George, the Outeniqua Mountains, the drizzle and the broken everything. The only place you're not scared of is the wooden bridge over the Gouritz River. You stare out of the window at the immense drop and for a moment your heart lifts out of your shoes, and you feel intrepid, crossing the Atlantic, the Pacific, the Romantic. This deep slice into the side of the world, this fantastic chasm, takes your breath away. The rickety bridge sings its frail and wonderful song as you cross.

Little Brak. Great Brak. You're almost in George. Rain beats down on the roof of Uncle Oscar's car, Eliot the Second. Eliot is Charlotte's husband. You married them outside Swellendam, when you went behind a tree to pee. What's going to happen to Charlotte? What's going to happen to all of us?

A train chuffs past you, going in the opposite direction, and there's a special van on the train, donated by South African Railways, carrying the coelacanth to Cape Town. Uncle Oscar read about it in the newspaper. The lady who found the fish is on that train, accompanying it to the South African Museum. Best Fish Story in Fifty Million Years, Uncle Oscar is saying, but you know it already. They called it Latimeria chalumnae, after the Latimer lady who found it. Latimeria chalumnae. Is that what Dad got on the train, the wrong train, a breath of bad fish, some spring tide from a million years ago that sucked him away, that stole him from his place behind the counter, selling beans and jam and umbrellas? Latimeria, malaria, a bite from a fish with teeth older than Moses. Or a sheepskin, its fleece gone sour, the man with the sopping wet eyes, the leaky boy. Nothing is clean or dry. Nothing is safe. You probably killed him yourself with your tap dancing and knobbly knees, all the worries you gave him and your mother, the basket of mystery and misery that came to them the day you were born. That's probably when he started dying.

It's four o'clock in the afternoon when you get out of the car in Meade Street, George. Your mother comes out of the house and says, Did you ever think this could have happened to us? She's standing in the rain, crying and shouting, and Uncle Herman and Uncle Oscar beat a path into the house, past the vale of tears. Mum is powder turning into paste, her shoes in a puddle, her hair lost and loose. For the first time you push her, a rough brokenhearted gesture. Better not get wet, Mum. Better not get a cold. The castle's collapsed and the party's over but everyone's there, under the same old roof. The commercial travellers won't come and the music's stopped but your suitcases are back in the room you share with bad brother, Bertie, who's suddenly old, a tiny man in suspenders sipping tea.

Maisie's mum now, unpacking the dirty shirts Mickey packed, his crumpled packet of cigarettes in the middle of the pile. Was it all that good anyway? She's got escape under her wings, an eye on the door, the waiting car, another life. Of course it was! Don't you remember how Mum laughed like a drain, how she peed on the floor and everything? Have you forgotten the stars under our feet, the laughing house, all the strangers that Dad brought home? Maisie's shrugging, not so. Mum didn't like it, you know. All the food and the money we spent. It's all over and now the till is empty. I saw it with my own eyes. Of course she bloody well liked it! You slap her in the face so hard that she falls on top of old man Bertie who yowls, and bites. There's a mark on your hand and Maisie's crying, and Bertie stamps his foot on yours. This is the way it always goes! Don't you remember? The flying bell, the smashed potato, smack after smack for bad behaviour. But suddenly there's light poking through the window, a stripe on the open suitcase. See! You hug Maisie. The sun's coming through the rain! A monkey's wedding.

Maisie lights one of the cigarettes. The smoke hangs in the air, bad breath over your father's dead body. He would have killed you, you say. Bertie takes a cigarette and breaks it open, dribbling tobacco. It was a happy home. You can see the words written on the floor, curling shards of tobacco telling the truth. Maisie nods, but the foghorn is bleating, and she's going, going, gone. To the chap in the yellow car. Bertie's telling you about him and how he smokes cigars and chuckles. He's short, but fast, and the car is a nice one, Harold. He's got the Ford dealership in De Aar and all across the Karoo. A knife is cutting off your other leg. Chicken Harold and Chicken Maisie are in the soup, but not in the same pot.

All the shops in George are closed because everyone's going to the funeral this afternoon, all the customers who bought mints and linens, the neighbours, teachers, the *dominee*, the brothers from the Outeniqua Lodge. The Coloured man who sharpens knives, Nettie's whole family, every labourer and hedge cutter and woodcutter and Kaaimans River fisherman, garden boy and maid, milkman and butcher's boy, librarian and hops grower, even an ostrich farmer from Oudtshoorn, and Harris Martens, one of your father's favourite commercial travellers who's staying at the hotel. They're English and Afrikaans, cream-coloured and Bantu, Jew and Malay, plump ladies who bought buttons and trinkets, poor Coloured children whose hands Dad filled with sweets, the old *smous*, Rafael, the enormous matron from the hostel, Doctor Brown, with his cracking black bag and delicate wife, no flowers, please, not for a Jew.

The doctor's the one who looks at you gravely, when you ask your medical student questions, peering down at you from his high horse. He saw you at the house, before, and influenza is what he told you. A dreadful case of influenza with multiple complications and exacerbations. His defenses crumbled, his guard was down. The disease bore down on him like a wolf on the fold. We did our level best. We administered tincture after tincture. We wrapped him and soothed him but nothing brought him back from the abyss, I'm afraid to say. He fell right in. The Gouritz is nothing more than a trickle, you're thinking, as your father falls and falls and falls. You're looking down from the bridge, trying to see him. Forty-seven! He was only forty-seven!

But he's at the bottom now, where it's quiet, and there are no more rivers. The cars follow his coffin down York Street, car after car after car. He would have liked to have seen all the models, the new ones and old, the Fords and Chevies, the farmer's lumbering vehicles, Wolfie's sports jobbie, slick and silver in the rain. Forty cars winding their way to the synagogue in the rain, Jew and non-Jew alike. Joseph Klein was everyone's friend. He gave away credit and penny dreadfuls, leftover lumber and free advice. Stupendous bargains at half price. A Grand Display in every line.

Yitgadal v'yitkadash sh'mei raba. . . . You're saying Kaddish for your father in the George synagogue and the words lump and crumble in your mouth, ancient stones scrambling on the riverbed as the water roars in your ears. Son of Abraham who begat Isaac who begat and begat and begat, and now you, son of Joseph, standing up for him because he can't stand up for himself anymore. *Yitbarakh v'yishtabah v'yitpa'ar v'yitromam v'yitnasei. . . .* Your tears are hot on your cheeks, and you can hear Uncle Oscar telling you, Pull yourself together, *Y'hei sh'lama raba min sh'maya v'hayim aleinu v'al kol yisrael, v'imru amen.*

The cars creep down York Street again, as the sun slowly curtseys, fanning lace-blue clouds in every direction, shafts of light spreading through the rain and mist.

Joseph Klein always dreamed of a Jewish cemetery in George, and now, oh God, it's today, and he's the first Jew who's going to be folded into the earth, right here, at the

Pacaltsdorp rail crossing. The Masonic Brethren assemble around the grave, placing sprigs of acacia on the casket and Brother O'Connell, the Irish land surveyor, murmurs, We are all born to die . . . we follow our friends to the brink of the grave. . . . Behind him, the sun shoots bolts of gold across the Outeniqua Mountains, anointing the hills. We see them sink into the fathomless abyss, Brother O'Connell whispers. You're watching him fall again, this time in front of your eyes, sinking into the damp earth of this new, empty place, where there are no other graves, no other fathers, mothers, brothers or sisters. Joseph Klein, General Merchant, Direct Importer and Showroom Specialist. Pioneer in the new burial ground. *Oseh shalom bi-m'romav, hu ya'aseh shalom aleinu v'al kol yisrael, v'imru amen.*

You drop a fistful of earth into the grave, your hand stiff as a claw. You're dizzy and sick with death, Mum burbling next to you, a fountain of grief, worry, fear of the future. We'll be alright, you whisper. We'll manage. (He was only forty-seven!) Goodbye to the ridge of pines, goodbye to the lonely plot in the new cemetery, goodbye to the town of Pacaltsdorp, a tilted open square above browning houses, next to the rail crossing. Goodbye to Dad.

At home, the dining-room table is covered with plates of herring—pickled, chopped, roll-mopped—liver, chopped and festooned with a mosaic of boiled, grated egg, gefilte fish and a garland of sponge cakes and sticky *taiglach.* It's a walled city of sharp, savory smells, with the Jewish mothers of George guarding the ramparts, their sleeves rolled up, aprons smeared with boiled carp, horse-radish, chicken fat. Wolfie penetrates, reaching over and plucking up a roll-mop. One of the largest . . . (the roll-mop rolls in his mouth) corteges . . . ever seen in George. How about that, Harry! He does his slip and pad, aiming for the solar plexus, but then drops his arms, remembering the day. He was a good man. The aprons come off, and the prayers begin. You're sitting shiva, and the cakes have just begun.

God Save the King on the radio, the first day of September, 1939. The six pips from Greenwich and then, This is London, here is the news. Wolfie came for prayers, and Uncle Oscar is rocking on his heels and whispering about money to your mother. In the early morning hours, German soldiers crossed into Poland . . . Ssssht . . . The apron mothers and Nettie, Maisie, Wolfie, Uncle Herman and even Bertie suddenly freeze as the voice from London, pukka Royal Southern British, describes how the Germans attacked from three directions, from the sea, from the air, with tanks. Across several borders, from Lower Germany, Slovakia and East Prussia, with the speed of lightning. And now Hitler's voice ranting, thunderbolts of German crackling through the air waves. *Blitzkrieg!*

Skiet en Donder. Donder en Bliksem. Bertie shouts out his rudest words, *poes* and *piel* and *donner. Bliksem! Blitzkrieg!*

Mum gives him a *klap*, red stripes on his left cheek, Hitler shrieking at all of you. Nobody wants any more herring, Maisie says, and starts moving the food back into the kitchen. SSSSHT*!* Uncle Oscar is spitting he's so furious. STOP WITH THE PLATES*!* Mum's stamping and champing. The sun is setting and it's time for prayers. The British man is back on and he says that the railway lines have been destroyed by the Luftwaffe, along with hundreds and hundreds of Polish planes. Stop with the planes! Stop with the planes! Bertie hops on one leg, as if he's got water in his ear. The plates crash in the kitchen sink and Uncle Oscar turns up the knob on the radio so that even the static roars.

Yitgadal v'yitkadash sh'mei raba . . . (Mum snapped off the radio, just like that, and told you to start.) Son of Abraham who begat Isaac who begat who begat and begat, and now you, son of Joseph, standing up for him because he can't stand up for himself anymore. Wolfie, Uncle Herman, Uncle Oscar, Mr. Wolk, Mr. Berelowitz, Izzy So-and-So, Harris Martens, the commercial traveller, Rafael the *smous* and Solly Shipman, saying Kaddish with you. Your father's still dead, the Hebrew words circling like moths. There's very little money in the shop. Mum will have to sell everything. Estate of late J. Klein. The public of George and District are notified that all goods in store are offered at marked prices with a special discount for cash. Come early to make your selections.

You have to go back on the train tomorrow. Uncle

Oscar says he'll pay for expenses, the dissecting tools, the white coats, whatever you need, my boy. And, of course, he'll pay for your studies, as long as you study, young man. You're going to be a doctor. The planes buzz in your ears, and there's fury beating in you, while Poland collapses and England declares war. Not your war, Uncle Oscar says. The money's short.

Whose war is it? There's a split in the cabinet right down the middle. The fuse is burning on the Fusion government. Hertzog wants to stay neutral but Smuts doesn't. The train puffs into the station, Mum and Bertie and Maisie silent in the billowing steam, a different goodbye. You're thinking about the coelacanth in the special railway van, and how it's in Cape Town already, being restuffed and remounted. It arrived on the same day as a foreign visitor, and there were flags waving in the streets, which Miss Marjorie Courtenay-Latimer thought were for her, and her dead old fish.

You know nothing's waving for you. You're neither fish nor fowl, not famous or foreign, just a boy flung into a man, *boytjie* into *mannetjie*. Sometimes you think they must have thrown the best part away when you were born, and kept the afterbirth. The real baby boy is gone. The one who would have grown properly, the one who didn't kill his own father.

Grave Crisis in South Africa, say the papers. And you can't help thinking of Joseph Klein, alone in his grave, alone in the new Jewish cemetery in George, with no friends or neighbours, no company. The man who invited strangers and travellers and cousins and uncles into his house, who gave away marbles and toffee and spades for two minutes of conversation, for a story, for news of a bigger world. He gave away everything and now they're selling the shop for a song. The government's in big trouble and the twelve cabinet ministers are meeting on a Saturday afternoon. The words in the newspaper wriggle across the page, jump into your lap, as the train rumbles back across the Southwestern Cape. Nothing's real anymore, and the mountains outside aren't skipping like lambs. You're cold to the bone, and you close the window of the train compartment. Eyes closed, you're counting ministers in the dark. Six are for Smuts, and five are on Hertzog's side. Smuts, Hertzog, Smuts, Hertzog . . . Choo . . . choo . . . Same old train, same old song, but now there's a war in the world again.

It's raining in Cape Town and you can't even see Table Mountain. Even Signal Hill is swaddled with rain clouds. The old monkeys are on honeymoon somewhere, and the new ones haven't even thought about weddings. They're still weeping at your father's funeral, wiping their eyes under the dripping pine trees. Hertzog believes he's going to win. And he's right! Yes, we'll all stay out of this war, and let the Germans march as they please. The Ossewabrandwag boys will be happy tonight. They'll break what's left of your father's shop. They'll break you.

You're back with Mickey and Maxie again, back

under the portals of Men's Residence. Maxie's drowning in newspapers and Mickey's a bit drunk but they're both sorry. They bought you gin and a bucket of oysters, shucked by the oyster boys. You don't like gin very much and you pour the gin in the bucket and the oysters down your throat, one after the other, like a ruffled seabird. Maxie's gone mad with the war and everything and he's forgotten about chem and bot and bio. He's six pips to the wind, Greenwich mean time every minute of the day, and now this. Smuts' amendment to Hertzog's motion, to "continue as if no war is being waged." Ja-nee, yes-no, the Union will declare war on Germany. The buggers sitting on the fence capitulate and Smuts wins, 80 votes to 67. Hertzog's resigned! Mickey's screaming as if the Ikeys just won Inter-Varsity for the first time in half a century.

Dorothy May is not in her seat anymore and her frog is gone. She's run off to the join the War, is what the boys say, but she comes back to class the day Hertzog asks Sir Patrick Duncan, the Governor-General, to dissolve the parliament and call for a general election. (Dorothy's leg still jiggles, and you want to take her thighs and hold them still.) Oysters change from male to female—or female to male—at least once a year, sometimes twice or even three times. The larvae are called spats. You remember the taste of the bucket of oysters as if it was still in your mouth, how you swallowed Mum's tears, Maisie's, Teddy's and your own, all that saltwater sorrow in one big gulp, the day you came back to Men's Residence.

Dorothy's still female and you haven't tasted her tears, not yet anyway, but she's the one who tells you about Duncan asking Smuts to form a new government. South Africa's at war, you know. Her legs twitch at you, shaking the whole world.

And then the letter comes, dated August 29th.

> Dear Harold, I feel a bit better this morning, as Daddy seems on the mend. We have had a very anxious time, as Dad flopped out completely. At times there was no pulse, and as for temperature, it didn't even register on the thermometre, it was so low. Before that, he arrived home very ill and feverish with Flu, and the train journey was definitely bad for him. The doctor was terribly scared of Pneumonia, and thank God that kept away, but then his temperature flopped from high to too low at one time, and then he was real bad. Well, I only hope it ends with the scare we had, and that now he is on the mend from hour to hour, as he needs it. He is delirious most of the time, and grumbles that he can't get up and go to the shop and the doctor won't even let him be shaved, and that is also a grumble. He doesn't even know what harm it is doing him to be so restless, as he must sleep as much as possible to gain all he has lost, but as he doesn't realize the state he is in, and you can't reason with him, we can only coax him and try and keep him quiet.
>
> Well, dear, I'll write on Thursday, and hope to report very good progress. Maisie is helping me, especially in the shop. It seemed to satisfy Dad that there

is someone in the shop. He really has that institution on the brain.

Well cheerio, wishing you well,

Yours lovingly
Mum

You read the letter over and over again, searching inside the words for pictures and cures. If only it had come the next day! If only you'd seen him before he flopped out and under, into the next dim world. You could have shaved him (he wouldn't have minded). You could have saved him from grumbles and Fever, and worries about the shop. He had that institution on the brain, Mum said. You can see the shop resting on his head, as he lies alone in the cemetery, the shop parked on top of the grave, keeping him under.

You fold the August 29th letter very, very carefully, and put it in the drawer with the first letter, dated August 22. The August 29th letter is on the top, with your father's letterhead on the envelope, The House for Value and Quality (underlined) then J. Klein, in bold letters below. Under his name, in lower case letters, quite small, General Merchant, Direct Importer and Showroom Specialists and then the address, c/o Hibernia and Meade Streets, P.O. Box 40, George, C.P. Phone 35. Your address reads: Mr. Harold Klein, Mens Residence, Groote Schuur, Rondebosch.

The postmark is quite symmetrical—two circles with

George uppermost, the date and time—29 VIII 39—11.15. You look at the stamp, with the five wavy lines of the postmark running through it. It's a tall ship in full sail, one of the old ships that docked at the Cape on its way to the Dutch East Indies. Suddenly you realize how carefully it's drawn, how precise the lines are, of the little grey ship against a carefully lined grey sky. It's sailing in an oval, with a deep pink border filled in with white leaves, South Africa in small white letters above, and the postage—1d.—below. The "one" is bolder than all the other letters.

Collector's items, you whisper, as you lock the ship in the drawer (with the other letters), and hang the key on a nail inside your wardrobe. You make a promise never ever to lose these letters, this envelope, with the ship in full sail, and never ever to forget the weather of the day your father's life ended (cold and wet), which was also the day before the Germans marched into Poland. No one is allowed to touch the key, or the letters, or the drawer. Ever.

CHAPTER 10

THE LIGHT IS so bright you can see the pores in Maxie's skin, each fine crease of his eyelid. The white coats are so white that they hurt. White coats against white tiles, glittering instruments hanging on the walls, instruments for slicing tissue, for sawing through bone. The bone saws make your breakfast lift, a buoy on the inner tide of fluids. Hold on, Harry. Maxie's gripping your elbow, as if he's going to capsize but then he says, Ulna, flexor digitorum profundus, flexor longus pollicis, pronator quadratus, supinator brevis.

Last week you had to come to class with your bathing costume under your clothes. Professor Clark told you all to take your clothes off and you stood in two lines, facing each other. He spoke quietly, chastely. A medical man, a scientist. Dorothy May had spots on, and you wanted to pant in her soft ear, you wanted to tear off the strap of her spotted bathing costume. But it wasn't your turn. One of the Ossewabrandwag boys got her, and you watched as he felt around in the acromial region for the deltoid, as he traced her humerus from the top to the bottom. You didn't even notice the chap who was fingering you, whose breath stank of sausages. Brachialis anticus, supinator radii longus, extensor carpi radialis longor. *Oseh shalom bi-m'romav, hu ya'aseh shalom aleinu v'al kol yisrael, v'imru amen.*

This is where the dead teach the living. The first week of Anatomy 1 is gone, behind you, a bright bubble of bathing costumes and bony (mostly boys') bodies, and Professor Clark's long line across the giant blackboard, ending up almost at the door. This line is the duration of human history, he bugled, gesturing at the white chalk stripe snaking across the room. At the end of the line, he stopped, raising his monkey-tail eyebrows. This part, he said, isolating a four-inch segment on the grand trail of history, chalk sifting onto the floor, is what we know about. (This was after he hopped like a toad, crawled across the floor like a crocodile, swung his arms like an ape and scampered behind his desk to emerge, walking erect, Australopethicus africanus!)

He's the chappie who found the skulls. He's rewriting the world, and all the things therein, Maxie was saying. You're singing "All things bright and beautiful, all creatures great and small." The girls' breasts are heaving under their tunics, lifting whole continents. You're on the other side of the Outeniqua Mountains. Maxie's in your ear, lips to lobe. Wake up, man!

But no crawling, man-bird Professor Skullfinder prepared you for the terrible smell in the long dissecting hall. Hell's teeth, man, you told Mickey, clinking beers in the Pig 'n Whistle later that day. It's a smell that has wings and feet. The sweet stench of the formalin settles inside you, inside your nostrils, at the back of your throat. It cloaks your socks, your notes, your hair. It stays with you, and it leaves with you. You're a marked man, Harry. Mickey pushes his chair back a little, as if he's downwind, catching a whiff of it. You're buggered.

The hall is so bright, your eyes squeak in their sockets. White tiles march from the floor to the ceiling. Inside this upside down chamber of tiles, are two rows of concrete slabs, with the dead resting on them, draped under formalin-soaked cloths, covered by rubber sheets. Professor Clark is barking like a seal in Table Bay and he wants you to sail in groups of eight, four at the bow, four at the stern. It used to be six men to a cadaver but now it's eight and some of them aren't even men. Dorothy's in your group, which is bad luck, since you would rather have her in her bathing-costume than at the helm, her leg twitching so fast it's making the rubber sheet jiggle. In fact, most of the chaps are twitching inside their coats, stricken with a sort of hysterical cold, an agitated ready-to-go. Most of them have never even seen a naked woman before, dead or alive.

There's a gutter around the slab, and your eyes rests there, thinking and not thinking, held in this bitter bright cold, held in the antechamber before the Valley of the Shadow of Death, thinking and not thinking of Joseph Klein, Merchant, stopped under the shop, here but not here.

A cherry-red Anglican priest, frocked and collared, murmurs The Earth is the Lord and the fullness thereof, and The Lord is my Shepherd, a funeral of sorts for the dead sheep under the rubber sheets. Professor Clark is next to him, shifting faces again, man to ape, ape to man, man-bird to jackal. The meek shall inherit the earth. And these poor buggers have inherited us, one of the white coats at your table speaks, a cracked thread tossed in the air, hanging loose, then vanishing. The red priest has his hands clasped around his King James Bible as if he's trying to press one of the stories back into life, as if he could make the blinding white tiles disappear and the dead sit up. But he's gone before they even try.

Professor Clark scrabbles for food on the veld, cowers in the wake of a thunderstorm, showing poor Australopethicus struck by the weakness of his jaws, the thinness of his hide. But then he picks up a piece of chalk with his curled opposable thumb and draws the brain on the blackboard, an organ the size of a small and intricate cake. Africa always offers something new. In this case, gentlemen, it was man.

There's a ripple in the white coats, a tide of shifting feet, disbelief, awe. That's when he asks you all to remove the cloths from the cadavers and the room is suddenly very silent. The cloths are lifted, and there's a very large, black woman on the slab in front of you, her head shaved, her pubus shaved. But there is no blackness left in her, just as there is no whiteness in the cadaver on your left, a very old, very thin man the colour of yellow rubber. You notice that the room is suddenly new, that no one's the same anymore. This is the first woman's body you have ever really looked at. (There was no looking at Koeka. It was all hurry, and blunder, bits of her racing past, in pieces you lost just as quickly as it happened.)

Dorothy is standing at the head, and she has her face tipped down. Maxie's winking at you from the cadaver's toes. The other five chaps, three English fellows, two Afrikaners, look a bit seasick although the boat is so still you could weep. You meet their eyes in the center, all eight of you arranged around the navel, your heads bobbing with the effort of looking and not looking, at the mountainous breasts, spread wide and flat, the ridge of the pubus, the deep set of the vaginal lips in their long unsmiling smile. The skin is a shadow, a blue-grey slide into a part of you that knows only cold, only terror.

Professor Clark tiptoes-triptoes between the slabs, motioning the white coats to cover their cadavers with the formalin-soaked cloths, putting them back to sleep all over again. Four of you are going into the upper body, the other four will enter below the navel. We'll uncover only those parts to be dissected. The body should never be allowed to dry out and the wrappings have to be renewed and moistened, as needed. Gentlemen, the tools of the trade. Inside your pocket, you feel for the leather container containing the picklike probe, the forceps, the scalpel and the scissors Uncle Oscar paid for. The *ghommas* are beating, and the carnival is about to start. You can see the white tiles dancing and tumbling.

Professor Clark is whispering, so you have to say, What? What? to follow. Lay down your traditional weapons, chaps. (One of the English fellows actually heard him!) Uncover the thorax. It's just a tour now, a trip from the costal groove to the xiphoid process, outlining the borders of the lungs, palpating the clavicles. The land surveyor is up on the breast with his instruments and he's looking you right in the eyeball. Don't worry, the pick hasn't picked a thing, and the forceps and scalpel are still. Professor Skullfinder is up your sleeve asking you, Present, absent, symmetrical? Present, sir, you say, Harry Klein, sir. I mean the mammary glands, Mr. Klein. I know you're here or am I bloody dreaming?

Mammary, mammalian. Mama, for short. He's looking at you, his eyebrows bent like seagull wings, as if he's observing a hairless primate on the veld. Mammary mammal. Her breasts (more like elephant ears) are on skew, the left smaller than the right, the nipples thumbing something rude that you can't hear. He's cutting into the skin of one of these shrunken flaps, and the chaps on the boat almost fall overboard but they laugh as they cling to the sides of the boat, calling her *Grootouma*, Great Grandma. Dorothy is now so sharp and thin she could cut *Grootouma* with her fingernails, and the thin, trembling wires of her hair. Professor Skullfinder is picking you with his pick, the instrument waving inches away from your own thorax. Yes, sir. You're going to show this bastard that you're not afraid of his picking, his poking, and his cutting. You saw how carefully he lifted the skin, leaving the fat behind, how he rested his hand on *Grootouma* as he sliced through. You're all eyes and hands now, and the rest of you is finished, something scooped off a plate and thrown into the rubbish bin.

These are the structures, Professor Skullfinder is saying, holding a breast in his hand which must be worth ten in the bush. None of you (except Dorothy May, of course, who wears her own strapped tight and hidden), has ever look-looked at a woman's breast before, let alone what's under the rest of the stinking sheet. The other lookings were secret and furious; your aunties' titties flipping in and out of their clothes inside the yellow hut at Muizenberg beach, the barely budded ones of girls at school, the blinding minutes with Koeka's rough ones, her sad walls, everything not hers.

You half-expect Skullfinder to put *Grootouma*'s breast on top of his head, and wear it like a beret, the nipple sticking up like a twist of black wool. But he gives it to you, and, as you hold this old woman's tittie, the world stops. The Germans even stop.

These are the tiny pathways carrying a mother's milk, the lactiferous ducts. They converge at the nipple, each one capable of spraying a thin fountain of milk into the mouth of a baby. Skullfinder tells you that there are between fifteen and twenty of them. You have to find each one, and clean it. He shows you how, with his fingers and the blunt end of the scalpel. The saliva pools in your mouth as you watch him work, miracle fingers trippling through these delicate feeding wires. There's Ebb 'n Flow, where the river begins, folded into the dense bush, the trickle curling it's way out of that lobe of glandular tissue. And here's where it opens into the sea. . . .

You carefully clean out each pathway, each root of this fatty, collapsed flower. Christiaan, one of the barefoot Afrikaner chaps, mutters, *Hy't jou klein handtjies gesien.* He saw your small hands. *Ek het die vet gekry.* I got the fat. Poor Christiaan is emptying out the breast compartments, tables, chairs and even the sagging old couch. The glinting tools are dull and slithery now and the liquid seeping out of the body is in the gutter around the slab. Now you can see what sort of a canal it really is. Something's in your mouth, suddenly, and you spit and spit into your hanky. Your lips clamp shut, locked forever in an airless grin that you will use every time you bend over a body, alive or dead.

Professor Skullfinder nods from across the room at Dorothy. Miss May is going to make the parasagittal cut through the nipple, gentlemen. You almost feel sorry for her as her shaking hand slices through the black knob but then it's all swept away by the blaze of understanding how the damn thing stands up on its own! Look at the smooth muscles, arranged in a circle. You're thinking of clams and sea anemones, and all the sea creatures that circle and tighten, circle and tighten and trap. The other chaps are glued to the nipple and Dorothy says, Excuse me, and she leaves. She comes back a few moments later, her face blotchy, her hair somehow knotted and pulled away from her face. I've got tissue in my hair, she says, but only *Grootouma* is listening. Serves you right, you're thinking. Already Skullfinder told her she was such a clever girlie that her leg almost shook off.

You're looking up into the air as you insert your fingers into the retromammary space. Girls like Dorothy will do anything to get what they want, to take what doesn't belong to them. You're feeling the breast from the inside out, finding the suspensory ligaments, in what direction the fibres run. She's poking at *Grootouma*, looking under the other breast, murmuring how you can separate it from the fascia of the pectoralis major. Doesn't she know that these are secret words, that you can't just say them like that? She's not the kind of girl you take to the Bohemian Club, whose skirts flap with promise, magenta lips circled around a cigarette, eyes slanted at you like a fake movie star. Dorothy's behind you, then she's next to you, and now she's overtaking you, carrying *Grootouma*'s jelly breast flopping all over her hands across the finish line.

When Maxie comes over and tells you what the other chaps have done, you don't even laugh. It's too funny. You twist your lips and two tight little dimples quiver in your fresh cheeks. Won't Skullfinder find out?

Ag no. He's too busy with what's left of *Grootouma*'s titties, packing them away nicely in a formalin-soaked bag, for future reference. He's talking about how much bigger they must have been when *Grootouma* was young, how they shrank, bit by bit, each time she suckled a baby. And how many babies did she have, gentlemen, by the size of what was, and what's now left behind? Two or five, or more than seven? He's taking you back to the Western Cape of a million years ago and you can't even imagine that *Grootouma* wore a dress, or cleaned somebody's kitchen. One of the Ossewabrandwag boys says that his pa shot the Bushmen on his farm like monkeys, and yes, it's now really true, he was right all the time except how could they be the first people when it was Adam and the apple in the beginning, not hotnots.

Next to you, a flurry of white coats swarm all over *Geelbek*, the next-slab-fellow, who is one of the few white bodies, except that he's more yellow-orange than white. Somebody says he worked on the railways because there's something black in his lungs, a kind of coating or fur. But that's not what the chaps are busy with. That's not the surprise.

You see Dorothy May outside afterwards, gulping air and smoking a cigarette. You almost tell her, because she's not the way she was in the dissecting hall, two feet taller than you and twice as clever. She's a girl again, and her white coat is off. You can see her long legs, and the soft, healthy skin of her throat. You imagine her naked on one of the slabs, alive not dead, more alive than anything else in the world. You're walking with her towards Main Road, the *cape doctor* sifting through the trees, cleaning your face, your hair, your heart. Still, at every corner, the bad smell waits, somebody's ugly pig-dog following you home. You want to shoo the bloody thing away but it won't listen. It sticks to your heels. It won't give up.

Dorothy won't give up either. She's talking about the test coming up next week, and have you started swotting yet and what questions do you think Skullfinder is going to ask and are you going to specialize one day and what did you get for chemistry last year. You watch her lips moving around and around, Table Mountain standing up behind her like a huge mantle of rock on her shoulders and you want to take her and lie down with her and put your smelly hair between her breasts, and suckle. You're going to ask her out, to the Bioscope, or to the Starlight or Bohemian, because she is the kind of girl you can swirl in the dark with a cocktail stick. The sky is so blue it's daring you.

"Don't miss the greatest adventure of all time. . . ." There's an army poster on the lamppost and Dorothy's eyes go from the words to you, and the daring is backwards now, and she's asking if you're going to enlist. You tell her about Uncle Oscar and how he's paying for everything because your father died the day before the war started. She's nodding but she doesn't really know what selling the house and the shop means, what happened on the corner of Meade and Hibernia.

Are you going to swot with me or not? It's hard to tell the difference between white and grey rami and have you found the greater splanchnic nerve? She's about to open her handbag to freshen her lipstick. You almost grab the shiny liver shape away from her. The chaps are chuckling in your ear. You've got to have the big match temperament, Harry. You've got to score the touchdown. There. She has the bloody thing in her hand now. *Geelbek*'s yellow *piel*.

The next lamppost is talking while Dorothy's screaming at you, You'll be sorry, Harry! You're a coward, Harry!

She's dropped *Geelbek's* penis at your feet. Dorothy's running, walking, sobbing, How dare you? She's growing again, and you're the one getting smaller. You never eat enough, Harry, and Maisie's healthy as a horse. She's as pretty as a primrose and as clever as that fox that ate all the grapes. The posters are coming at you, Join up now! The only dress for non-key men is a uniform! (Dorothy's around the corner and gone, lost smoke, something else broken that can't be fixed.)

Even *Geelbek*'s penis is telling you to enlist. You pick

it up and it's cold in your hand, not circumsized. You're going to have to return it to the Valley of the Shadow of Death in case Skullfinder comes looking, in case Dorothy tells. This is a balls-up.

CHAPTER 11

THE NURSES ARE here to bathe you and change your bed linens. One is very blond, with red-fresh lips and a quick glance at Simon, who turns to me as if I can help him, as if he's the one she's going to strip and roll and pat dry. Ma is talking to her oldest brother, First Prize the surgeon, and we follow them out of the room into the wide hallway, with its glistening floor bright as a river. As Ma and First Prize walk slowly away from us, Simon's muttering about science and medicine, and how the doctors are dabblers and tricksters and none of these bloody gods in their white coats is telling the truth. In his voice is the old fury, the scorn at what he had and lost, when he left medical school and became a scientist.

I'm thinking of the nurses in your room, the blond one with the full lips and the other one, brown-haired and mousey, clips in her hair, eyes downcast. They're touching you as if it's nothing. I've stood at your bed for hours and hours, your words rattling and running ahead of me, behind me, all around me, everything you ever told me, streaming back to the source before it's too late. In all that listening and talking, I haven't reached out a hand to touch your hand, or the top of your black-and-grey head. Si-Si, I say. Have you touched him yet? Simon looks at me as if I've gone mad. What the hell are you talking about? You should touch him, I tell him. At least one of us should. Why don't you? he asks. Since it's your bright idea.

If he was awake, he'd be flirting with the blond nurse, reaching for her. Ma would be telling her, He's just a dirty old man. We'd be looking away, pretending not to see or to hear, I say out loud, even though the words are hard to speak. We'd be very embarrassed.

Simon nods, his eyes filling up. And I wouldn't even mind.

We've drifted back to the door of your room, and the blond nurse motions to us to come in. He's ready now, she says, as she plumps the pillow behind your head, as she tucks you in. A grey cloud is filling you up from inside, and your face is darkening and changing. Life is the miracle! you once said, coming home in the early morning after delivering a healthy baby boy, drops of blood like roses on your shirt, blood on your tie. There's nothing miraculous about death. When life goes, the body is just a piece of meat, a thing on the table.

How long . . . ? The rest of the sentence writes itself on the empty walls. The brown-haired nurse catches the two words in her fist and says, A day perhaps, maybe shorter. It's hard to say. But she pulls out Ma's chair and tells me to sit, to rest. Maybe she'll bathe me too, and brush out the knots in my hair if I sit quietly enough, if I pretend to be you.

Simon is at the window now, watching the boats bobbing in the harbor, a plane in the far distance. I look at his curved back, brown hair touching his collar, and I'm remembering the model aeroplanes he built and hung from his ceiling, on translucent strands of nylon thread. The Spitfire next to the Hurricane, the Halifax tailing the Mosquito, another Spitfire slowly spinning by itself. Simon's building a Meteor now, and he lets me watch him, his hands careful with the small parts, deliberate with the dabs of glue. He wants to be a doctor when he grows up, just like you. He's going to be a good doctor, I think, as he glues the wing to the body.

A GOOD DOCTOR just like you. It's years later and you can't help it but damn it all, man, you're proud of Mrs. Boshof's porphyria because you're the one who finally diagnosed it, beating all those fancy specialists in Cape Town to the finish line. They thought it was her appendix, her brain, her stomach, her skin, her nerves, always her nerves. Come on, chaps. For crying out loud. I delivered all four of her babies. I know this woman has nerves of steel.

The term just ended and Simon's on his way home from medical school, driving over the Du Toit's Kloof pass. The Hurricane's up on his ceiling clinking against the Spitfire in the breeze. Ma didn't have the heart to take down his planes.

I'm thirteen going on fourteen, standing in the kitchen in our house in Worcester, smelling freshly ironed sheets, the hot cement of the back stoep, when Simon drives down the driveway, the branches of the loquat tree scraping the top of his car. Yesterday I heard muffled conversations on the phone, saw Ma's face drawn tight at the corners. You slammed the front door, rattling bones.

Something's wrong. The snuffling terrors are marching down the passage, a bestiary of two-footed, three-footed and even ten-footed creatures. Some of them are as old as I am, some are much younger but they all have names and faces, they all clamor for attention. Fear of the Terribly Black Dark stabs Little Fear of My Own Death who's chasing Fear of Everyone's Death who's being led by the nose by Fear of the Powers That Be. Somewhere in the middle of the pack is Fear of Failing, desperately holding hands with Fear of Singing out of Tune, who looks like a bandicoot with a crooked snout. They can't even march properly, which is Fear of Doing the Wrong Thing's very worst fear.

When Simon slams the car door, they all fall silent, pressing themselves against the wall, not gone but flattened. He always had a way with them, his lopsided, rueful smile vastly shrinking their numbers, disarming the fiercest of the lot. When you'd lose your temper, screaming, I'll give you something to cry about! Simon would show me how to stay still, watch the storm unfold and pass away. Let it wash over you like water off a duck's back, he'd say.

I'm happy to see my big brother but he hardly notices me as he walks through the back door into the kitchen, empty handed. He gives me an odd little squeeze around the neck, his face turning away from me. He's lost something that's bigger than a suitcase or a record album or a bag of laundry. The snuffling terrors shake themselves off, start up a low cackle, talking amongst themselves. Simon's presence does nothing to calm them down. I decide to stay in the kitchen, close to the ironing table where Maria, our Coloured maid, is ironing shirts and listening to stories on the radio. There's always a serialized drama in Afrikaans every afternoon at around three, ruined farms and broken marriages, jealousy between the sisters-in-law, a stillborn child, a terrible car accident and endless, burning drought.

I can hear Ma summoning you on the office telephone system, prying you loose between patients. What follows is a film dismantled by the projector, one melting picture on the screen and then several long strips of celluloid alive and curling on the floor. There's Simon, vanquished for the first time by the Snufflies, bawling his eyes out. You're shouting at him so loudly that I stuff my fingers into my ears. Maria turns up the volume on the radio as two lovers are magnificently reunited in a whirlwind of stars and bells and Christmas music on Langebaan beach.

Johannes! Marietjie! The lovers swoon. In the next room, I hear seven different kinds of crying, yours, Ma's, Simon's, and four Snufflies who have shown up, just to make things worse—Fear of the Neighbours' Hearing, Fear of the Maid Hearing, Fear of the Whole Town Hearing, and, worst of all, Fear of the Patients Knowing Everything.

It sounds like Simon failed first year, I whisper. And they won't let him go on. *Ag*, shame, Maria says. Your daddy so wanted him to be a doctor, you know. *Ja*, I answer. Steam puffs out of the top of the iron, the smell of your lightly baked shirt searing my nostrils.

The sliding door between the kitchen and the dining room bulges, the grain of the wood suddenly grown large. How could you do this to me? How could you? The sentences are lassoes, cutting through the air and roping poor Simon. It sounds as if he's sinking to his knees, the words driving a stake through his heart. I can see Fear of Failing stamping and cheering, dancing up a storm on top of the dining-room table. The word Bertie explodes like gunshot, and then there's a loud crash, a broken dish, a flying chair, Stop It! Flung into the air, water from a twisting hosepipe.

I'm not going to ask Bertie! Your voice is pure black. Bertie's a big shot nowadays, a fancy shmancy cardiologist on Chris Barnard's team. He drives a Jaguar and he lives in a glass house in Camps Bay with a pool and twin girls my age, who like ballet and want to be models when they grow up.

Ma doesn't know when to stop. Maybe Bertie. . . . FUCK BERTIE! The words burn right through the kitchen door. Jeez, there's even a brownish stain on the white shirt Maria's ironing. She quickly tosses the singed shirt into a basket under the table. *Ag nee*, man, she clucks, lightly tapping the underside of the iron with a moistened finger, steam hissing back at her.

When has Bertie done me any favors? When? This is different, Harry, Ma says. It's for Simon. (The ill wind falters, then changes direction.) You didn't tell me what was happening. You didn't tell me he wasn't swotting. I didn't know, Harry. Of course you bloody well knew. You know everything! Now you're going to tell me it's all my fault. (Of course it's all your fault.) Ma gives a long-suffering sigh. It's all my fault. You're paranoid, Stella. No—YOU'RE paranoid!

Stop! Simon's cracking, broken voice rises up above the fray. Johannes is whispering into Marietjie's ear, My *liefling*. Maria lifts her iron, anticipating the next kiss. My heart sits in my throat like a bullfrog. The phone burbles, breaking the spell. You answer it, clearing your throat first. Champing? you ask the receptionist, your code for Are they champing at the bit? Are the patients tired of waiting for the doctor? She's supposed to answer Champing, or Not champing, doctor.

Instead, she connects you with Mrs. Boshof, and now you're clearing your throat again, almost laughing. *Wragtig, mevrou*, you're saying, followed by a stream of Afrikaans. She calls you Dr. God, this lady with the rare disease that you love so much and now you're laughing out loud again, loving her name for you, and how you saved her and how all those doctors at Groote Schuur could learn a thing or two from you, a country doctor whittling wood all day long like a peasant. Because that's what they think, don't they? The whole damn lot of them including Bertie, too-fucking-big-for-his-boots Bertie, towering above you as if he's going to take a piss on you.

Why don't you ask First Prize? you ask Ma. Your bloody brother knows all the senior chaps at the medical school. He can help us. No! Simon bellows, a raw sound from deep in his chest. I don't want to be a doctor anymore! He slams the French doors, almost breaking a pane or two. The next thing we hear is the revving of his car engine, the car backing up, turning, then heading down the driveway, the branches of the loquat tree scraping its roof, a final parting shot.

I help Maria fold a crisp white sheet as the church bells ring for Johannes and Marietjie. Here comes the bride, big, fat and wide. He'll change his mind, Ma says. We'll ask First Prize to put in a good word for him. How could he do this to us? Your voice is naked now, and I cover up my ears barely hearing you say, He's bloody lucky to have a father! Ma sighs, Here we go again. I'm squeezing my ears so hard that my head feels like it's in a pulsing tunnel. Your words go up my nose. We were allowed to repeat in those days. It was different. He knew it was different!

Betsy, you ask me later that night, pouring yourself a glass of Cabernet, watching the deep red liquid swirl a third of the way from the top of the tulip-shaped glass. Do you know what they're doing to District Six? I move the wine bottle away from you, and you grab my hand fiercely. Don't, Ma admonishes, fixing me with a long, tight stare. I let go of the bottle, stretching my numb fingers. Simon's absence yawns. The last and most fearsome of the Snufflies glimmers from the French doors, a blurry, tearswept figure I know as the Fear of Being Alone.

Do you know what the bloody bastards are doing? They're tearing the heart out of Cape Town. My spidery fingers crawl across the tablecloth, closing around the base of the wine bottle, inching it away from you, Fear of My Father Drinking Too Much sitting on my shoulder like an engorged owl. Ma's eyes are scorching, and she crosses her arms, tightening the mantle of disapproval around her shoulders. To the secretary, president and treasurer of the Worcester Teetotallers' Society. . . . You lift your glass. Cheers! You haven't noticed the basket of my white knuckles around your bottle of wine.

Constitution Street, Hanover Street, the fish market, the British Bioscope, it's all gone now. They smashed it all to pieces. All those tumbledown double-storied houses with the *broekie* lace are gone, bulldozed right down to the ground. The *skollies* are gone, and the *nonnies* and the children and the old people and the fish-horn and the smells of curry and the sea, it's all finished. Group Areas Act. Finished and *klaar*. Over and done with. Goodbye to Picadilly, goodbye to Butler Square. Remember Harrington Street? When I was a houseman, I once had a Malay patient who lived at number forty-five. Head-on collision. You shake your head from side to side, a lion with an earache. What a mess. Took us hours to stitch him up. His wife was sitting right next to him in the passenger seat. You shake your head again, remembering blood, glass, a dead woman's lacerations. We had to tell him when he woke up.

You reach for the wine and this time my hand scuttles back into my lap. I'm not going to play games anymore. I promise. *Ja*, you turn and look straight through me, past me, out of the house and into the street, all the way across the railway bridge, through the Du Toit's Kloof tunnel and over the mountain, all the way to Harrington Street and beyond. I am the tunnel, air quivering in front of you, a trick of the light, a phantom.

When you stand up, sniffing a plummy Pinotage from a second bottle, you give a little burp. I'm in my cups, Madam, you announce, the generality of the statement washing me backwards, into the sea with Ma. She's settling down with the newspaper, a kind of house she builds for herself out of paper. It floats surprisingly well. She's knee-deep in the section she calls Hatch, Match and Dispatch.

I'm in my cups, you tell us again, asking for a response. Ma crinkles the newspaper, Fear of Terrible Things Happening who likes to sit on the windowsill shrinks into his feathers.

Maxie's dead. Best friend I ever had, you say to the wineglass. Dropped dead of a heart attack just like that. Don't you think this wine has good legs, Betsy? You swirl the glass in front of me. Harry, Ma says, putting down the newspaper. You never heard from Maxie after you graduated. He sent letters, Stella, from Tristan da Cunha, the Bering Straits, Spitsbergen. Harry, they were postcards, once every ten years! I don't care what you say, Stella. Those were the best years of my life, Stella. We were always laughing in my mother's house! What years are you talking about, Harry? You've spent more years with me than you spent with your mother, with Maxie, with Gertrude, with Sonnie and Morry and Bunny and Wolfie and Maisie and the whole damn lot of them! That's the whole point, Stella. Those years, I mean THOSE YEARS, George and the girls in the boat and medical school, Maisie before she got married, Dorothy May and Maxie and Mickey and the dancing, always dancing, those were the best years of my life. Even though we were poor, we had a lot of laughs. We danced in the moonlight at the Fairy Knowe Hotel. Hell's teeth man, old man Dumbleton knew how to throw a party. And everybody would be there. I mean, everybody.

Your mother never stopped talking. She talked-talked-talked-talked. And what about *your* family, Mrs. Goddamn High-and-Mighty? Your crooked bloody . . . Harry! Don't Harry me, I've had enough of you! You take another long sip from your wineglass.

Daddy! I pull the bottle away from you and suddenly your hands are on my chair, shaking me, shaking the chair, the whole room shaking. My head hits something wooden as I go down, my fingers grab at emptiness. The floor feels right, somehow, my natural place. Get up, Miss Teetotaller! Get up off the floor! When I stand up, you're not much bigger than me, your eyes at my eye-level, burning black.

Get out, you whisper, a blast of wine-breath in my face. Both of you!

And then Ma's voice coming from miles away. Betsy, look what you started. Are you happy now?

CHAPTER 12

"LAMBETH YOU'VE NEVER seen. . . . The sky ain't blue, The grass ain't green." "When the lights go on again all over the world . . . and the boys are home again all over the world. . . . " Your blackout isn't very black, Dr. Dad, if feet are still marching, all over the world. I can hear the planes flying low, I can see the bombs falling in the dark, and you're in this very same hospital, learning how to fix a broken leg, pump out a poisoned stomach, drain the pus out of the train boy's wrist. You're peering in, and the ravines are slippery and red, and sometimes, in the hours and hours after your reason has slithered into the corner, you feel like you're going to fall right in, that you're going to die inside someone else's dying body. There are so many of them here, dying fast and dying slow. And this isn't even the real war. This is just Groote Schuur.

The brand-new building, with its red roofs and cream-coloured walls, cost nearly a million pounds to build. Within two months after it opened in 1938, all of its 628 beds were full. The six-storey main block has wards with twenty beds in them, as well as smaller rooms, with one bed, or two or three. It's supposed to be divided symmetrically and equally into White and non-White sections with the same treatment for all but everyone knows how many non-White cases pour in, and how few beds there really are for them.

It's right here that you're learning the world of difference between the body preserved in formalin, and the body alive, surging with juices, glistening, beating, demanding every ounce of your attention. The yellow-grey flesh clinging to quiet bones is suddenly dressed in scarlet, black velvet, green, orange, puce, and nothing is still. The shop doesn't close, everything keeps moving across the factory-floor, blood, salt, water, waste and a thousand chemical compounds sweeping from one complicated structure to the next.

You were just getting used to *Grootouma*, who taught you about the worm in the brain and the circle of Willis, the intricate bundle of tubes and wires right in the centre. She lay still while you entered the vestibule of her vagina, the brightest of bright lights burning overhead.

She didn't flinch when you cut into her, making a nice straight line between her anus and her vaginal orifice. Another chap got to make the midline incision from your transverse one, up towards the mons pubis.

It's nothing like that when people are broken, sick or crying. They twitch beneath your scared hands, breathing, moving and smelling like fish or fowl going *vrot*, a different, fiercer smell than the dead sweetness of formaldehyde. The surgeons don't even go near the children's ward because of the terrible smell of infected burns and osteomyelitis. You're learning how to clean burns with one nurse or two or four, and you holding the burnt child who dreads fire and now dreads you. It's your own tiny wriggling body there, except this one is scraped and scrubbed, all the loose, burnt skin removed until the wound is raw and red, the brightest colour in the world. Charlotte was in a house on fire only she wasn't a car. She was not much older than Bertie and got burned up to her eyebrows. You're the one who has to peel her skin back, and put on the gentian violet. She's screaming and biting and you almost hit her, you're so upset.

Then there's Frikkie, one of the osteomyelitis boys, whose left femur got infected by the raging staphylococcus aureus, Marcus Aurelius riding through his blood and attacking the longest bone in his body. You were there when the surgeon exposed the bone, cleaned out the infected and dead areas, drained the pus, and said, We have to pray, gentlemen.

Another stinking flower in bloom all over the children's ward is empyaema, pus filling up a body cavity, a lung, a gallbladder. Antjie has pleural empyaema and she struggles to breathe through the pool of pus in her chest. She cries all night for her mother, in between breaths. One of the giants, Professor Osgood from Scotland, will operate on her one windy morning, entering her chest to drain the pus, and she'll die on the table, his hands still inside her.

There's draining and mopping and cleaning into the organs, cutting the bad bone, treating infection after infection as they rain down on you like a thousand different insects. You wear your white coat like a lucky charm, a magical barrier of brightness that's supposed to keep the germs out, and your soul in. It doesn't always work and here and there a white coat gets TB and has to go home. Most of them come back, after long months of bed rest and artificial pneumothorax therapy. They've crossed to the other side, walked with the sick and helpless and now they're wrapped in white again, almost inviolate. You hold your breath and tiptoe between the staphs and the streps and the syphs, listening to the senior chaps talking about the patients in Latin, writing prescriptions in Latin, because what you don't know can't kill you.

The profs whisper Luetic Disease, the Great Imitator, and you're supposed to learn all the colours of syphilis—primary, secondary, latent and tertiary—as you follow the Greats on their ward rounds. A chancre in the genitals is usually the first clue and then comes the rash. In non-Whites the rash is black. In Whites, the spots are pinkish, pale red. But rashes are legion, and you have to have an eye for the right spot, the right blotch, on the right skin. Sometimes you look at your own wrist, your thigh, and the top of your arm, for the mark of syphilis, the Destroyer. The *ghommas* were beating for you too, my boy, and Koeka wasn't quite white. But the spots aren't there, nor are the lymph nodes involved. (You've checked those too, feeling carefully in your armpits for swelling.) Of course it was years ago but there are always the marks you might have forgotten, the fever you missed. You could be latent now, mere months away from General Paresis of the Insane.

It's all Mickey's fault, the bugger who took you to the Blue Lodge. Mickey's a rear-gunner now, bombing the hell out of the Italians in Abyssinia and Somaliland. When he comes home on leave, he has girls hooked on every arm and there's even someone climbing all over his eyebrows. You're making sure that your nose isn't being eaten off your face while he's sleeping with one girl in the afternoon, and a new one at night. The varsity girls are falling like leaves in an autumn wind. They flutter in the arms of the boys in uniform, in their organzas, their crepes and their taffettas. Maxie says they'll even fall for you, when the soldiers go back to war. Let's finish up what Mickey started. It's open season.

Famous last words, you tell him, as you stare at a syphilitic spirochete on a slide under the microscope. The spiral shaped bacterium thrills you, in a nameless but chilling way. Be my guest, you say, as you offer Maxie a look at the slide. Pinta and yaws, he whispers, fondling the names of other terrible diseases caused by spirochetes. There's nothing to stop the curling, curving, flat-headed, club-tailed, spiralling armies of bacteria from marching up your pants and eating you alive.

But it's coming, he tells you, Mr. Maxie Bloody Know-it-all. Penicillin is going to save us all, if the Krauts don't get us first. Never mind the arsenicals for syphilis, the emetine for dysentery, the quinine. A miracle is just around the corner. Maxie reads *The Lancet*. He's light-years ahead of you, a true scientist in the making and a *feinschmecker* of the highest order. You call him F.S., for short. He says you're a mysophobe, and you say a What? Someone who's afraid of picking up an infection, he says, Sir Lancelot Lancet Reader and World Expert. Your nose sharpens, draws in on itself, and your eyebrows double knot in the middle. Don't be so paranoid, old chap. I was only pulling your leg. You're the one who's paranoid, you mutter, but even the spirochete is ruined.

The bloody buggers are ruining the war too. The coffin in the ground and the shop on the coffin, Mum, Maisie and Bertie on top of the dead shop. Your dead father's hands are locked around your ankles, holding you down, keeping you here while the other chaps fly around the world and back. You're missing the greatest adventure of all time. Uncle Oscar won't listen because you have to become a doctor. You know that, don't you?

But right now you're just a house officer learning to take histories at the bedside, watching the great Professor of Medicine, Professor Man-Bird, whose pointed questions can unravel a man's life and chart the map of his sins, his habits, his desires. Often he makes his initial diagnosis by asking, and seeing, before turning the sheet back, and touching.

The test is the doctor, not a machine, and his dream of what's inside a body racked and turned by sickness or accident. You've prostrated yourself before the all-knowing Man-Bird, like all the other house officers, and you're hoping to learn what's inside his fierce head, under the shining big top.

He's got all of you around him this morning, all the lucky bastards in his firm. Dorothy May, you're happy to say, is in another firm and with any luck she's with the ladies and babies, where she belongs. A Coloured nurse, her white uniform lacquered onto her firm breasts, wheels in a patient from the non-White ward, a grizzled Coloured woman, her toothless mouth downturned with pain, a faded, rose-patterned hanky twisted between her fingers. Today Man-Bird is not asking any questions. He goes straight to the patient, and exposes her abdomen to the staring, sleepless group of ten housemen. He's not doing the usual tap and shuffle about the art of medicine, the magic wand of beribboned words, Hippocrates here, and Sir William Osler there, telling you that it's more important to know what sort of a person has a disease than to know what sort of a disease a person has. He's not shouting about the olden days where anatomy students were sent to executions, so they could see what's inside the body when it's drawn and quartered, so they could watch and take notes when the four pieces were separated and the internal organs pulled out. He's not screaming, You chaps have it easy! Too bloody easy!

There's none of that today. He's a lamb, his voice fallen and soft, his gestures small. It's the most dangerous show of all. You know that, just as the other housemen do. You can smell the sweat that's starting to prickle in armpits, palms, behind necks. Man-Bird palpates the woman's abdomen and there's a thick silence in the ward, as he draws the vast body of his knowledge into his fingertips. In your mind's eye, you're back in Gross Anatomy, lifting the lettuce leaf of the Greater Omentum and looking at what's under the apron, rifling through the organs you named and labelled. This time they're not out but in. They're neatly packed and tucked into a Coloured woman probably from District Six, with roses looped between her fingers. You're looking all over her for clues, at her sunken jawline, her swollen arthritic knuckles, the soft fabric that she's teasing and kneading over and over again. You can hear the fish horn's whine, and she's selling flowers on the parade, her hands dipping in and out of big buckets of water. Nettie's wiping your bottom. It's raining in George and she says her knee hurts, and don't be *onbeskof*, otherwise your mother will give you a jolly good hiding.

Man-Bird's eye almost catches yours but then it washes past you and lands on Maxie. Maxie is summoned to the patient's bed and now it's his turn to palpate the organs, and feel all the treasures and horrors buried under the skin. Do you feel the spleen, Mr. Sloan? Maxie puts on his best palpating face. Yes, sir, I feel the spleen, sir. Posterior to the stomach, sir. In contact with the diaphragm. Not a big love affair, you're thinking. A letter once a month, maybe a phone call on the spleen's birthday.

Maxie goes back to the group and another houseman, Sam Katzenellenbogen, is summoned to the bed side. Sam is from the Orange Free State, a Jewish chap who grew up near the Big Hole and walked to school without shoes on his feet. He has a brown moustache and hooded eyes and Man-Bird makes a big fuss out of his name, Katzenellenbogen, Cat's Elbow. Again Man-Bird asks, Do you feel the spleen, Mr. Cat's Elbow? Sam's hand crosses back and forth over the woman's abdomen like a pale crab. The crab has dirty fingernails, and you're hoping Man-Bird doesn't notice. He's looking away, thank God, and finally Sam's crab-hand stops in the general vicinity of the stomach. Sam nods, Yes sir, I feel the spleen, sir. Man-Bird waves him back to the group.

Mr. Harold Klein! The whole ward just lurched, an

ocean liner rolling on a tremendous wave. It's a wonder all the trays and instruments and beds and patients didn't roll down the shiny floor and land in a big heap against the wall. Now it's still again and you walk the gangplank to the starched white bed, the soft, brown abdomen in the centre, its surface crosshatched with lines and folds. The belly button is saying something rude but you don't listen. Your fingers have a life of their own as they press into the softness, rifling through the layers of tissue, hunting the liver, the stomach, the colon. You're looking for jellyfish in the pitch-dark, diving for golf balls from the railway bridge and all you're coming up with is a fistful of mud.

Do you feel the spleen? Man-Bird's voice freezes the sweat on your upper lip, it locks your jaw. All you can do is shake your head and search. The woman in the bed raises herself a little, and then she sinks back. The hanky falls from her fingers onto the floor. For a hideous second, you imagine that you've killed her with your ignorance. The pages of your anatomy book whir in your head, next to an endless parade of the organs and ducts. Right, left, right colic flexure, left colic flexure, left, right, ascending colon, descending colon, right, left, jejunum, secum.

DO YOU FEEL THE SPLEEN? No, sir, you whisper, and you can almost hear everyone behind you begging, Just say you feel the spleen. Tell him you have it. She's going to die anyway. We're all going to die. Just tell him you feel the spleen!

Mr. Klein! You've got to be able feel the spleen! He's

hissing now, and you're the one who is being drawn and quartered, whose insides are spilling out all over the floor. That's your gallbladder rolling under the bed, and a nurse just stepped on your pancreas. All that's left standing, is your penis, and it bobs its circumsized head at the housemen. I'm sorry, chaps. You wish someone would pick you up, put you in Dorothy May's handbag and take you out of this glinting, evil place.

More than anything, you hate the spleen, this stupid mouse of an organ hiding behind the stomach somewhere, tricking you like this. You'd like to pull it out and squeeze it to a pulp between your fingers, then trample it to death. Maxie catches your eye and he looks like he's struggling to breathe. All the housemen look like they're drowning, like their bloody ship is sinking. You hate all of them, and you want to scream and cry at the same time.

Mr. Klein was the only honest one, Man-Bird intones. The patient does not have a spleen. The woman in the bed bursts out laughing, suddenly, a mad noise from a completely unexpected source. She turns her head into the pillow, overcome with embarrassment, as she tries to stifle her cackles.

Now it's Maxie's and Sam's turn to feel the rack and the screw, Man-Bird's talons around their necks. He talked them into feeling an organ that wasn't there and now they're sitting in the stocks, two chumps on a log. Man-Bird is flying high, dropping diseases down on all of you, malaria, tuberculosis, leukemia, thalassemia.

Schistosomiasis, anemia and glandular fever. All of them cause the purple mouse to grow into a purple kitten. But why isn't it there, Mr.Klein? Why is this spleen not enlarged but entirely absent from the scene? What happened? All you can think of is the train, the colon-train and a terrible accident, sir. She must have suffered a fall from a dizzy height. Or something must have fallen on her, like the bad hand of a bad husband. A train or a car, a big mistake and she came in to the hospital bleeding like mad and she almost died, sir. But she was spared because her spleen was removed and the artery supplying it was tied off. She was saved!

You're tap dancing down the wards one week later, long after even the nocturnals have turned in. "Hey, *tjoekie*, it's a quarter to four . . . there's a stripe of moonlight pointing right at my door . . ." You're dreaming of taking Matron in your arms. . . "*Tjoekie*, don'tcha know that I'm nude . . . You mustn't keep me waiting when I'm in the mood. . . . " You haven't slept for days and days, and even the windows have started to dance.

The lights are ringing all over the world, the doors are flying all over the world. The Coloured nurse collars you because you're the house officer on duty. What? You're watching her mouth move, and you can't figure out if she's speaking English or Afrikaans. But then she makes a choking gesture and you follow her like the wind down the corridor to outpatients, where there's a brown man going blue, his lung collapsed, pneumonia squeezing him to death. The senior house officer has taken a powder. The non-White wards are too much for him, especially on a Saturday night. Too many knife wounds. It's like a bloody abattoir, you heard him tell one of the other senior chaps.

But you wanted moonlight in the hardest part of the hospital. You're right in the broken heart of Groote Schuur feeling the glimmer of war, something huge you can help to fix.

The button of a nurse whispers trake, and you take the scalpel from her. You've never done a tracheostomy before. Yes, the metal tube is there, you have the scalpel in your hand, the lights are burning bright. You're ready to jump into the forests of Normandy, the valley of the Rhine. Your parachute is sharp and it glows in the dark. "When the lights go on again all over the world . . . and the boys are home again all over the world. . . ." The song leads the scalpel into the trachea, breaking and entering, a full-scale invasion. The body shoots back, a stream of blood that leaves you drenched, right down to your socks.

You're suddenly wide awake, more awake than you've been for weeks and weeks. Jesus Christ, Harry, you forgot his thyroid! You sailed straight into the isthmus and punched a hole in his superior thyroid artery!

The patient's painting the whole town red! Streaks of scarlet stripe the walls, the floor, the ceiling. The nurse's uniform has gone from white to ruby. She's in a bright evening gown now. You've slid through the Valley of the

Shadow of Death on your bottom right into the jaws of hell, into the howling flames. The man on the stretcher reaches for you, his face twisted in agony and surprise. *Dokter!* You hold him, trying to close the hole in the dyke with anything you can lay your hands on but this leak is impossible. His life-force sweeps over you like a tidal wave. He's taking away everything you've learned. You're going with him into the abyss.

With a gurgle and one last spluttering sigh, his dinghy capsizes and he sinks like a stone. He didn't even make it to Ebb 'n Flow.

You're still here. Pinch yourself but don't look at the nurse. She's dead quiet and you want to kill her. It's all her fault. She should have called someone else, not you. Didn't she know that you're so tired and so small that all you can do is clappety-tap down the halls by yourself? Didn't the nuns tell her that you still shit in your pants?

There's a group of Coloured nurses in the room now and they're all over the place with buckets and mops. The water is soapy and red. They don't tell you what they've seen before, that the isthmus of the thyroid is a trap, a bridge over the throat that comes in many shapes and sizes. Even if you hadn't forgotten all about the thyroid, even if you'd found the isthmus, you still could have jammed right into it. You're going to have to pay for your mistake like everybody else does. A bubble of blood trickles down from the corner of the dead man's mouth, and pops on the way to the floor.

The man's name is Fanus Meintjies and his wife, Sara, is on the other side of the swinging doors. Go tell her that her husband is gone, that his temperature flopped from low to high, from high to low again, that all he wanted to do was go back to the shop because he had that institution on the brain. Tell her any story you can think of but just don't tell her that you killed him. You wash off the blood that's caked your eyebrows and you change your coat for a fresh white one before you swing through the swinging doors.

You're pretending to be Trevor Howard in *Brief Encounter,* taking soot out of a beautiful woman's eye, passing a camel through the eye of a needle. Sara Meintjies is crying and you're floating just an inch or two below the ceiling, bumping the back of your head occasionally. He said he loved you, and goodbye. So sorry, Mrs. Meintjies. Bump goes your head every time you tell a lie. Bump bump.

She's blinded by your fresh white coat, so blind that she's saying *Dankie, dokter. Baie dankie.* Thank you, doctor. Thank you very much. She's a small Coloured woman, smaller than you, and you could pick her up and carry her out of here, and it would be over, at least this part anyway. But you have to keep acting and telling her about his collapsed lung and how it was all too late. Even though you did the tracheostomy he had already stopped breathing. *Ek is baie jammer, mevrou.* I am very sorry.

Maxie likes to say that these are the people we get to

practise on, the poor people of Africa. The Strandlopers, the Hottentots, the Xhosa and the descendants of Malay slaves. The Cape Coloureds, the Bantu, all the shades of non-White, all the different language speakers who come here and bleed here and die here. You might as well have pulled your wagon into the *laager* at the Battle of Blood River and shot your own Zulu. At least you wouldn't have had to lie to his wife that he'd died before you killed him.

You might as well have joined the Ossewabrandwag and marched across the Great Karoo reenacting the Great Trek with a flaming torch in your hand. You could even be in Hitler's Army right now, killing your own people all over Europe. There is no pit deep enough for you, no jail that will hold someone who forgot about the thyroid gland.

CHAPTER 13

THE SUN IS slipping, laying a place for itself at Bertie's table, ready to dress his house in dazzling colors. We're on the other side of the mountain, in the shadow of Devil's Peak and the light is fading on us, the day is almost done.

Simon's outside your room and he's shouting in the corridor at someone about your IV. Is it morphine and is it too much because now your breathing is getting harder and harder and the old *chorrie* is fighting to get up the hill, even though you're in first gear. Ma gives me a full tray and I'm eating brown meat and gravy and a tower of mashed potatoes as Simon's voice starts to sound more and more like yours.

Ma's talking about the night and the carjackers and

the thieves and the *skollies* that come out in the dark and I'm staring out at the hunched mountain, with its baboons folded into the crevices, waiting for the spray of stars to come out. I remember how you tumbled down at the end of the day William and I got married, how you lay on the ground and I thought you were dead. I ran away from you into William's arms. Protect me, protect me, I said, pulling his arms around me like a cloak. His lips were on my hair, and he held me until I was calm, until you got up and brushed bits of gravel from your wedding suit, laughing as if you'd just heard a good joke. Now William's on the other side of the world and you're not getting up this time. I'm hugging myself in the half-dark, hugging the baby floating inside me, wishing William was here to hold me and steady me, in the storm that's beginning to break right over our heads.

He didn't want an endotrachial tube, I hear Dr. Daniels saying. And the laryngeal mask usually works perfectly well. Simon's voice is getting louder and louder, And you listened to him!

Look here, I don't know how you chaps do it in America, but we were working with him, we were doing what he wanted. He's practiced medicine for over forty years! We had to take that into account.

He was his own doctor! And you didn't think there was something wrong with that?

Ma gets up and she's shouting too. Simon! How dare you! And the two men are in the room, the row is moving right to your bedside. You always liked a *lekker* fight and now it's happening right here and this time I'm sure you're going to wake up. You wouldn't want to miss it for anything in the world.

He didn't want the tube, Simon! He was terrified! Ma's almost spitting. Why don't you leave your father alone? There's nothing more we can do!

That's the point! Simon shrieks. He was operated on and he struggled through the night without getting enough oxygen and then Dr. Daniels moved him here where they could finally intubate him! But by then it was too bloody late!

How do you know what happened? You weren't even here!

We were following your father's wishes, and with that, Dr. Daniels swirls in his white coat and is gone.

Is that true? Simon's eyes are burning and his voice is thundering and you're still quiet as a mouse, even now.

Ma's crumpling and she's telling us that she has angina. We're ringing for the nurse and by the time a new one comes, with greasy hair this time and mottled skin, she's bent over in the chair moaning. The pain is here, and here, she says, pointing to her own heart.

How does that song go again? I whisper, as the nurse takes Ma's pulse. "Love, love, falling in love. I wasn't thinking of you but now I am. She loves me, she loves me not. She loves me?"

* * *

Stella Sacks' arms, face and throat are covered with tiny brown freckles. She wears her reddish-brown hair twisted up and there's always a halo of cigarette smoke above her head because she smokes like a chimney. How far down do the freckles go? You whisper to Maxie in the Groote Schuur student dining room, as the fat lady behind the counter pours gravy on your chop. He shrugs, makes a quick calculation, as you both watch Stella sit down with her tray, rummage in her handbag for her cigarettes. Oops! She dropped something. She looks at the chap who's with her and now he's bent under the table looking for her matches. She has them all over, Maxie breathes. I'm not so sure, you tell him. But I'm going to find out.

You make a bet. If there are freckles inside her brassiere, or folded between her thighs, you owe Maxie a shilling per freckle. If she's lily white, he owes you. C'mon, old man, you say, how do you expect me to count them all? Okay, he says. A shilling for the first five you see. You can keep counting if you like, he grins, his mouth as damp as a puppy's.

Stella's laughing now. Maxie's craning his neck, telling you that the chap next to her said, Can I eat while you smoke? He's one of the senior men, going into pathology. She's still laughing, her mouth wide, her head thrown back, a big, open laugh that makes you want to see her laugh again and again.

She's a radiography student, learning how to tell

patients to lie absolutely still, and hold their breath, until she takes a shadowy picture of the oceans and continents inside their bodies. Suddenly she catches your eye, and you swear she has X-ray vision because she can see inside your cowering heart, to that silly bet you made with Maxie, all the way down to Fanus Meintjies shooting his blood all over you. You want to back out now, forget the whole damn thing but it's too late, old chap. A deal is a deal. She seals it with a look into her powder compact, a dash of scarlet onto her lips, and click, the mirror snaps shut and lunch is over. The serviette on her chair has the red trace of her lips on it. You're up the river all over again, with the stained tablecloth and the yearning burning, all over the world.

Look down when she passes your table, pretend you're talking about the war. Maxie's checking his teeth in the butter knife. Watch out in case she sprinkles you with her cinnamon dust, her brown paper freckles. Her legs are pencil thin, and her brown shoes have straps around her narrow ankles. She's nervy, and slim, with buttons marching all over her breasts, wearing a tight-topped dress that's closed up like a soldier's uniform. Maxie looks up, as she stops a few feet away from you, and the senior chap lights her cigarette. Du Maurier, my dear Watson, in case you didn't see. But she's gone now, freckles and all.

It's only two days later, a slow Saturday afternoon slipping into dusk. You just got off duty, and Stella's climbing into the front seat of Charlotte. You can't help noticing the tiny brown spots all over her feet and her calves, marching into the car with her like an army of ants. In the house called Chantry, she was all flurry and promise, a scarf fluttering between her hands, dropping her du Mauriers in her handbag, kissing her ma goodbye, a mother bun sort of mother, solid and greying, floating a wan smile in your direction. There were boys all over the place, taller than you, one young and soft, one on leave, the infantry man, and another freckled one, the oldest, studying to be a surgeon. The father, you were told, was in shul, a *macher*, a Zionist, a religious man from a religious place, practising his religion religiously. He stared at you from his wedding picture, next to his much younger bride, new missus Bun before all the boy babies got to her. Stella is the rose among the thorns, the one and only kitty cat, the prize girl.

You leave the double-storied house with its pile of rooms and Persian carpets, the aura of something immoveable your house never really had, the commercial travellers coming in and out, and ma's flying bells and bad moods. Stella's lighting a cigarette again and you lean towards her, mock-whispering the advertisement, Didn't you give me my first du Maurier? I shall always think of you, who-who-who, you hoo-hoo-hoo. She's not quite Jeanette MacDonald and you're not Nelson Eddy, but wait, she's calling you, who, who, who, that Indian love call across the Canadian gorge. You shade her with your Mountie hat, then you slip the clutch and Charlotte lurches towards Paarl and beyond, to the secret place you're taking her to, almost as good as Ebb 'n Flow.

This isn't what she was expecting, she tells you, a bit cross. It's not the Bohemian Club in the misty dark, an omelette or a sandwich before midnight, giggling with the other powder puff girls in the cloakroom, a long dance in the arms of a new stranger. You can't really tell her about the freckle-hunt, how you need light to see, and a reason to go swimming. I hope you brought your bathing costume, you say, as smoke streams out of her nose. What? She's not really laughing now, a play-play sneer curling her upper lip, a funny spoiled girl attractive. You brought Maisie's costume just in case, you tell her. Maisie who? Maisie, my sister, you tell her.

The road winds through vineyards, the Hottentot's Holland mountains retreating into the far distance, Du Toit's Kloof up ahead, where the Italian prisoners of war are helping to blast a road through the mountain, which will replace the old Bain's Kloof road. They're the chaps captured in North Africa, you explain. I saw one once in casualty. She's interested, suddenly, and her half-sneer drops into a half-smile, not the full-blown rose you saw in the cafeteria, but a smaller flower.

You're driving towards your story, the place where your Italian prisoner of war, Enrico Carretoni, helped four of his friends carry a painted wooden cross to the top of Huguenot Kop, a mountain near the farm where they are stationed. If you squint on a clear blue day, you can see the cross glinting white at the top of the mountain, small as your thumbnail, the Holy Ghost sitting up there all by himself. Of course you don't believe in the Man, the Ghost or the Cross but there it is, and those chaps carried it all the way up to the top of the mountain. A couple of the farm boys went with them, chaps they've befriended since they've been living in the barracks near Keerweder. The Afrikaans boys bring them fruit and fresh eggs and the Italians teach them to swear. Eat my fig. Your mother's pancake. Stuff ten birds with your goat.

She's laughing now, and you could almost do it, one fell swoop, off with the white shirt she's buttoned up to her nose but Charlotte would mind, and drive herself off the side of the road. Instead, you tell her that one of the farm boys, Hendrik, brought Enrico into casualty the day it happened. What happened? You tell her about the baboon that climbed up Huguenot Kop behind the Italians and the two Afrikaans boys, the baboon that grabbed their sandwiches, stole their cigarettes and gave Enrico a swipe on the arm that peeled the skin and muscle off the bone like someone rolling back the lid of a can of sardines.

The baboon was almost as clever as Professor Skullfinder. He exposed all the woven parts, the warp and weft of nerves, the long head of the biceps and its smaller brother, the short head. You could see the humerus and it wasn't even funny. You slowly park Charlotte at the side of the road. He wasn't the usual Friday night pile of stab wounds, the chronic ones with TB, syphilis, kwashiorkor, beriberi. (She smiles when you say beriberi.) Roma, he said, when you asked where he was from, and his black eyes flashed with pride. It took you hours to stitch and clean up his arm, and you worked slowly, and carefully, the saliva pooling in your mouth. She's smoking again, and you climb out of the car, looking up at Du Toit's Kloof. See what those chaps built, you tell her. Look at the new road! I want to know about his arm, she says, and you're the baboon now, chasing her and holding her thin upper arm between your teeth. She's screaming and laughing, a last hint of smoke escaping from her mouth.

You see freckles on top of her shoulder, a line of them on her acromion, two or four or forty nestled in her scapular notch, and at least a dozen lurking in her supraspinous fossa. The sleeve of her dress balloons up above your hands, and you can see right in. She jerks her arm back and away, with a sharp snapping motion. I have four brothers, she says, with that snarling smile she has, spoiled silly with boys.

You point up to the cross, white as your nail. You lunge again, and she dodges, almost falling off those strap-happy shoes. Let's climb to the top, Stella Bella. The wind has started sighing and whistling through the protea bushes, silver trees and pincushions, above the jagged line of the new road. There are fir trees below the line, a windshield for the farmers protecting the vineyards in the valley. You tell her what Hendrik the farm boy told you, his flat blue eyes watching you as you sewed up his friend's arm. When you stand and look out across the valley, the mountains make the shape of a man's face. You see small buck hopping over the bushes, and beautiful flowers you've never seen before.

I was stuck on a mountain once, she says. And I couldn't go up or down. I was frozen. They had to carry me. She can barely light her next cigarette the wind is so strong. There's a big grey cloud covering the cross. You're thinking of the Wilderness and Wolfie's boat and raindrops in the river. Your boyhood comes tumbling out, faster than the blood spurting out of Fanus's neck, stories to patch up the broken faces and oozing limbs, your mother's tablecloth to mop up the pus, Nettie and the chicken called Harold, the house on the corner of Meade and Hibernia, Ebb 'n Flow and the rocks under brown water, golf balls in your pockets when you least expect them.

Stella can't believe how much you miss the Outeniqua Mountains, the waves at Victoria Bay, how many orange fan shells you've collected at Lentjiesklip and how you know the difference between spring tide and neap tide, and which moon is which. Let's go to Ebb 'n Flow, you tell her. I'll take you to the source. She pretends to know what you're talking about, the way girls do sometimes, when they like you.

By now, it's too late for Bain's Kloof. You haven't seen all her freckles, although you've counted up to seventy-three so far. For every brown fleck on her nose, her hands, her arms, you've told her about a person, a house or a car, something real from the place you've known all your life. You even told her about the story of your father chasing the train, how he got the engine driver to stop at the crossing, so he could put Maisie on board, bound for a holiday in Oudtshoorn, with a rich feather-farmer's daughter. There's a jerk in your voice because of the last train, the one from Johannesburg that gave him the fever and the terrible sickness, his temperature flopping from high to low, his life suddenly snipped short, a gardening accident of the highest order. The Germans invaded Poland and my father died, and we almost died too, you know, of confusion and grief and being so poor, so suddenly. Faster than cats, quicker than scorpions. (We have a lot of those, climbing out of the bath at night.)

She's living your life, cigarette after cigarette, a giggle for the river, and a big laugh for the sea. All she knows is the city, her brothers in every room of the house, and the garlic her mother puts in her coat pockets to ward off evil spirits. The two of you are sitting on a pile of rocks near the side of the national road. Charlotte is watching, and you swear her white coat is turning a faint green with jealousy. You're not going up or down. You're just talking, in case Stella gets frozen again, and you can't carry her down. And anyway, the cross is all bandaged up with clouds, and the klipspringers have probably gone to Hermanus for a dip.

The Hottentot's Holland mountains are a purple

ripple in the distance. The sun is falling quietly tonight, no sweep of orange and pink, just a slow, sullen bruising spreading across the sky, a giant hematoma. Charlotte coughs when you try to start her. Do you want to spend the night on the mountain, sulking? She sputters nnnn . . . oooo. Rrrrrh! With a few tries, you manage to get her going. Stella gets back into the front seat, checking her nose in her powder compact, as if it was missing and just came back.

We shouldn't be driving, Stella says. We're not supposed to use motor cars for pleasure purposes. Or buy new clothes, you answer, rubbing the brown of her skirt. She triple-sneers at you, and then you lean over, almost in her lap, your voice rising. Oh, I shall remember! Didn't you give me my first du Maurier? You have one of her cigarettes between your lips, and she's lighting it for you. I shall always smoke them—and always think of you. . . .

But the war is between you now, and how guilty you are because you're not dying somewhere in Europe, burst into pieces by a bomb or a land mine or a rattle of machine-gun fire. Stella's just as bad, eating hot lunches in the Medical School dining room and wearing soft clothes from her father's shop. When you tilt the world, so that it's Europe on top, not the southernmost tip of Africa, Jewish girls are standing naked, their clothes in toppling piles, their shoes becoming history.

There are very few other cars on the road, black ghost

ships with masked headlights because of wartime regulations. Charlotte's lights are taped too, with just a crack of light in the center to poke through the darkness, through the valley of the shadow of your fears, and Stella's. You've driven through the countryside, past sleeping vineyards, and livestock tucked in for the night, and now you take her through Athlone, and Elsie's River, Grassy Park and District Six.

You show her the places where so many of your patients come from, the tumbled down houses and shacks and *pondokkies* where you can pick up TB, dysentery and syphilis in every garden, where stab wounds proliferate like stars poking through the sky's night-blanket. She's staring out of the car window, at the *skollies* and the nightwalkers, the gamblers and street fighters and she tells you to slow down. I get carsick, she says, Stop! You park next to an empty lot full of whispers and menace, two men watching your car with hooded eyes. The women and children are upstairs or downstairs, sleeping in boxes, on floors, ten in a bed, two at the window. You're looking for Fanus's house, for his widow and his poor children but you can't tell Stella. You pull on your white coat, as she bends down next to the car, and vomits. At first, you try not to look and then you see she's reeling a little. You hold her shoulders, trying not to get splashed. The two men walk past you, and they tip their hats. *Dokter*, they say, in the dark. *'Naand.*

When she's finished, there's a tear glinting in her eye,

a reproachful diamond. You help her into the car, and she tells you she's seen her fair share of brokens too, in the radiography department, under the giant X-ray machines. She sniffs, and then she lights another cigarette, her own private smoke signal. You forgot the freckle-hunt. You got lost on your way to Ebb 'n Flow. You took the Serpentine by mistake and now you're nowhere near her softest parts, the lilt of her breast, the slope of her abdomen. It's not funny anymore. The car smells of her shame, her curried lunch, your shame and all the sprats you never ate. It's salt air and leather, cigarettes and bile. She's steaming with tears at what you didn't give her, the tea room that wasn't there, the nice place to stop for scones and cream and jam and a pot of tea. She didn't mind District Six. She just wanted something hot to drink at four o'clock.

You drive her back to Chantry in silence. Nobody says sorry. Other cars lurch towards Charlotte in the dark, rolling forward like blind tanks. Out of the blue, Stella announces, I want you to come for Friday night supper and you say, When, because I'm at Groote Schuur this week and the next and the next. When the cows come home, she says, you can come too.

CHAPTER 14

MA SWALLOWS A nitroglycerine tablet the nurse gives her, chasing it down with a mute sip of water, her lips flattening. The glance she gives Simon and me over the top of the glass is full of reproach.

I'm back at the window again, losing myself in the moonlit cloud wrapping itself around the dark mountain, as if it's the caul I was born in. You told me that you came into the delivery room when Ma was about to give birth to me. She and the obstetrician were both smoking cigarettes. You waved your arms furiously in the smoke-filled room. What the hell are you buggers doing?

Suddenly it grips me, the one fact I can't think about. This child of mine is a face you will never see.

Simon's out in the hallway again, and Ma takes a long

sigh. You think it's all my fault, don't you? she says, and I can't speak suddenly, looking for your murderer in every corner. Maybe it was the night nurse at the other place where they did the surgery, who watched you struggle for your life not wanting to call up the doctor in the middle of the night, because she knew he was booked back-to-back all the next day. Maybe it was the ambulance driver, who was feeling hungover from the night before, and took an extra twenty minutes to get you here, where they finally hooked you up to the right machines and got you breathing properly again. And who made the decision to operate on you in a place without the right resuscitation equipment, without an ICU? Was it you?

Your breathing is more ragged now, and I can feel the tightness spreading inside my own chest. Perhaps I have angina too. Simon is back at your side, stricken. Ma's eyes are shut, her cheeks have lengthened and she has her legs spread out stick-straight in front of her. We are all dying too.

Outside, the sun finally drops out of the sky, and there's an even deeper chill in the room. Ma gets up, shuffles out of her chair without talking to Simon or to me, leaving a maze of ridges on the plastic seat. I'm going for a walk, she says. And she glances behind her, at a spot above your head, as if she can't be caught loving you.

I'm hearing your music again, and you're dancing with Ma at the Wilderness Hotel and she's just as tall as you, her eyes fixed on your hairline. Your face is turned inwards, searching the past, and you're examining an old picture of yourself, dancing and swaying to the sweetest of sounds.

I USED TO be quite a dancer, old chap, you say, shaking William's hand, minutes after you meet him. Later that evening, over a Cabernet Sauvignon you've brought with you in your hand luggage, you initiate him into the brotherhood. It isn't the Royal Arch. It's a royal, loyal KWV red you introduce him to. William tells you about his travels all over the world, and you gasp and laugh and shake your head with penguin amazement. He listens to your stories about the wine-farmers and their vineyards. On our first trip to South Africa together just after we're married, you have William drive you all over the Hex River Valley, to Robertson and Paarl, stopping to taste wine at every vineyard. With Medieval courtliness, William says, You are the master. And I am your young apprentice.

Danie de Wet is the Chardonnay King! You make William take you to Danie's estate, De Wetshof, in Robertson. He follows you into a building that looks like a chateau, gleaming white against the blue flamed sky. Susanna, the girlie with the big breasts, is standing behind the counter. She must have seen you come in, the little doctor and his towering son-in-law. Of course you make her blush, your eyes clapped onto her boobs like magnets, but she says *Goeie môre, Dokter*, a good girl scraping her desk back and saying hello to the teacher.

You're chattering nonstop to William about the oak, and the fruit and then, as you lurch towards Susanna, it's her fresh nest that catches you, her wrapped-up cuckoo birds. They don't come out of the nest, do they? You look pointedly towards the shelf of her bosom and William, a gentleman's gentleman, feels the blush going down all the way to his heels. He isn't going to say anything because that's not his way, but he feels Susanna's shame, and he tries to steer you back to the tasting table, with its rows and rows of tulip-shaped glasses. I'm not in my cups yet. I'm still trying to get into her cups!

You pour glass after glass for William, toasting and tasting, the wine, the grapes, the bloody blue sky. It's a helluva country, this, you tell him, swirling the pale yellow Bateleur Chardonnay. Danie always selects this one from his barrels. *Waar's Meneer* de Wet? You call to Susanna and she flushes apricot, delicate peach, all the hues of the wine itself, marmalade and smoke, oranges and nuts.

You barely see the man in front of you, William with his mop of red-gold hair and luminous skin, eyes the colour of storms. You can't imagine the places he's lived, the books he loves or the wide open plains where he was born. You don't think of us dancing at dawn under a fluttering maypole in Riverside Park. You don't notice me looping through his crooked arm laughing so hard I'm afraid I'm going to burst, on that first day of May seven years ago. You don't hear us speak in the chilly air, stamping feet, massaging cold hands. And you don't see William looking into my eyes, seeing me.

So he listens and you speak, and he pours and you drink, the Finesse, the Bon Vallon, the Lesca and Danie de Wet's Call of the African Eagle Chardonnay Reserve. You shout for Susanna, A case of the Limestone Hill! And a case of the Chardonnay D'Honneur! And, then, to William, The Eagle is bigger than the Hill, don't you think? The Finesse has more curves, just like Susanna. William takes you (and shakes you) and says, What about your boat? Betsy told me all about the Wilderness. You push your chair back and look at him and say, You know what? You're a *lekker ou.* A nice chap. A case for Mr. William, Susanna. *Hy's 'n lekker ou.*

Betsy told me that she was alone with you in the boat once, in the rain. You remember, whistling through your teeth as you dislodge something. *Ja*, she was curled up like an animal in the front of the boat. I'll never forget how small she was. You stop, caught outside the circle, and William sees for the first time that day that you are my father. But then you wash it away with the Edeloes, Danie's best dessert wine.

William loads up the back of your white Toyota with a case of the Limestone Hill, a case of the Chardonnay D'Honneur and two of the Bon Vallon, one for you, one for him. That's the last he sees of the Bon Vallon. You bury it in the back of the cement room where you keep your bottles. He doesn't ask for it and you don't give it to him.

Joseph Klein gave everything away and he died with a leaking pocket and a hole in his till.

But you keep both halves of every wishbone you ever snapped, all your old socks, medical samples and broken pens and stamps and envelopes and newspaper clippings. Every time you visit Danie de Wet, the Chardonnay King, you make sure you save every bottle because no one does it like Danie.

On the way back from the De Wetshof Estate, you tell William about the Kanonkop Pinotage, the Meerlust Rubicon, the Allesverloren Tinta Barocca, other great wines of the Cape. William drives and you talk and your words weave themselves into what he sees spreading out in front of him, on either side of the national road: vineyards, farms, mountains, wind pumps, telephone lines. You tell him which farmers still use the *dop* system, paying their workers in alcohol at the end of the week, which winemaker killed one of his workers, which grape-picker beats his wife, which *klonkie's* wife drowned her tenth child, which mad Alsatian bit a farmer's son. Which farmer was that? You don't hear William. You're too busy telling him that you always ask your patients to lock up their dogs when you come on house calls. Those bloody Alsatians, man, they eat a Jew for breakfast every morning!

Ma and I are back at the house when you and William drive up the driveway, the branches of the loquat tree scraping the top of your car. After you unload the car,

I'm there waiting for you for to take out the old photos you took when Simon and I were little. I want them for a painting I'm working on. Wait a minute here, you say. You can't just go through them like that. You have to make copies, copies of the copies. I've found some other pictures that aren't of me or Simon, given to you by one of your patients who bought them in an estate auction and I've made a big pile of the ones I want to take back to America. I'm holding up one in particular, an engraving of equus quagga quagga. I'm painting one right now, I say, shaking with excitement. Look at this poor animal's face and those sad eyes!

You can't have it! you scream. It's mine. I need it for my work, I say, knowing you can sense how much I want it. I'm standing right next to you, looking straight into your black eyes, at the inflamed beak of your nose. You're just like the girlie in *L.A. Law*, you hiss. You'll do anything to get what you want!

That's when I run out of the house shouting the way I used to when I was a teenager. I hate you, I hate you. I never want to see you again. I wish you were dead already.

Bloody little bitch! You lock up the quagga picture in a drawer in the bedroom and hide the key.

Dinner is horrible. You drink a whole bottle of Rubicon you've been saving for a special occasion but you feel so bad you open it anyway. William and I decide to cut our trip short and go back to Cape Town. The only reason we haven't left already is Ma, whose face is so hard and pinched you can squeeze battery acid out of it.

William stops liking you, the way a car just stops on the road and won't go anymore. The whole bloody world's gone to pot, you say, and get up from the table. You want to say something about the women wearing the pants but William's long, folded hands and the way he looks at you stops you right in your tracks. You're a big chap, you mumble, taking the bottle of Rubicon to bed with you.

You sit in the half-dark with no one to talk to. These bastards don't know what it's like, you keep thinking, to work like a dog the way I do. Jesus Christ, forty plus years of seeing people dying a million different ways, the human body just conking out, finally. You remember the chill you felt for the first time in Anatomy 1, surrounded by corpses, the sweet, bad smell, the bright cold, the prickling fear of death climbing up your spinal cord into your brain. Jesus Christ, man, I have seen so much pain. You take a sip of Rubicon and look at the drawer where you locked up the pictures I wanted and it reminds you of the other drawer, the other time, at Men's Residence just after the Germans marched into Poland and your father died and your mother's late letter came and you locked it away, along with the first one, wishing you a happy birthday.

Where are those letters? You leave the bedroom and go into your study, rifle through papers and files and letters and old envelopes, the dust and the crumbling paper making your head spin. You search and search until you find them and then you read them and you remember everything about that day and the trip in the car and the end of it all. You feel very, very sorry for yourself, still young, still alone, nobody's son.

And she wishes I was dead already. You people don't know anything about death.

The next morning Ma hands me the pictures in a brown envelope, just as we're about to get in the car and leave the house with the loquat trees forever.

You don't say goodbye. You look straight through me as if I'm not there, as if you're hearing music in another room.

BOEM, PFFF! *BOEM*, pfff! The sound of the *klopse* coming, the drums, and the shuffle of their feet, and it's New Year's all over again. 1945 Hurray!

Without any warning, BOOM! It's not a sparkler, or a Catherine wheel. It's a bloody V-2 rocket, flying at 3,500 miles an hour towards the heart of London with murder in its belly, and gosh, golly gumdrops when it strikes its target, there's hell to pay.

Overseas is where the action is, and you're desperate to get started, to fight the good fight, flying away from this horned continent to the real theatres of war, to scrub and patch and sew all the demented bodies flung this way and that, broken and burst by the enemy, the enemy of all enemies, the evil legions of Hitler. There's a race on, and you can't even whisper a word to Maxie, even though he's probably dreaming the same dream, yearning just like you to leave the southeaster behind, syph and sniff, staph and strep and strap, in exchange for a real uniform not a white coat over your mother's fears.

You've read in *The Lancet* about debridement and you can't wait to explore a wound and see the gaseous magic of the dreaded Clostridium bacteria for yourself, and not its black-and-white cousins in the pages of the *British Medical Journals.* Each marching footstep into France brings you closer finishing your housemanship and you're not sure who will reach Berlin before you. All you want is to get to the war before it ends, before you miss the greatest adventure of all time. Sometimes, in your darkest dream, in your smallest hour, you know just how wicked you are, wanting this dreadful war to wait for you, so that you can join in. Have a heart, chaps. Wait for me before you break down the gates of Hell. You bastards don't know how good I am at stopping gangrene. I've read up on it, volumes of the *British Medical Journal* going back to World War One. I've treated diabetics with festering feet and blackening legs. I've opened and cleaned their suppurating wounds, snipped off dead tissue, removed all foreign bodies one by one. Look at my hands. They're the hands of a tidy monkey, a primate who tends flesh instead of gardens.

With a snickering, sickening thud, your fiercest dream comes true. The Germans burst through the American lines, and they're a bulge in old Europe's pants. The Allies wade through thickets of death. When the *klopse* sing, *Daar kom die Nuwejaar! Ons is deurmekaar!* they're not joking. From the silver trees on Table Mountain to the pines of the Ardennes Forest, the earth shivers, as the Battle of the Bulge holds everyone's fresh new year by the throat. There's a lock on joy. The ships in Table Bay are buffeted by a sudden squall, a whiff of misery from the North. How many wars are you going to miss, *boytjie*, before it's too late?

Maxie, infernal, bloody genius, hands you a note during a ward round at Groote Schuur. Where do the spots end, Doc? Never mind the Krauts. Stella Bellicosa.

A houseboy answers the telephone when you call. How about that! Stella gets on the line and her galloping laugh is in your ear. What did you say that was funny? It isn't you, she screams, it's my little brother, tickling me to death. Little brother, my foot. You know he's a head and a half taller than you. Shush! she giggles and she tells you which Friday to come, and how strict her father is. You might as well walk because he hates Jews who drive on the Sabbath. I'm going to put on my shoes, you say. I'll start right now. *Vat jou goed en trek*, Fereira. *Vat jou goed en trek.* Sssss . . . phhhhh. . . . She's smoking one of those du Mauriers. You can feel the earpiece getting hot and smoky in your hands. Can I breathe while you smoke?

Can I drive while your father eats? Can he hold his breath under the table? Why don't we just forget his strings and his prayers. My family cut up ten rugs, long after it was dark.

You're scraping your feet on the mat outside the house, when the voice-on-the-telephone houseboy opens the door. You almost fall into his arms, before he disappears like a coffee-coloured shadow into the *derms* of the house. The wall next to the door is cold, and the glinting floor gives you the evil eye. There's a giant grandfather clock facing you at the foot of the spiny stairs, chiming loudly in your ear. You're the mouse running up the clock, a tailor house mouse who can sew very tiny buttonholes, thank you very much. Hello Stella, you greet the Queen of Smoke, a white ribbon trailing after her as she comes down the stairs. I can do ruffles and lappets. And then, squeezing your eyes together and tipping your fingertips, My stitches are very, very small. She smudges her red lips against your forehead, a quick blurr on your cockle shell.

My father won't like your muddles. His father's father was a *gaon*, a learned man, and his father's father's father was a *gaon* too which makes my father the *gaon* of the *gaon*'s *gaon*. Now you're in the dining room, a chamber of men, except for Stella, her mother and the tawny manx cat twitching her orange-and-black coat behind your knees. Shabbat candles twinkle on the table, Mother Bun fusses with the houseboy and a row of dishes steam on the sideboard. You plant your coccyx in the chair closest to Stella, the cuckoo's beak pointing down, down. The brothers fan out on both sides of the long table like beanstalks. You're not quite sure if there are four or five or only three. They're all twice your size, oddly patrician for yeshiva *bochers*, talking about the cricket scores and the Old Man, how the Allies are closing the Bulge, and what perfume does Stella have on tonight. Cat's water? Dog's whistle? Or is it bred in the bone, something a little closer to home?

The Old Man enters, in the middle of Stella's squealing and sticking out her tongue at the boy-boys. He's tight and fat in his suit, his chest and abdomen puffed like a pigeon's, every part of him swelling with pride. You're shocked that he's as short as you are, but so full of his own gifts. You can't help kicking Joseph Klein under the table for all the things he gave away: the brooms and tins and old postcards and nails and bags of flour as well as his life's blood. There's a tear prickling in your throat as the Old Man winds up for the kiddush and raises his cup, twin billows of self-congratulation holding up his right arm, and his pudgy right hand. Even his lips are full, two plump fish moving ever so slightly with each loose, warm breath he takes.

His eyes are a mix of soft and sharp, the same piercing cocktail Stella has, the eyes of a judge, a noticer of defects, flaws, inconsistencies. Now they're resting on you, son of poor dead Joseph and East End Yetta, the shop that stopped with barely a penny to its name. What do you have to say for yourself? What do you have to offer?

God made the world in six days and on the seventh day he rested. The Old Man blesses the Sabbath wine, the covered bread, this holy penetrating moment as his eyes flick from the dancing Hebrew letters on the page to the quivering half-smile on your face watching Stella and her pouts and all the nonsense going on with her brothers and the sister-in-law who is missing, mind you, the oldest tallest brother's wife, pregnant and upstairs, lying in. There's a lot of muttering and chair-scraping and sardonic eyebrow-raising, the cat's back arching, as she sidles behind everyone, counting feet and faces and who's going to pay her with a nice long stroke.

Ahh. Friday night was never this iffy in George, with the commercial travellers putting their hats on the table and the music lifting the edges of the carpet, a night to plan picnics, and find the right high tide, to remember the old roads and when Joseph stopped the train and the Model T Ford got stuck halfway up the Montagu Pass. At least that's what you remember tonight, on this night of judgment, the Old Man's gaze scraping you like sandpaper. Are you good enough? Are you big enough? Your name and college, sir. This warden of all wardens has cracked the shell of this year's confidence, shaking the fragile mannikin of selfhood that you've patched together on the eve of becoming a doctor.

You've forgotten all the knife wounds you've stitched

and cleaned, the broken bones you've set and the babies you've held, fresh to the world. He doesn't think much of you, this roly-poly ball of a man, Stella's father. There's a quick prayer for the rear-gunner, the middle brother up in the air over Europe. The war suddenly swoops into the room and the rear-gunner might as well be there, in his bloody uniform, stretching his hands inside his Air Force gloves, stamping his cold feet. It doesn't matter that you want to be in the air too, or fighting on the ground, from a ship, in a tent, cracking codes behind enemy lines, using every ounce of what you've learned as a doctor, as a man, as someone with a heart. None of that matters, because you're here and you're poor and you have to wait until Uncle Oscar says you can go.

There's a blast of fury in your chest that withers the fat Old Man and the sneering brothers and supercilious Stella. Remember the colon-train that brought you here from George, and the other old man who thought you were less than fifteen? The sunset bursting in flames on your face? And the night with the rough blanket as you rubbed Gertrude's thigh between your legs? These buggers have never travelled on that train. They've never even been up the Swartberg Pass. All they know is here, the rude cat and the long table, Friday after Friday. They've never seen what happens when they take the furniture away, when everything you can see and touch and sleep on gets sold for a song.

You keep all your old envelopes and carefully put

them, one by one, in a saucer with water barely covering the bottom. You watch the stamps slowly loosen as the radio plays sweet music, and then the news comes on. Maxie comes over and he's also excited by your new stamp collection and guess what, so is Stella's youngest brother, the greenest beanstalk, the only one without a moustache.

I wish you were here, Maxie, even though this man-boy says he has the first day cover of King George VI's coronation. There are giblets in your soup and you scoop a tiny chicken heart into your spoon, the dark-grey blood vessels a tangle of words you can still count off on both fingers. Vena cava. Left innominate vein. Innominate artery. Left carotid. Left subclavian. Vena azygos major. Look, there's a major general standing on the potato! He's about to lob a grenade at the carrot! Psshewww . . . Poof! The heart falls into the bowl. Dead again. Mother Bun is at your side in an instant, pouring another bucket of chicken soup into your plate. Stella said you were too thin. Ma! Stella growls at her, I never said that. Yes, you did. No, I didn't.

Buff! The forks jump and so does the moon and your spoon. The Old Man has his fist on the table. Don't argue with your mother. He's shouting at Stella but his eyes are on you and he knows that you hate potatoes, that you shun carrots, that you despise anything cooked and soft and formless. You can't finish what you haven't even begun.

Leonard, the fresh face, shows you his *Voortrekker* stamps, printed to celebrate the centenary of the Great Trek. Thank God the wagons are moving, and the Old Man's eyes have shifted north, to the promised land. You know I was there, you tell Leonard, when they wore all the old costumes and rolled through the Little Karoo for the second time around. There's a happy family on the stamp: bearded Afrikaner father, bonneted mother and God-given child. They're standing on a rise and looking at a rainbow spreading over the new country. Above their heads is a banner, *Voortrekker Eeufees*, 1838–1938, in mouse letters.

That's not our holiday, your father said and he went and bought Charlotte. Whose country is it? you asked, even though you knew whose bread was afflicted. I sell to everyone, Joseph Klein told you. Everyone comes to my shop.

Stella's Old Man bulges as he talks about the Bulge. You can't help think about his innards and the layer of orange fat filling him up like a cream puff. He says he visited Prague and Vienna and London before the war, buying lace and fur-trimmed jackets and slippery negligees for his salon, where *Ouma* Smuts buys her suits. His shop is better than your shop ever was. Your father never sold anything that was slippery, not like the Old Man's sliding gowns and silk blouses, satin skirts and soft pants.

The stamps flutter on the table after the dessert is long gone. Pictures of tanks, soldiers, a sailor, buck, the

Red Cross, thorn trees, aviators, an old sailing ship rounding the Cape. Stella's smoking like the devil and the Old Man is provoking her. They're arguing about what hat a Jewish woman should wear, and how many times Stella didn't go to shul with her mother, and who she didn't talk to, and what sort of life she won't even think about living. She won't bother learning how to bleed a piece of meat, how to brine a chicken but she will make pickled herring, when she's in the mood. What sort of a daughter is this, Mr. Klein? Who smokes when she's not sulking, and sulks when she's not smoking? And sneering! Why, she sneers from morning till midnight.

Then he chuckles through the fog of her smoke, and his cigar, floating, mingling, above their heads. But she likes my clothes, Harry. Ask her to show you her buttoned kid gloves, her embroidered Hungarian blouses, her cut-velvet evening dresses. There's no joy like the joy of dressing your own daughter.

You can't help thinking of the Old Man's fat hands pulling Stella's panties over her navel and hooking her brassiere, stretching silk stockings over her thin legs and lacing up her shoes. I love a good frill, you tell him, especially when it's in the right place. My father sold combinations and one day I didn't get them off fast enough. Ha. Ha. I was only joking. I'm not the little boy you think I am. You know I can sew ruffles and lappets, hemstitches and ha-stitches, cross stitches and bobbinets. I can turn lace into skin and skin into lace, and back to skin again.

The Old Man loads his cannon with his eldest son, First Prize, also F.P. and sometimes Jack. He's so brrrrilliant that even the professor of his professor's professor wasn't clever enough for him. Do you know how brilliant that is? Here, First Prize, ask this *boytjie* a few questions. Check if his anatomy is still grey or if he's forgotten everything he learned.

First Prize is tall and speckled, variegated like Stella but not so pronounced. He's got a quirk or two up his sleeve and of course his first question is female. Where is the canal of Nuck? The floor creaks as you get off in the basement and *Grootouma* is there, tapping you on the shoulder, all the dissected parts of her face put back together again and tied up with string. *Hy is 'n skelm!* She whispers in your ear. He's a cheat! *Myne was glad nie daar nie.* Mine wasn't there at all. It's the tale of the disappeared spleen all over again, the lost canal of Nuck, a tiny copy of the peritoneum which, in the foetus, turns into a little tube, an infinitesmal horn that protrudes into the inguinal canal.

They threw the boy away and kept me, the placenta, you tell them. I don't have any real nerve endings, and you can take me on cruises as your handbag. You sidle up to Stella. I'll breathe in all your smoke. I'll sit on your lap at the captain's table.

This is when all the sons and their father turn into one big dragon, each head a different spiny plate, Fresh Face holding up their spiked family tail. That's our Prize

Female, the only one who can carry a foetus with its very own Nuck. You have to do quite a bit of swimming for her, not to mention studying. You might as well throw away all those stupid golf balls. The Old Man is slowly crawling towards you, a fish with legs. This I can manage, you're thinking, your brain talking back to you like someone on the other side of a telephone. One fish is better than the whole family dragon.

I am a coelacanth expert, after all. Remember when the specimen came to town in a special railway van? The Old Man pulls out a deck of cards. Do you play *klawerjas*? You can't play but you can talk and the coelacanth is an old friend. I've seen J.L.B. Smith's boat on the Knysna lagoon. First Prize is telling you about Professor Skullfinder (as if you didn't know!) and the first ape man and how they're scared, those Afrikaners, of evolution, but they're proud of the coelacanth and all the hominids, large and small, that keep sticking their elbows and knees and rib cages and jaws out of the South African sand.

You don't know any card game, not even rummy? asks the Old Man. No, you answer, becoming a no-man yourself. But I like all the fish in the sea, salt water up my long nose, and tap dancing so hard that my knees knock and the chandelier falls down. Talking about chandeliers, you're now in the lounge with the tinkling, winking light above you, and the brothers swirling, Fresh Face and First Prize playing mock rugby inches away from the table with the honeyed *taiglach* and crystallized fruit in cut-glass bowls. The *taigel* sticks to your teeth and your hands and you're sorry you touched the damn thing. Where's the bloody tablecloth when you need it? The embroidered baskets and bows that you left under the bush at Ebb 'n Flow must be stitched to the bottom of the river by now.

The Old Man rocks back, a glass of brandy in his hand, and he sees a screw in the centre of the dangling, maddening chandelier. He reaches up, and his arm is longer than you ever imagined, with an opposable thumb a monkey's monkey would be proud of. I wonder what that is, he says, twisting the screw. There's a cracking sound, and a stupendous crash as the crystals fall, an avalanche of glass which misses the Old Man's cranium by a sip of brandy, the whisker of a mantis.

It's all my fault, you're thinking, staring into the pile of broken glass. I said it. I brought the house down just by talking. Why did I have to tell the Old Man about tap dancing?

His sons are all strangling their laughs, lifting their faces to the giant hole in the ceiling, from whence cometh our help. A stream of smoke pours through Stella's nose. She tilts her head, trying to untwist the smile in her lips. You're counting the seconds before the Old Man says NO! And then, NO! But he's quiet, as the houseboy comes in with a broom and a dustpan to clean up the ruins.

The smell of a bad joke is in the air, all that broken

glass clinking and clattering as Sam, the houseboy, sweeps and sweeps. The crystals that fell didn't fall on us, thank God. Mother Bun is dusting the Old Man's shoulders looking for slivers of glass, specks of glass, tiny crumbs that can cut you to pieces. She's chattering and so is Stella, lucky birds as they circle the Old Man, who still isn't talking. The rest of the family dragon is lying on a couch, six long legs in a row, or is it four? There's hissing about you and Stella and how you stepped on the chandelier instead of the wrapped-up glass, putting the cart before horse, Charlotte before Stella, tap dancing before cricket. Did anyone say cricket? Because there's one chirping behind the curtain and crunch, the orange-and-black cat just ate it, cricket legs cracking in its mouth, folded cricket wings snapping like mangled umbrellas.

The frogs are out on the edges of the lagoon and there's a moon in your eyes when you look at Stella laughing into the hole above your heads. I'm glad it fell down, she says. I never liked it anyway. Your heart is a bubble rising, a balloon on a string in her hands. You lead and I'll follow. She takes your hand and you twirl like a girl.

You lead and I'll follow.

CHAPTER 15

My Dear Harold,

Please accept my heartiest congratulations and very best wishes. You gave us all a wonderful surprise with your high marks and made us very happy and proud of you and your achievements. I am enclosing a small cheque for a celebration or to pay for any medical instruments you may be buying or needing.

Permit me also to put in writing some of my thought, anxieties and hopes for your future. Sir Lionel Whitby defines the "Ideal Medical Student" and for that matter the "Ideal Medical Practioner" as "Cultured, broadly educated in Humanities, Intelligent, Humane and Sympathic, and above all one who will love his profession as well as his fellow men, together with all their weaknesses, joys and sorrows."

I am sure you possess all these good qualities and you will be a blessing to Humanity, but I have always found that you suffer from an inferiority complex, you always get in with the best, in the finest positions, but you are also kept down in spite of your superior knowledge, your experience, you are sometimes pushed aside in account of your kind nature and humble disposition. Now when you have proved yourself I hope that that inferiority complex will disappear.

I find that the General Practioner or what we used to call the "family doctor" who qualify in South Africa is found wanting. Very few doctors are born "General Practioners," the rest grope blindly in the dark, in spite of the fact that some of them possess superior knowledge and are far above the average. In England, on the other hand this handicap or drawback is not so prominent. The average English General Practioner possesses polish, manner and poise, the English Doctor's bedside manner is well known and appreciated, they may be born doctors, but I understand students in the Medical School in England receive training, they go out with a General Practioner and acquire the special knowledge and practice.

I would therefore suggest that you try and get in with a General Practioner, work with him and get the experience and the manner of a General Practioner in England. I am not sure whether London itself would prove a good place for that type of experience you require, as the "Panel" system may somewhat reduce the qualities the English doctor displays, but a provincial town or even Scotland may prove a good field, and I am sure you will be able to fit in, in a position. Needless to say any expense attached to it will be borne by me in full. I won't say anything about Stella, you know her best, but I feel sure that it may have a great influence on your future, and the sacrifice of a month or two may be worthwhile. I believe that to acquire the experience I am suggesting would be of a greater benefit to you than any special course you might take up.

I hope then you will not mind an old man's heart to heart talk, and will forgive me if I am intruding, but I mean the best for all concerned.

With love and best wishes,
The Old Man

Stella climbs into Wolfie's boat. She's your bride of two days ago, and there's a dot of confetti caught in the up draught of her red hair. She doesn't know anything about the Old Man's English letter, in its brown envelope with a love stamp, a man and woman caught in profile, their faces floating above the sea, staring at a lost star. You read the letter, and you looked at the stamp and couldn't tell which was which, love or the war, England or South Africa. You read it again and then you folded it carefully, under your socks, remembering your own father, Joseph Klein, Merchant of Quality. He couldn't write like the Old Man but he had the milk of human kindness flowing in his veins. But the Old Man was trying in his own bossy way, wasn't he? England's not quite out of the question, I might add.

Stella's wearing a brown tweed skirt and a jersey the colour of butterscotch toffee, all things from her father's shop, part of her grand trousseau. Her lips are a flare of scarlet, against the tangle of bushes, the tall reeds and the sulky sky. It's not summer and nobody's slipping into the water. There's a couple in the boat with you, Margie and Ike, a marriage as new and shiny as yours, rings gleaming, faces stunned with hope, and loss of hope, all the todays and tomorrows packed in tight, making the little vessel sit low in the water.

You're on honeymoon at the Wilderness, a freshly baked groom to Stella's pointed bride. The land is all yours, each twist of the Touw river carrying your life's blood. A long-necked black bird lands on a bare branch, and it's your heart he's standing on, caught in the V of the tree. I'm the captain! you shout at Stella as she stands and trembles, afraid of falling into the water, or the sky falling into the tree, or the tree collapsing under the weight of the bird. Sit down, for Chrissake! She's lighting a cigarette under her arm, into the wind. Margie says, She can't swim. Stella blows smoke into the sky. No, she says, No, I can't. You'll drown your cigarettes, you say. You'll pour water down the wrong end of the chimney.

Here's where J.L.B. Smith might have brought his boat, all the way down the Serpentine. You know the coelacanth chappie, the man who's swimming all the way back to the beginning? Of course it's a sea fish but we can pretend. Have you ever been to Ebb 'n Flow? Ike says no, and you dip the oars and lift them, you dip them and lift them, and the boat makes a soft pleat in the water.

You're under the pylons of the railway bridge for two strokes and a breath and then it's in front of you, as you lean back towards Ebb 'n Flow. You reach forward, into the past, then pull your arms and the boat back into the longer future, the older beaches. The canvas tents at the municipal campsite are ghost-grey, and spotted with mould, and nobody's there. A big tree stretches its top branches over the river. A long rope hangs from it into the water. Simon and I are taking turns at the gnarled base of the tree. Simon goes first, his cockeyed smile the best thing the river has ever seen. There's a whoop before he lets go and dive bombs into the water. Then he's out of the water helping me, showing me how to hold the rope high up, and climb as far up as I can at the base of the tree so that the swing over the river takes me far and away, past the muddy little beach and the other children. I swing into the light and I'm so pale and bright that it's impossible to see me. Stella shades her eyes from me, and so do you.

There's a fine mist that sifts water through your hair, and a rainbow arches over the railway bridge which is now a miniature, with a toy train going over it, puffing toy smoke. Whooo . . . whoooo. The monkeys are all up at the top of the river, you tell Stella, dancing and drinking Scotch, toasting the bride and the groom. The banks are drawing closer and the water is turning to amber. Here's where the water level used to be. You point up at the long green beards trailing from the branches. That's lagoon slime caught in the air, from the days when the river was almost up to the sky. Rubbish, Ike says. That's a tree fungus.

Stella checks her lipstick in her compact and there's nothing but red. She can't see me winking back at her, swinging on a strand of Meibomian glands, plonk! into the middle of the mirror, a twinkle in my mother's eye. Maxie's here and not here, whispering *Gray's Anatomy* into your ear. The eyeball is composed of tunics and humours, humics and tuners. Remember the nummular layer and the liquor Morgagni, elixir of death? Stella snaps shut her compact, and you're back in the boat again, out of the patient's deathbed. Margie's leaning out, near the prow, staring at *miggies* skittering across the surface. She's shy and her brown jersey is thick, so thick that you can't see her breasts. You almost smack her with the oar. Ike gives you a gentleman's frown. That's my wife, my house, my whole life making the boat tip like that. Margie, sit in the middle, it's my turn to row.

One day I'm going to have my own bloody boat, you say to the monkeys. If you want a turn, you're going to have to apply for one, in triplicate. The trees are coming closer and closer, as Ike pulls the boat towards the river's source, its first breath. Ssssh! Stop! Ike pauses, oars akimbo.

Stella and Margie sit with their arms folded over their chests, and look at you. You point to the ragged cliff, pocked with holes and stumps of bushes, growing sideways. The buggers are sitting in those holes, and watching us. They're watching us watch them, and they're not amused. Sometimes you can see the Knysna *loerie*, a rare tree bird. Today there's silence. Nothing moves. None of the monkeys have anything to say. The *loeries* are buried in the trees, branch-hopping.

Ike is a land surveyor and he's been all over the place with his instruments, measuring and looking. He's climbed the Drakensberg mountains. He's seen elephants, on horseback. Poor bloody horses, you say and Stella giggles, shifting the plume of smoke between her fingers. You pass the small beach where Gertude scratched her thigh getting out. Stop, you say, but Ike wants to go to the very tippy-top of the river, to the beginning of the beginning. You can't. It's far too shallow. We'll scratch the bottom of Wolfie's boat.

You're trying to explain the memories in the orange-brown water, of Maisie and old picnics, the tablecloth and Gertude's soft skin, your pals chopping up the water as they laughed all the way upstream but no one's listening. This is becoming honeymoon dreadful, all the actors on stage and no one in the audience, everyone waiting for the show that never begins. You can't tell Ike or Margie or Stella about the tangled love that's hanging from the trees. There's a lump in your throat the size of a river stone.

The war will wash it down. The Bulge was closed months ago, in your summer, their winter. The Germans are toppling all over the place. Stalin just arm wrestled Churchill and Roosevelt at Yalta and twisted Roosevelt's arm so hard that it drove his clavicle straight into his heart and killed him. Churchill almost got eaten by his own black dog. I'm itching to fight, you tell them all.

Margie says, Poor Ike. He can't go because he's got bad feet. Look at them, dull knives, flat as pancakes. Silence again, all of you bent forward listening for monkeys. Ike keeps rowing and rowing until the boat gets stuck between this bank and that bank.

Wolfie's going to kill me, you shout. Look what you buggers have done! There's a screech of white paint on a long flat rock sitting under the water like a bloody torpedo. All you can do is pull Stella and her cigarettes out of the boat, before the hull cracks and you're all stuck here forever and ever, at this impossible place where the river ends and there's nothing to see. The ebb is an eking, a backwards yearning and you can never tell which way the river goes. When the bush started burning, there was nothing before and nothing afterwards, you say to the reeds and Ike's back, as he helps Margie lift her skirt out of the water.

Stella's telling everyone about how you took her to the mountain and the cross she couldn't even see because the mist was so bad. What are we supposed to be looking for, Harry? She slips on a slime-covered stone and almost falls flat on her bum but grabs Ike instead. He steadies her, and leads her onto the pale beach, ringed by giant yellowwoods and stinkwoods. Margie's smiling at you, and gosh, her big speckled eyes and her brown hair are old friends. She grabs your arm and her hand is so big that it wraps around your Humeral Region like a tourniquet, slowing the blood to your heart. This is a bridal bower! Margie says, looking at the ferns higher than your head, the ancient trees with their mottled trunks. Where time begins, you whisper, and suddenly her hand on your arm drops. There. Down. To the left. Careful. The words make a circle like a silent O. She can't tell what you're thinking. Her eyes are on Ike, who's right behind you, a gemsbok waving his horns, pawing at the ground with those ridiculous feet.

There's the crisp smell of cigarette smoke in the air as Stella leans against a knot in a tree, her arms closed over her chest. Hey! I'm over here. You brush past the gemsbok to get to her. The beach is much smaller than it used to be. We used to have picnics. Now it's so overgrown you can hardly sit down. You told me about the picnics. Stella picks a leaf from your collar. A hundred times.

There's a twig cracking, a muffled thud behind you. The buffalos are making a bed, Stella says. You have to inhale her last breath in order to hear. Gemsbok, you answer. Look at the twist of the horns. There's not much space between you and the red-hot coal glowing between Stella's fingertips. You take the cigarette, crunch it, and grind it into the ground between her feet and yours. Now they're back in the boat, Stella says, her voice soft. Over there! But you don't turn your head. You don't want to hear the wobble in the water as Ike presses against Margie, as Margie lifts her eyes to the leaves, sinking into the sky without birds.

They're wrestling inside their clothes. All their buttons are locked. Their shoelaces are so tight, their eyes are bulging out of their heads. Stella's telling you this, fumbling for her du Mauriers. You catch her hand and bite her little finger. When she screams, you cover her mouth and kiss it, pinning her head against the tree, the rest of her slowly slipping down until she's below you, so far down that she's the size of a nice brown hen, a chicken for the Sabbath. You bury your head in her feathers and she pecks at the air in the middle of your ear. Ouch! You reach up and she almost lights another cigarette but you grab her hand and hold it between you like a trophy, as you lean towards her and kiss her properly, without words, or smoke, before God created light or dark. There is no sound but the drip of the river and it comes to you then, you cannot heal the sick, or bring back the dead but you can hear the beginning of the world. You follow the beat of Stella's blood, the gush of fluids in her bowel, her kidneys flushing the tea she drank for breakfast, in the little cottage facing the lagoon. At last she's swimming in your waters, tasting your salts with the tip of her tongue. You touch her face. The sky turns and she's dark in your hands, the colour of her own soot. Her white skin with its cinnamon freckles is now ash brown, with shifting white spots, so many spots that you can't keep counting them. Maxie's laughing, because you lost the bet. You gave up, old chap.

You're bursting to tell him the truth, stars flickering in her dusky armpits, all the blackness that's fallen on you, as you sink into the mud, the primeval slop of the river around your knees, stones rubbing your ankles. The freckles never ended, Maxie. The leopard changed her spots. I couldn't keep up. I'm sinking, Maxie! Stella's satin petticoat slithers between your fingers, whistling the same scared song that's in your ears, that's dribbling and gurgling around the next bend, and the next bend after that, and the next one after the next one after the next one. The terror of living is the same as the terror of dying. They're dancing together, the Peanut King and his awful wedded wife, hitched to his side, forever and over.

It's only greasepaint, Stella whispers. I switched colours. You stare at her, in the dappled light, spots in your brain. She unbuttons her shirt and faces you in her brassiere, her brown-painted stomach stippled with white dots, like a faun. Maxie told Leonard, Leonard told First Prize. And of course, First Prize told me. Here, she hands you the box camera Uncle Oscar gave you just two days ago. Take my wedding picture. Tell Maxie I won. You take a close-up of her abdomen, a slab filling the frame. A pox of confetti, a new rash for *The Lancet.* Palloris Tenebrae.

Maldoris Outfoxedyou. Give one to Maxie and please let me sign it.

She poses with her shirt tied in a knot, and then you pose with a handkerchief over your eyes and then she sticks her tongue out at you, and you take a picture of her standing like that, arms crooked on her hips, blowing a rude noise. You clasp one of the elder stinkwoods and swoon into its broken leaves. Stella wipes mud on your cheeks, and you cross your eyes, and pant like a puppy. You throw a hand full of leaves into Stella's hair and she shakes her head in quick bursts. Cooo . . . whooo. . . . Margie's calling you, hoo-hoo-hoo, from the bumpy boat.

Stella brushes the mud off your face and you brush the leaves out of her hair. Thank God, the terror of happiness is behind us. Bliss isn't sitting in the boat when the four of you get back in. Stella lights a cigarette, blowing smoke upwards at the ghost of the moon dangling in the upper afternoon. Margie's cheeks are raw from kissing and Ike isn't finished yet. He tried, though, and so did you. It wasn't everything. Everyone's still dying, all over the world. With every dip of the oar, another set of knees buckles, another young chap pitches forward, biting the dust.

CHAPTER 16

IF HE WAS awake, would he say goodbye? I ask Simon, who's sitting in the chair Ma was in, almost falling asleep. His eyes flutter open and he looks stung, as if I put those alligator clips on his ears and he's the one who's going to leap into the air now.

He wanted to drop down dead, Simon says. At work.

What about us? I say this so quietly that you've got to hear me this time.

Then Simon bends over to you, puts his mouth close to your ear. Remember the third test-match in 1965, when the Springboks snatched victory from the jaws of defeat?

He's crying now and the tears are dripping all the

way day to the edge of his nose, and he rubs them with his hand and I'm on your other side and I don't know what to say and then the machines start hissing and beeping and talking to us, and there's a picture on the computer screen right next to your bed of Simon and me dancing and singing.

For he's a jolly good fellow, for he's a jolly good fellow, for he's a jolly good fellow, . . . and so say all of us.

SIMON AND I are waving sparklers because it's almost your birthday, your forty-seventh one. For once, you're feeling very chuffed with yourself. This is going to be a happy birthday after all, goddammit!

Mahmoud Kafaar just jumped off a Coca-Cola lorry stacked with bottles of Coke and caught his shiny, new wedding ring on one of the bars. He came to you at ten o'clock in the morning with a giant, reddening bandage wrapped around his hand. You slowly unwrapped the whole bloody mess and saw that he'd almost sliced through his finger. That's marriage for you, you told him, touching the slippery ring. He gave you a weak smile.

So you spend hours and hours carefully sewing his finger back on, working your way through the digital arteries and nerves, the dorsal interosseous muscle number 4, clamping and stitching and cleaning all the way to the fourth metacarpus. You hold your breathe around the ulnar nerve, the one that goes all the way up to the elbow.

By the time you finish, two shifting grids of black spots pulse behind your eyes.

You come home for supper and pour yourself a nice Scotch, steadying yourself. I'm in bed with a temperature of a hundred and two and Ma brings you into my bedroom, and you lay a cool hand on my hot forehead, steadying me too. It's my birthday, chaps, you tell us. I'm forty-seven, the same age my father was when he died, when he stopped under the shop with the train on his brain, when he left me and Maisie and Bertie and Mum at the top of the river with a boat but no bloody oars to row home. Don't be so sorry for yourself, Ma says. You take your hand off my forehead and it looks like you're going to give her a *klap* in the face but you don't.

Ag, it's later, much later, and you've had most of a bottle of Bellingham Shiraz when somebody rings the doorbell and you feel a tugging inside, an upside down heartbeat.

Tell them I'm not here. Take two Disprin, call me in the morning. Go away. *Voertsek*. I'm forty bloody seven years old! Ma is pursing her lips as she takes the bottle away from you. Mahmoud Kafaar got into a fight. He buggered up his left hand.

You meet him at Coloured casualty and what you see makes you blind with fury. His finger is black and swollen and the circulation isn't there. You bloody bastard!

I have to cut off your finger! He almost falls down he gets such a fright. Some of the patients in the waiting area start to cheer. Come on, *dokter*, get him! Someone ululates, whoops. Mahmoud shifts away from you, sullen.

The only way you can get through this is to to keep swearing. For each stitch you have to undo, each mangled piece of tissue you have to cut through and clean up, there's a motherfucker and a son of a bastard, a son of a gun, a son of a bitch. Eventually it's time for the bone saw and now you're really the hell in. Mahmoud is out like a light, of course, and even the anaesthetist is out of the theatre, busy with the next patient. The room is brighter than hell and you pick up the saw which you once borrowed from the hospital to cut a nice neat circle in the pointed end of an ostrich egg. Simon and I watched as you removed the disc from the top of the egg and poured all the thirteen yolks into the sink.

This time you're not pouring egg down the drain but all your years of training, all that time spent trying to save and fix and patch and heal. You never ever liked bones, remembering with a sick thud in your nether regions the time Professor Beaton knocked a pin into a man's femur—thock, thock, thock—and the floor suddenly swept up to meet the ceiling. Everybody had the one thing they hated. For some it was blood. Others hated pus. Fluids never bothered you. It was bone that sickened you, more than anything else.

In a bigger hospital, a bigger town, you wouldn't be the one doing this, undoing what you just did, chopping off the finger of a boy you delivered from his mother's womb, a boy who could almost have a bright future if he wasn't Malay and it wasn't South Africa, and if he didn't have nine fingers now instead of ten. You bloody bastard! You can't stop shouting as the bone-saw whines and whines. When it's over, your voice still echoes, coming back to you like a ghost whispering, it doesn't matter, it doesn't matter. Everybody gets it in the end. We're all going to die.

You stop to talk to the nurses for a while on your way out, their teeth flashing white with embarrassed laughter at your jokes, brown nurses in their white, white uniforms, on the other side of the hospital. Give him hell when he wakes up, you tell them. Make him pay. I still remember the day that *klonkie* came into the world. What am I going to say to his ma?

By the time you get home, Simon is closed up in his bedroom doing his homework and Ma gives you the evil eye. Betsy's fever just went up to a hundred and three, she says. Were you talking rubbish to the nurses again?

The grid behind your eyes pulses once, twice, then it shatters, a cascade of all the bones of the finger and hand that you memorized and studied, that you crammed into your head, and then unwound, on a long spool as you stitched Mahmoud's finger. All the phalanges and metacarpals scatter, rolling under the table, behind the couch, under the chair Ma is sitting on. I'm losing my marbles, dammit!

Here. I saved you some fruit salad. You take the little

bowl from her with its nicely chopped chunks of paw paw and pineapple and apple, and the cosy little dollop of ice cream nestling up to it and throw it all on the floor, where that bitch made you drop all the bones of the hand. You jump on the fruit salad. No bones here! You stamp it into the ground. The bowl shatters, the ice cream is all over your shoes, the fruit seeps into the carpet. It's your wedding all over again, glass shattering under your heel, but this time there's something extra. A nice big mess to clean up. And I'm not going to be the one to do it! Stampety, stampety, stomp, stomp.

My fever goes up, up, up as you jump, jump, jump. Ma! I can hear my own voice, my own little bone-saw, thin and insistent, calling for help. I'll Ma you! you shout back. Ma hisses at you, the girl's very sick. You go into my room and I'm suddenly very afraid of you but I sit up anyway, my black eyes flashing into your black eyes, my cheeks red with fever. The whine of the bone-saw turns into the putt-putt of the engine of your little red-and-white boat, and I'm curled in the front, your very own fox. I grit my teeth at you, Go away. I want Mommy.

You pull the blanket off me and it's freezing. I'm shivering, fighting back tears. You know what, my girl, you say, your teeth clenched. You know what I'm going to do one day? I'm going to kill myself! I look at you, sucking in my breath. A wheel spins off your old car, CW 4545, plowing right into me, knocking me flat.

You lean in even closer, your face blotting out the ceiling, the walls, all the edges of the room.

I'm going to kill myself, you whisper.

BUT YOU NEVER do. In the mornings, I brush my teeth in the only bathroom in the house as you shower and soap those goat thighs, that chest feathered with black, springy hair, Ma seeping in the bathtub, all of us stung with steam. I'm sixteen and using your razor to shave my legs and your tweezers to pluck my eyebrows in the long, boring afternoons. I pluck and pluck and pluck until the hairs almost all disappear, till I have an Elizabethan ghost forehead, without the extenuating crown.

Jesus Christ, the girl's got trichotillomania! Ma isn't impressed by your diagnosis. She looks at you over her knitting or her sock-darning or her cross-stitching, She's just plucking her eyebrows, for God's sake. Can't you see holes she's digging into her own skin to get to the hairs before they even appear? Severely disturbed children pull out their hair, schizophrenics pull out their hair. Sometimes they even pull out their pubic hair. Tell me, is she plucking her pubis?

Go see for yourself, Ma says. She likes to tell you what a miracle our bodies are, bursting into adulthood. There's nothing more beautiful than a girl whose breasts are just starting to grow, or a boy turning into a man.

Keep the bathroom door open. Let the steam peel off the mirror. Look at what you've produced!

I float in the bath, closing my eyes, my wild hair spreading like ink in the water, while you both stand at the door, watching. Ophelia, Ma whispers. That's right, you say. Sent into the world to drive her father mad.

Get thee to a nunnery! Off with your head! You catch me kissing Marius in the kitchen on top of the ironing table late on a Friday night, after the flicks. I'm sorry, Dr. Klein. I'm sorry, I'm sorry. The poor chap blushes so furiously he almost bursts into flame. At least he isn't a rubbish like some of the other ones, the ones you won't let me see, small town *skollies* with their half-smoked cigarettes and chipped teeth or the chap who paddled down the river at the Wilderness in a canoe, more than an hour of paddling just to see me, sweat on his bare chest, a signet ring gleaming on his left hand. You sent him packing and I spent hours and hours weeping big, salt tears which fell into my tomato soup like rain.

Sometimes children eat the removed hair, which turns into a hairball, you tell Ma. I'm drifting to sleep on the swells and troughs of your voices. A Trichobezoar, you announce proudly, remembering a word you learned at least thirty years ago. No wonder she's always complaining of a stomach ache! Bezoars can cause all kinds of complications, from constipation to loss of appetite, vomiting to severe abdominal pain. Ma loves it when you speak disease, viruses and ailments and symptoms pouring out of you, not to mention the stack of medical journals in the lav, with their photos of ulcerated legs, bulbous tumours and disfigured faces. She stops her knitting and asks, What's the treatment?

First you have to find the hairballs, either by doing a barium X-ray exam or a gastroscopy. Then you do a gastric lavage, a thorough washing out of the stomach. I can smell the grimace on your face, your sour down-twisted smile. Is she eating the hair on her head as well?

Remember when she was two or four or six, Ma says, clucking over a dropped stitch. How she'd twirl curls around her fingers, playing with her hair endlessly. Perhaps that was a dress rehearsal for the terribly plucked brows, the scabs and the sores and the stomach aches? If it goes on, you say grimly, we should definitely look into it.

You don't wait longer than that night. You and Ma tiptoe into my room and creep towards me in the sleeping dark, an advance of the Shapeless Snuffling Night Terrors. I'm lost in the black cloud of hair on my pillow. You stand over me, watching my sullen mouth, tongue finally quiet, the swaddled baby you brought home from the nursing home suddenly grown immense. You have a small flashlight in your hand, the kind you used to look down sore throats. I lie very still as Ma runs her fingers through the dense cloud, searching for holes, bald spots. The moving circle of light from the flashlight turns my hair into a field of billowing grass and you are the field mouse darting between long stalks, trying to find a clearing. You don't see my half-tickled smile as I moan and shift, sinking under the mountain of your shadows. The light moves down, down as Ma lifts a corner of my nightie and you shine the flashlight onto my Mons Veneris, my rounded eminence. My eyes are squeezed shut now, and there's a sudden draft of icy cold sweeping over me, beginning where you are, at the root of my tightening thighs.

Ma steps back. You flick off the switch, put the light in your pocket. Exactly how many candles did Betsy blow out on her birthday cake? Sixteen? Seventeen? Mrs. God beckons and you leave the room as I pull the covers over my head the way I used to when I was five, six and seven.

You can't count anymore. There were too many candles crowding the cake, too many inches between us plus the thousands and thousands of unaccounted for hairs. You shake your head. There are no holes on my head or my pubis that you can clearly see but you remember the groaning, my hand drifting over my lower abdomen in the dark. Perhaps there really is something there, yesterday's hairball or the large colon tying itself into a granny knot.

In the morning you tell me about the barium X-ray. You shouldn't have breakfast, my girl. We have to clean out your large intestine. I take the laxative you give me, just as I always take your medicines and treatments, trained from infancy to be a good patient, excellent at succumbing. Ma writes a letter to the school which says that I have pain in my lower gastrointestinal tract. I spend hours and hours in the toilet, reading Regency romances, a lost world filled with upswept dos and Empire waisted dresses, phaetons and fops. The next morning you and Ma take me to the hospital at the crack of dawn, to get it over with.

Star-spangled stairs, the nurses of yesteryear floating past in their capes, singing "Silent Night." I sat on your shoulders like a prize, an important hat. Today I'm still special, the doctor's daughter, the same nurses bobbing and smiling at us as we walk the halls. That's Sarie Boshof, Ma says to me as we turn a corner and practically bump into a white uniform.

The nurse has a crisp part in her brown hair, a careful ponytail. She's a patient of your father's, Ma says. Her mother was the one with porphyria, the royal urine. I look at Sarie as if I'm as old as Noah. Hello Dr. Klein, she says. Hello Mrs. Klein. You must be Betsy. Your father is always talking about you and now here you are, in the flesh. *Sy's baie slim, nê?* She's the clever one.

She has pain in her abdomen, Ma explains. The pain's pain lifts me onto its shoulders. I can still see everything just the way I used to, but from a position of vast superiority. Hey, remember how you used to bring her to the hospital on Christmas Eve, to listen to the carol singing? *Ag,* shame man, she was just a *lightie.* You give her one of your special Christmas box smiles, trimmed with that special ha-haah laugh. Of course I remember, nursie.

I walk into one of the X-ray rooms between you and Ma, a prisoner of my own plucking. She hands me a hospital gown, always the drabbest, saddest kind of dress. My hands shiver as I tie a long bow in the back. I'm still shivering when she tells me to climb onto the table and hold myself in the foetal position. Sarie flits around the room like a black-and-white butterfly, in case you need her. I can see her out of the corner of the eye pressed closest to my right knee. Funny how body parts drift apart, disassemble, how the foot is a stranger to the ear, how the eye won't have anything to do with the buttock.

I lie there as still as a quagga, turned into a fascinating skin for someone's floor, the very quietest of Snufflies. When you insert a tube into my rectum for the barium to pass through, the table sinks beneath me, my mouth falls down. In the close dark, I find myself looking at a giant squid in a giant case in an immense museum. The museum guards are all nurses, singing "Silent Night" silently as the barium spread like a red tide. I close my giant squid eyes while Ma takes the X-rays, just the way she used to when she worked at Groote Schuur.

Sarie Boshof, sampler of my shame, denizen of my knee cap, mote in my sad squid eye. She could be in the room with you right now, counting your bad numbers, watching the clicking, spitting machines draw pictures of your heart. *Ag,* shame man. *Ag foeitog.*

Later, when you and Ma examine the pictures, you notice a slight distension in the splenic flexure. You end up taking me to First Prize, a fancy surgeon by now and Chief Family Operator. He's removed a benign cyst from one of Ma's breasts, cutting and sewing his way through brothers and sisters, uncles and aunts, nephews, nieces and in-laws. He welcomes me with his trademark, a shrill whistle right into the ear, echoes of Uncle Wolfie. Then he examines me and spends several moments staring at the X-rays. If it is a hairball, maybe it will pass right through, he says, in his soft, sing-songy voice. Keep an eye on it.

For a few days, you inspect my stools but you can't see anything. I stop complaining about the pain in my abdomen. All my animals are in perfect order, thank you very much, the Snufflies mixing nicely with the squid, the quagga and some of the lesser vertebrates.

When I go to have my hair cut, I ask the hairdresser to cut it very short, like a boy's.

The animals prefer it that way and so do you. Ma says I look more beautiful than ever, and that she can see my eyes, finally. My eyebrows are almost gone by now but I can see my whole face in the mirror, white and luminous like an egg.

What about the gastric lavaaage? I ask, making my voice plummy and droll. It sounds like a special beauty treatment. Am I going to have one of those too? You say, No lavaaage for you, my dear.

Off to the nunnery!

CHAPTER 17

THE SPHYGMOMANOMETER IS whispering secrets to the ECG machine, and the ECG machine is spitting out swear words on paper in between globs of black ink. The IV stand and its hanging plastic bag jiggle in time to the sighing of your blood pressure cuff and the catheter is the biggest moany-groany of the lot, saying over and over again, you left me high and dry, *boetie*. You gave up the ghost.

Simon and I are posted like sentries on either side of your bed, and now the machines are shooting at us, spit balls and paper planes that land on our eyebrows and in our hair. You've finally had enough.

When I bend over to see if you're still breathing, the blood-pressure cuff slips from your arm onto mine, and pulls my arm back so quickly and fiercely that I hit myself in the face. Simon's struggling with the cords of the IV wrapping his legs and his feet and pinning his arm to his sides. He's pulling the tubes with both hands but it's hard to break free.

Your pillows are filling up then emptying out, like giant white bladders. Your sheets are shifting and flapping, sails on a boat that's coming around. I can hardly see in the blizzard of spit and piss that's flying around the room. Simon, I'm shouting but he can't hear a word I'm saying. The sphygmomanometer is hissing and wheezing like a child with croup.

You're in the eye of the storm, a wan smile playing on your lips. Look, Simon! I'm pointing at your amused face through the gauze of fluids and solids floating past. But Simon's buckling over, stumbling out of the room, the largest spitball landing squarely on the back of his head.

You are my strongest child, you once said, handing me a case of wine to carry into the house. Well, I'm going to show you all over again. You put the machines up to this, and I'm not afraid of them or of you.

In the half-dark, the cords twirl one last time, and then finally shudder and settle. The air is clear now, and a deep quiet flows into the room. All the machines are shinier than ever before. You're still alive, even though the spaces between your breaths are longer and longer. I notice that my teeth are chattering, that my hands and feet as cold as blocks of ice. "Not talking = madness," you wrote, and now it's come true.

* * *

THE OLD PAIN is spreading, a spring-tide covering the beach, edging up the shoreline, lapping at the rough grass, finding its way onto the stoeps of the beach houses. But where's Maisie? The tide is rushing towards you and you're running now, looking for her everywhere. There's a plane roaring overhead and you look up and there she is in the sky with Ronald, her husband, and they're flying over the Du Toit's Kloof mountains.

Everybody else drives over the mountain but Maisie's different. She flies. The chicken is stringy and Stella's upset, pacing and shouting because they're late, late, late. She's a woman who eats by the clock, a woman who respects the twin needles of time. Maisie and husband Ronald land at the Worcester aerodrome and we're all there to watch them land. No, we're not staying for lunch or for tea or for supper, they say. We have to fly before dark, before the sun goes down and we crash right into the side of the mountain. They don't even offer you a ride, a loop-de-loop over the Breede River, and the patchwork farms. They plop me on the wing and take one, two, three pictures which they send years later in a foreign envelope, airplane wing girl with bow in her hair, nine years old. You and Ma, Simon and I stare up at the sky like village idiots as they disappear again, with a bellow from the plane's engine and a breezy wave.

She loves me, she loves me not. The sound of the sea is deafening, and you can hear Arnold Toynbee above the noise, with his grand pronouncement, The Jews are the fossils of history! Bloody anti-Semite, sticking it to the Jews like that. We're not a dead civilization, no matter what Mr. Hitler tried to do to us!

Your voice is coming out the old wireless radio at Chantry. She loves me, she loves me not. I'm a fossil, I'm not a fossilwww . . . Sssssh. . . . zzzzz. . . . Wheeee . . . V for Victory! May 7th, 1945. Germany surrenders! But the war's not completely over. England's on the air, all ravaged and torn. "The evil-doers are now prostrate before us . . . But let us not forget for a moment the toils and efforts that lie ahead. Japan, with all her treachery and greed, remains unsubdued." If I live long enough to eat Mother Bun's chopped herring and sticky *taiglach*, none of you buggers are going to stop me from fighting this war, from going as far east as I can.

AND YOU'RE NOT going to stop me from taking the boat up the river either, you tell Stella, who is watching you from her beach chair on the lawn of the Fairy Knowe Hotel, her face set in an attitude of grim concern, a plastic-covered library book rustling in her lap.

It took you almost an hour to get the boat into the water, Dumbleton's grandson, directing you from the little beach, as you backed your car with the boat-trailer hooked onto it towards the river. The wheels of the trailer slowly inched backwards into the mud. It took all your strength to release the winch and let the boat glide into the water. You wouldn't let the boy help you with that although you took his arm as you climbed into the boat from the jetty. Fuel-pump check. Oars check. Oarlocks, check, check. Once you left one behind.

It's May 7th, 1997, old chap. Fifty-two years to the day after Germany surrendered! You tell this to one of those black, long-beaked birds sitting on the skeleton of a tree on the opposite bank, watching you as you gear up to start the engine. Simon used to do this, in the old days. His kids must be old enough to help you by now. You can't remember when last they were here. Was it before you got sick? Before the operation to take out the bad piece of your colon, the inflamed train, hell on wheels?

You pull the cord to start the motor. It doesn't snap tight the way it used to, and fire the little five-and-a-half horsepower engine. There's no putt-putt, no whiff of petrol, no sound of churning water just the empty, whirring of the cord, motion without action. You look up, briefly. Even the clouds are stacking up against you. You take the handle in your hand again, inhale, pull . . . downstroke, upstroke, downstroke . . . The motor's still dead. You bend over, squeeze the bulb on the petrol tank, giving the engine a little more juice. Stella gets up, leaving the book in the chair. She stands at the edge of the lawn, a few steps away from the wooden jetty, her arms folded across her chest. She doesn't want you to go. She doesn't want to worry about whether you'll come back or not.

The river is very full, you tell her. I wonder how far up Ebb 'n Flow I can take the boat. She says, I still don't think you should go. You take the cord between both hands and pull as hard as you can. Stella bites the dust. She has to eat her words. Downstroke, upstroke . . .

Dead. Rage is blackening the sky, the river, the other boats. Get away from me! Go sit in your bloody chair! The Dumbleton boy, who's been working on a boat at the other end of the jetty, looks up at you, as if you called him. It's flooded, you pant. Have to wait. Stella's back at her post, the book in front of her like a shield. For an instant, you see a column of smoke rising from her. Jesus Christ! She's smoking again! Remember that slip of a girl, smoking like mad, a laugh as big as a house. I'm going to grab in and take those tonsils out, you used to say. I can see them from here.

Then you remember that she hasn't smoked a cigarette since 1965. Not that you miss the cigarettes, mind you. You were one of the first doctors in Worcester to tell your patients to stop smoking. You grew to hate Stella's cigarettes, the sour ashtrays, stale air in every corner of the house. She got so sick one winter, wheezing and coughing for weeks, that you finally said to her, You have a choice, Stella. Smoke or breathe.

She gave up, and gained inches and pounds for all the lost smoke. Maybe that's when her laugh evaporated too. Or maybe it happened when the last child left home. Was it when they stopped having New Year's Eve dances at the

Wilderness Hotel? The fire that burned down the old buildings? The new management? Maybe it was the new management everywhere, shopkeepers, salespeople and chemists younger than your own children, not to mention women doctors, women lawyers, women everything. Remember how you hated the way Dorothy May's leg jiggled, how it was never still? She became professor of medicine somewhere, didn't she? You pull the cord in a fury. Bloody fucking bitch!

There's a sharp pain on your left side. Dammit. You sit down on one of the wooden seats, your legs crossed under you, purpling varicose veins threaded through your calves. All I want to do is take the boat up the river, putt-putting between the canoes and the swimmers, the rope-swingers and the same old birds on the trees. Have a heart, chaps. Have a heart.

Stella is talking to the Dumbleton boy, and she's pointing at you. Jesus Christ, woman. It's not that bad. She's still pointing, as if you're lost at sea. I'm still here, chaps, alive and kicking. You almost wave and make a face at them but that would let her know that you noticed. You make a point of staring at the sky, folding your arms. I could be swotting for the seventh degree. I could be writing my speech for the annual Lodge dinner. Stella hates those dinners. She hates it all.

Now the little bastard is coming over to tell you something. He's still wet behind the ears, but he towers over you already. He's going to be at least six foot two,

Marfan syndrome or not. In two long strides, he's in the boat next to you, folded over the engine. With a quick flick of his arm, he gets the motor started. There are tears in your eyes. Thank you, old chap. He gets out of the boat quickly, ducks away.

He bloody well saved my life and doesn't even know it. I wonder if old Dumbleton is a Freemason. In Stella's old house, the orange-and-black manx cat twitches in front of the wireless, rubbing against the corded fabric of the speaker, listening to the Yanks roaring The War's over! in Times Square. Now she's behind the cabinet, looking for Americans buried in there. An unearthly yowl erupts. The heart of the city is breaking. Stella, her brothers, her uncles, her aunts, babies and grannies, the Old Man and Mother Bun stop in mid-sentence, mid-thought, mid-everything. The cat leaps out from behind the wireless, its stub of a tail still smoking. So that's where the smoke was coming from. The wireless crackles and dies.

The orange cat's gone too, along with so many of the chaps who graduated in 1945. Maxie died in his forties, a sudden myocardial infarction in a fancy house in London, with a world-class job and a world-class wife, blond up to her armpits. You had no idea what you were in for, did you, when you became a doctor. Of course Maxie's world was science and he didn't see naked women year in and year out, young and firm, old and sagging, every kind of breast you can imagine, every pubus in the universe. You always wanted to talk to him about that, about the years of look-and-don't-touch, but then it was too late. Maybe he wouldn't have understood anyway, doing his experiments in the Arctic, testing how the human body reacts to extreme changes of temperature, and then back in lovely London, with his blond, not-one-bit-Jewish wife. He flew out of your life and never came back. Here today, gone tomorrow. Old Wolfie's kicked the bucket too, more sheep than wolf at the end. Even the war died before you could get to it.

The engine purrs louder than a thousand orange-and-black cats, as you steer the boat under the railway bridge. The water mark on the pylons is very high this year, and it fills you with an old happiness, a love for this river that goes all the way back to George, to your mother and father's childhood thrill at their new world, away from the cold of England and Eastern Europe, winters forever and ever.

You keep to the left side, just as you always told me and Simon. There are no more cowboys on the river the way there used to be, big men in powerboats pulling skiers. The George Divisional Council banned them, turning the lagoon into a wildlife sanctuary. You have to cut the engine around the next bend, observing the same rule. Oars, check. Oarlocks, check, check. You have to row soon, and there's a pang in your right shoulder, a blinding glint of sunlight on the blade of a knife. It's the same knife that poked you on the right, when the boat was moored, and you sat and waited, long minutes dropping into the water and sinking like stones. Bloody bastards let you sit there all alone. No one came to help until it was almost too late.

The high-water joy is gone, and you feel so sorry for yourself that you can hear the monkeys laughing behind their hands at you, a pathetic old man in an old boat going up the river all alone. She wouldn't come with you. She hates the water. She can't even swim. Now she's sitting on the lawn looking at her watch every five minutes, waiting for you to come back so that she doesn't have to worry whether you're dead or alive, animal, vegetable or mineral. I'll show her. I'll stay out on the river until the sun rolls over and plays dead, hiding behind the mountain like a charred dragon.

You cut the engine and the air is suddenly quiet. You sit in the silence for a moment. Then you lift the left oar, carefully inserting it into the left oarlock. You do the same with the right oar. You sit still again, the oars lifted out of the water. There's a twisting just under the surface of the river and you peer in, staring straight into the eyes of something you have never seen before. Jesus Christ man, it's a fetus fish with legs and a big head, a bloody coelacanth's uncle. You can even see nails on its fingers and toes. Before you can recite the Five Points of Fellowship, the swimming thing is gone, buggering off downstream.

Can't help remembering when I was just a candidate, before I was inducted into the third degree. Gosh, those were the early days, weren't they? You were just learning the ancient mysteries of the Craft and you were never sure whether to laugh or not, watching the jeweller, the land surveyor, the car dealer, the wine farmer, in their dinner jackets and Masonic aprons, acting out their parts. It wasn't so funny when it was your turn to be blindfolded, hit on the head and rolled up in the canvas, three Brothers playing the roles of ruffians in the muffled dark. Easy with the heavy maul, you told Brother Lategan before the proceedings began. *Versigtig, asseblief.*

Later, it was your turn to be one of the ruffians, and you practised and practised so much that you could say, ". . . My tongue torn out by its roots, and buried in the rough sands of the sea, at low-water mark, where the tide ebbs and flows in twenty-four hours . . ." quietly to yourself, as you scrubbed up before going into theatre, ". . . My breast torn open, my heart plucked out . . . " whispering as you tied off an artery, ". . . My body severed in two, my bowels taken from thence and burned to ashes, the ashes scattered to the four winds of heaven . . . " delicately closing up the incision, hoping for the best.

Downstroke, upstroke, downstroke, backpedal, backpedal. The water is so high that the lower branches of the trees are submerged, long fronds of moss under the water, the hair of a green girl pulled backwards by the tide. Each stroke hurts your right shoulder, the pain travelling across and down into your lumbar region where the vertebrae are thickening, turning into bamboo. Paget's Disease. Paget's Disease!

But it doesn't have the same ring as porphyria, or trichotillamania. It isn't as salacious as Luetic Disease, as grotesque as acromegaly. Each dip of the oars in the water is an initiation into the exquisite mysteries of the spine, an invitation to count the rings of the ancient yellowwood tree.

The green girl is shifting, slowly spreading her legs so that you take your mind off the pain in your back, and you turn your attention to her. The surface of the water is the silky skin of her breasts and her hair catches the blade of your oars as you row. You stop to take a breath, and you almost fall overboard with longing. Gertrude's floating under the water, an Afrikaans Ophelia, along with Dorothy May in her spotted bathing costume. Your aunties are taking off their brassieres all over again. Nurses are rising out of the water, mermaids in wet white uniforms, their capes and hats drifting on the water's surface, like giant black lilies. Now it's the heavy fabric that's sucking on the oars, making them hard to lift.

As you breathe, the river empties. The boat drifts into the hissing of the afternoon, insect noise and monkey echo. Your oars are up finally, and still, except for the delicious plink-plink of water dripping from the blades.

Just as the breasts, long legs and wet bodies begin to fade, the patients float towards you, upended leaves turned into boats, an armada of naked women flat on their backs with their legs crooked, their vaginas open wide. Here are all the women you could have had, you might have had, you wanted to have had. Here is your undoing. *Grootouma* and Koeka are sitting on the rocks, laughing and cackling obscenities. *Grootouma* is in one piece again, as she crouches forward and points at the water, her breasts hidden by her knees. Koeka's a blur of faded colours, her dressing gown so thin you can see her jagged hip bones, her low-slung belly. She's less distinct than *Grootouma*, a figment of the dappled shadows, a girly whirl.

Koeka's smoking, the air fuzzy above her head. Ash dribbles into the water from the glowing tip of her cigarette. There's a lost girl holding her breath beneath the surface. She's younger than the other patients. She's too *skaam* to get out, to show her nakedness. Koeka offers her a Lucky but the girl won't move. Her face is blood red. She looks like she's going to burst or die. Come on, *meisietjie*, Koeka is whispering, I'll help you. She drops her cigarette into the river and unties her gown. This is the cruelest cut of all. In all your years of practising medicine, you have never seen breasts so perfectly formed, a waist so supple, legs that curve and bend and twist in all the right places. Koeka's nipples are miniature roses and there's a green, mossy beard between her legs. Wait a minute, you're thinking, That's not her!

They're going to get me. They're all in it together, the whole bloody lot of them. Go away! You pick up the oar and try to smack Koeka with it. She disappears and all that's left on the rock is a rainbow stain, burnt into the stone. The girl under the water bursts through the surface, her face the colour of Cabernet. She's going to fight you because you scared away her only friend. Koeka was waiting for her, ready to cover the girl's nakedness with her very own dressing gown.

I am that green girl, swaying with the tide, drifting up the river with you, now and forever. It was me holding my breath like that, reddening my red face. It's me, Betsy, standing at the prow of the boat. I'm not going to hurt you. Just sit back and relax. You don't have to row anymore. I'll do all the work.

I climb into the boat and sit right next to you. Your hands are still on the oars, as I take them up. My hands cover yours, my fingers slightly longer, gripping for both of us. I can feel you tensing. Remember, catch and pull? Catch and pull?

That's better.

Look! The other patients are capsizing all around us. There goes Ma, both her sails buggered. Mrs. Boshof is face down, just the small of her back showing, the last hump of her before she sinks to the bottom. Lizzie April is waving at you, trying to ask you something but it's too late. You can't help her anymore. You can't help anyone. She's asking you if you know what's wrong with her blood but all you can see are her brown breasts, two holy places.

Your breasts are killing me, you whisper to her as you float past, inches away from plucking them out of the water. How many times have you touched but not kissed, palpated but not fondled, fondled but not squeezed, decades of feeling for lumps, your cool hands rubbing and smoothing the flesh like a baker, looking for the tiniest crumb of a tumour, the briefest wink of disease buried in all that softness. It's agony when you find what you're looking for, and it's agony when you don't because the examination is over and Mrs. So-and-so turns away from you and snaps her brassiere in the back, three clasps and the prison gate slams shut. *Baie dankie en totsiens.* Thank you and goodbye.

The girls today don't care anymore. They burned their bras and then they put them back on again but in smaller sizes, in brighter colours, with lace and flowers and mesh all over them, throbbing black, howling pink, juicy green. You don't know what someone's going to do to you behind the row of buttons, underneath the zip of a jersey, what maddening trick they've got up their sleeves, looped over their shoulders, what little bomb strapped to their heart is about to blow up in your face.

I'm not going to save you. You have to save me, Dr. Dad. Isn't that why you became a doctor? Leave the women in the river behind. Leave your wife and your mother, Maisie and the girls with their purple bras, their purple hair, their candida, cystitis, spastic colons, the Afrikaans ladies in their foundation garments, the farmers' wives with their nerves and their pills, all the nurses you have ever loved and hated. Leave them soaking in the cooling water of the lagoon until their skin wrinkles and becomes old.

Duck when the branches come at you, threatening to poke out your eyes. You're going to need to see between the bushes, through the web of creeper and tree trunk. You have to see through my face into the world below. I want you to take this river stone, roughened with fossils, and rub my white-faced shame with it, sanding it down so that the skin sloughs off. Underneath the topmost layer, the stratum corneum, you'll find the stratum lucidum, with its closely packed scales. You'll know them like the back of your own hand. Keep rubbing through the stratum lucidum until you penetrate the granulosum. Glide through the eleidin all the way to the stratum Malpighii. Push on through the stratum germinativum until you reach the prickle cells.

That's where the truth is, woven into the violet and red grass of the epidermic fibrils, buried deep under my shameful cheeks. Remove me from my skin. Peel me like a banana.

The boat is filling up with water. Scoop it out with your hands. Don't go down with the ship. You're not even listening to me anymore. You're looking for *loeries*, your eyes glued to the tops of the trees. We're here. This is the crack in the mountain that feeds the river. This is the source. You've got to keep breathing. Downstroke, upstroke, downstroke, rounded wave. You can't stop at the top. Downstroke, backpedal. Watch out for that *gogga's* nest. You don't want to choke on a mouthful of spider's web. Upstroke! Upstroke! We've got to finish before the sun comes up.

I'm putting the stone into your hand, closing your fingers around it. I am your very last patient. Remember when that chappie passed out during his wife's delivery? Remember how you stepped over him? You said you wanted to die in the middle of seeing a patient. You wanted to be the one on the floor, out like a light, everyone waiting for you to give the injection, stitch up the jagged wound, shaped like a smile gone wrong. Cut me with this stone, and we can both rest. Look, I've got your hand in mine. I'm doing all the work for you. There's blood all over us, all over the white sheets, all over your rocky face. The morning nurse is going to be as mad as a snake.

I'm basting you with my liquor sanguinis, coloring you with my heart. There are red tears streaming down your cheeks. I can't stop now. I'm wading in the river, pulling the broken boat up through the carotid artery and it's choked up with paper and wine bottles, all the mess that's collected in every corner of your body. The only way to keep moving is to cut through the undergrowth, to let all the solids flow. There. It wasn't so hard to find the right place, the only way through. Now you're anointing me with your history, the fountain of old salts, metals, nitrogenous extracts. All the old doctors are riding the waves, Hippocrates, Galen and even an old witch doctor in Zimbabwe, who cured a rapid heartbeat by putting a locust on a cut in the chest, and let it drink up the bad blood and fly away.

I'm soaking your pillow and you're spraying my face, my hair, my breasts. Death is fierce after all. It's not a muddy river but a volcano. You're not sinking anymore. You're blowing your stack. We're walking up the old road together, and the sunlight is divine.

The End

ACKNOWLEDGMENTS

I would like to thank all the medical and mental health professionals who helped me in the course of writing this book: David Goldblatt, Trevor Kaye, Morris Karnovsky, Alan Katz, Anne Katz, Jack Katz, Jeffrey Katz, Carol Keohane, Samuel Kennedy, Cynthia McDermott, Jerry Pomerantz, Samuel Shapiro, Mel Singer, Joel Wagman, Gerry Wein, Steven Wein and Neil Zilberg. Further thanks to my mother, Ruth Landsman, my brother, David Landsman and my aunt, Lillah Phillips, for providing details of life in South Africa. My thanks also to those who read the manuscript and offered helpful suggestions, Melanie Fleishman, Cheryl Sucher, Jill Bialosky, Carola Luther, Nancy Greystone, as well as Maria Massie, my agent, for her unflagging support and Laura Hruska, my editor, for the depth of her editorial insights. Thanks also to the Ucross Foundation, for the gift of peace and time, and to the Writers Room, where much of this book was written.

And finally, an enormous debt of gratitude to my husband, James Wagman, and children, Tess and Adam, whose love means everything to me.